TRUST
TERRITORY

TRUST TERRITORY

JANET ᴬᴺᴰ CHRIS MORRIS

A ROC BOOK

ROC
Published by the Penguin Group
Penguin Books USA Inc., 375 Hudson Street,
New York, New York 10014, U.S.A.
Penguin Books Ltd, 27 Wrights Lane,
London W8 5TZ, England
Penguin Books Australia Ltd, Ringwood,
Victoria, Australia
Penguin Books Canada Ltd, 10 Alcorn Avenue,
Toronto, Ontario, Canada M4V 3B2
Penguin Books (N.Z.) Ltd, 182–190 Wairau Road,
Auckland 10, New Zealand

Penguin Books Ltd, Registered Offices:
Harmondsworth, Middlesex, England

First published by Roc, an imprint of New American Library,
a division of Penguin Books USA Inc.

First Printing, March, 1992
10 9 8 7 6 5 4 3 2 1

 Roc is a trademark of New American Library,
a division of Penguin Books USA Inc.

LIBRARY OF CONGRESS CATALOGING IN PUBLICATION DATA:
Morris, Janet, 1946–
    Trust territory / Janet and Chris Morris.
        p.   cm.
    ISBN 0-451-45126-0
    I. Morris, Chris, 1946–   . II. Title.
    PS3563.O87435T78   1992
    813'.54—dc20   91-27329
                                                                         CIP

Printed in the United States of America
Designed by Eve L. Kirch

TRUST
TERRITORY

CHAPTER 1

$\triangledown$

The Ball

Between Mars and Jupiter, beyond Threshold, humanity's artificial port and portal to the stars, Spacedock Seven sat like a discarded Tonka toy on a street corner.

Joe South's spacecraft was nearly alone in the traffic lane as he approached Spacedock Seven. The whole area was cordoned off as off-limits to civilian traffic, because of the sphere parked there. People in the know out here called it "the Ball."

The mysterious sphere at Spacedock Seven was laced with scaffolding that made it look, in *STARBIRD*'s monitors, like some Christmas ornament tangled in metallic icicles.

Captain Joe South, late of U.S. Space Command, leaned back in his spacecraft's acceleration couch, pulled down his own suit's visor, and said, "Birdy, give me a close-up, real-time, of what's going on out there." He designated the resolution he wanted and *STARBIRD*'s artificially intelligent (AI) expert system imported the relevant flight-deck data to the heads-up display on his helmet's visor.

Good enough, considering that South and his ship, *STARBIRD*, were both antiques, "Relics" five hundred years behind the times. Only Birdy, his AI, had so far been retrofitted up to twenty-fifth-century specifications.

1

South's newly augmented milspec display was light-years ahead of the capability he'd had when he punched out of an experimental spongespace jump to find that "home"—the early twenty-first century—was five hundred years in the past and "now" was the world of his own future.

Still, he was adapting. Making points with the local government of Threshold, the United Nations of Earth (UNE) installation out here between Mars and Jupiter. He'd gotten himself assigned to this Top Secret program, hadn't he? He'd gotten into the Threshold Customs Service, hadn't he? He'd gotten title to *STARBIRD*, the spacecraft that had once been an experimental "X-class" test vehicle but now was just an antique. He'd gotten his ship, if not himself, aftermarketed into some kind of serviceability.

He ought to be damned proud of how far he'd come in six months of living in Threshold society. But he wasn't. He was uneasy. And he knew why.

The silvery ball displayed on his helmet's heads-up gave him the willies. Sometimes it changed colors. Sometimes it reminded him of things he didn't want to remember. Sometimes it seemed about to open up and show him all of its secrets. But most of the time it just sat there, seamless, smug, and inscrutable, reminding Joseph South of his exploratory mission to nowhere.

Joe South had jumped X-99A *STARBIRD* into spongespace because his country had asked him to, and done a flyby of an unexplored solar system then designated X-3. He was—had been—a test pilot. He didn't resent outliving his whole culture as a result of living through that test flight. You didn't become the top-rated test pilot in your time by playing things safe, or by kidding yourself about the risks of your job.

But South had seen things out at X-3 that bothered him. And nobody in this century would talk about X-3 with him. He hadn't been able to get anybody who was cleared to look at his report to discuss it with him.

X-3 was classified. So were his memories of what had happened to him there. So were his goddamned dreams. And so was this sphere of silvery metal that changed colors some-times, and that had seemed to open up before South's eyes, once.

Joe South had taken the salvager who'd found the Ball out to its quarantine site at Spacedock Seven, and the Ball had opened up for South. Or seemed to. He couldn't corroborate what he thought had happened to him there. Not even Birdy's scans had recorded the event.

The seamless Ball had opened up and South had seen inside it. Or thought he had.

He'd seen . . . things . . . he wasn't supposed to have seen. Things like sad-eyed aliens that nobody would admit existed. Things like lavender sunsets and ringed planets in the midst of a world he'd supposedly never set foot on. Things that were connected, somehow, to the mysterious sphere that had become, even in Threshold official docu-ments, "the Ball."

South resented the fact that Mickey Croft's Threshold gov-ernment thought it could classify his dreams and his memories along with his test-flight log of *STARBIRD*'s trip to X-3. He resented it more than he resented the fact that, coming home and finding home relativistically displaced by five hun-dred years, he'd become a charity case, until the Ball turned up.

And he resented the Ball most of all, because it made him sweat when he looked at it, even through his heads-up display.

On his helmet's visor, the Ball was small. It should have been less imposing, reduced to manageable proportions. But nothing made that image manageable for South.

When you had a personal demon that was a physical reality, not a psychological phantasm, you had to confront it. So he was out here confronting it. He was nearly nose-to-nose with the image on his heads-up. But he'd been closer. He'd been right alongside the Ball. He'd touched it.

Now even looking at it made his stomach churn. Over the scaffolding surrounding the Ball technicians in white space suits crawled, purposefully, busily, like warrior ants in Extravehicular Activity (EVA) suits. The United Nations of Earth government called the suits Manned Maneuvering Units (MMUs), not Extravehicular Mobility Units (EVMUs) as they'd been designated in South's time.

Everything was different here in the future. Just different enough to make everyday life a minefield. Just different enough that he still couldn't bring himself to accept that he was stuck here. But for now he had to live here. He had to adapt, like Birdy had. But Birdy was an Artificial Intelligence. South had hired an aftermarketeer to give Birdy whatever additional capability she needed.

He couldn't retrofit himself. He had to learn to live in this world the old-fashioned way: by hard work, by trial and error, and by making survivable mistakes.

Getting involved with the Ball project was one of those mistakes, South was nearly certain. But he hadn't known any better, and now he was enmired in a classified project that had him rubbing elbows with heavies in the Threshold government.

He couldn't have avoided becoming involved, even if, then, he'd known all he knew now. Which wasn't much.

South had ferried the old salvager known as "the Scavenger," Keebler, out to view the Ball, because Riva Lowe from Customs wanted it that way, and Riva Lowe's way was the only way he was going to secure title to his ship.

Now that he had title to *STARBIRD* he could get the hell out of this part of space, go somewhere among mankind's three hundred colonies throughout the stars—once he could figure out where to go and how he'd make a living once he got there.

Once he'd finished with this Ball business, that is. South was stuck here, with the classified information in his head, until the sphere gave up its secrets or somebody closed the project. Somebody like Mickey Croft himself, the UNE Secretary General.

Sometimes South felt as if he were one with the Ball,

imprisoned in its scaffolding, with all of those techs poking and prodding at it, milling about on it, and scurrying in and out of the science station constructed there.

"Birdy, give me a patch through to the science station. To Remson, if he's there. Or to his XO." Vince Remson was a Special Assistant to Threshold's Secretary General. Remson or his executive officer would know what all the activity today signified. The Ball was now South's job. He'd never wanted this kind of job. He wanted to fly spacecraft. Riva Lowe had promised South that someday he'd be able to pilot again—not just his own spacecraft, but test craft and sponge-capable craft.

Until then he was a Customs jock, with a restrictive security clearance that gave him some clout but put him on a long leash.

The stars were as far away now as they'd been when he and Birdy pushed that first button and punched the X-99A through the skin of spacetime in search of eternity.

Birdy burbled to herself, then connected South to Remson back on Threshold: "South, where the hell have you been? The Scavenger's on the rampage. He's barricaded himself in the science station. Maybe he'll listen to you. Otherwise . . ."

The comlink buzzed in South's ears. Otherwise? The Threshold bureaucracy was very tough. The Scavenger, Keebler, had discovered the Ball and towed it in. By rights it should have been his, according to the Salvagers' Guild to which he belonged.

But Threshold had confiscated the Ball and now it was classified government property. Just like Joe South.

South said, "I'm nearly there. Keep a lid on. Customs Special *STARBIRD*, out."

Then he jacked his acceleration couch upright and watched while Birdy, on command, negotiated the sensitive spacedock procedure with her fellow Spacedock AI.

You didn't fly these twenty-fifth-century spacecraft, you gave them suggestions. When South had been flying testbeds in his native time, the most dangerous portions of any flight were always takeoff and landing (for aircraft and single-stage-to-orbit vehicles) and parking maneuvers for orbiting vehicles.

Now those procedures had been freed from human error. The AIs did all that. You just chewed your nails and watched, or filed your reports, or played with your sensoring packages. Hell of a note.

This time South needed the interval to figure out what he was going to do about Keebler. Keebler, a filthy old reprobate with greasy gray hair and green-scummed teeth, shouldn't have been out at the science station in the first place.

Whoever'd decided he could be ought to have his butt kicked.

South watched the docking schematics that Birdy put up to comfort him, so that he'd feel like part of the process, and tried to come up with a plan for enticing Keebler out of the science station.

Under him, the retrofitted *STARBIRD* waltzed toward the precise coordinates of the tube docking assembly as if Birdy had been doing it all her life.

Maybe he couldn't have made that matching orbit manually, not without destroying lots of expensive spacedock equipment. He hit an auxiliary function and used his helmet's redundant gear to patch through to Threshold Customs while Birdy talked to Spacedock Seven Control.

When he got his comlink he was put through to Riva Lowe right away. That security clearance he had, and Remson's name, opened lots of doors.

He could see her sharp-featured, exotic face on a window centerpunching his visor display, if he wanted. He wanted.

She couldn't see him, because he didn't want her to. He said, "Director, we've got a mega-mess out here. Keebler's holed up in the Ball science station."

"I know, Commander South." She liked to call him that. It reminded them both of how much she'd done for him. "Have you any ideas?"

"Better than talkin' him out with promises, the way you did me when I first got to Threshold? Nah. How about I tell him he can expect to have the Ball back when we're through with it?"

It was a long shot. Threshold didn't tend to bend. It broke you over its knee when it had to, instead. South had seen that for himself.

Riva Lowe's tiny image chewed a stylus. Her intelligent eyes narrowed. "If you must, I suppose, you can tell him that. Just don't give Keebler any time frame. No ammunition he can take back to the Salvagers' Guild. As a matter of fact, maybe you'd better tell him that he can have *access* to the Ball when we're done with it. Not possession. It's government property, remember."

So was South, or so it seemed to him most of the time. He almost told her that he could see Keebler's point. But it wouldn't do any good. He said, "I'll do the best I can. But you've got to back me up."

He knew that Lowe was lying to him when she said, "Of course I will. We're as good as our word. You know that."

He got off-line just as Birdy finished docking procedures with an audible thump. Then a chime told him his lock was mated to Spacedock Seven's.

Air pressure in the tube leading to the habitable hub of Spacedock Seven was, according to Birdy, nominal.

Inside Spacedock Seven's main concourse, three Customs officials and two ConSec (Consolidated Security) types waited for him. South ordered, "Just take me to him. I'll do the best I can. But I'll want plenty of backup."

The Customs guys peeled off, and the ConSec officers half ran beside him to their little space-to-space cruiser.

The wonder of Spacedock Seven's huge hub was already lost on South. You can get used to anything.

The space-to-space cruiser had kinetic cannon, A-potential grapples, and lots more armaments that were going to be useless in this situation.

UNE peacekeeping forces didn't tend to get aggressive.

They stood around and flexed their muscles and, generally, it worked. Whether it would work with old Keebler, the Scavenger, South wasn't sure.

He'd never even seen a hand weapon on Threshold, so he was startled when one of the two cops pulled something that had a pistol grip out of a console compartment and slid it across the cockpit bumper to him. "Know how to use that?"

"Nope." He slid it back. "Get Lieutenant Reice out here, will you? If he's available. If anybody's going to start shooting anything in that science module, I want it to be on good authority—and that's Reice, not me."

No way was South going to discharge any weapon anywhere near the Ball. His instinct on that point was unshakable.

And Reice and South had an understanding of sorts. Reice had been the contact officer who'd brought South and *STARBIRD* in to Threshold in the first place.

The little cruiser disengaged from its slip and headed for the Ball. South could see the sphere, larger and larger, in the real-time monitor.

The closer they got to it the less South wanted to go there. It was all he could do to keep his seat. His suit couldn't cool him with his visor up.

So he sat and sweated, in an uncomfortable, contagious silence broken only by the ConSec pilot's attempt to contact Reice.

Come on, Reice, South prayed silently. *Get out here. We can't let this thing get out of control. We can't.*

The closer South got to that silver sphere from nowhere the more certain he was that something terrible was going to happen if they didn't get Keebler out of there, under control.

They didn't know what they were dealing with here. Threshold didn't. Secretary General Croft and his assistant Remson didn't. Riva Lowe didn't.

Even Joe South didn't. So the Scavenger sure as hell didn't. But Keebler, the Scavenger, was sure that the Ball was going to make him rich and famous, and the crusty old codger didn't care about anything else.

But Joe South, approaching the silvery ball, found that he cared desperately about getting the Scavenger out of that science module and away from that mysterious sphere—alive.

CHAPTER 2

▽

A Funny Feeling

The science station was a prefab module, thin-skinned and no place for a fracas. Reice dumped the schematics and floor plan from the ConSec cruiser *Blue Tick*'s display console and got into his combat EVA suit while his ship parked herself by the science station.

Reice checked everything twice: his life support, his com systems—including his visor's capability to display data on its heads-up that was patched through from Threshold to him by *Blue Tick*—and his weapons.

Funny, there hadn't been many times Reice could remember when he'd wondered if he had the right weapons. Usually he chased smugglers, dope addicts, or common criminals. For that kind of action he generally needed his ship's KKDs and electromagnetic weaponry.

Hand-held kinetic and electromagnetic weapons just weren't part of normal ConSec duties. Consolidated Security for Threshold might need the occasional sniper rifle, but you didn't usually go in for close-quarters combat when that combat was bound to be inside the thin skin of some sort of life-supporting module.

Reice finally chose a pistol that shot calmative flechettes (in case the Scavenger wasn't fully suited) and a pocket infrasound generator that would handle things if Keebler was suited up, even if he wasn't using his com system. For good measure Reice took an HPM (high-power microwave) gun about the size of a sawed-off shotgun.

If he had to use the HPM gun, the Scavenger would never be the same afterward—if Keebler lived long enough to be any way at all afterward.

Damned fool Scavenger. Reice should have known something like this would come of everybody's being so polite where Keebler was concerned. Even the crazy old white-hole fisherman should have realized that you can't keep possession of an alien artifact that might well be the first indication of a superior civilization—not if you're a civilian.

But too late to say, "I told you so." Even if there were a couple of people Reice would have liked to say that to. He toggled through his suit's capabilities one more time, ported his ship onto remote so that he could control everything in it from his heads-up display (HUD), and stepped into his two-stage air lock.

When the light turned green in front of him and the outer lock opened, Reice was facing a short space walk to the strutwork where a dozen suited figures waited.

His Manned Maneuvering Unit took its cues from his neural firings as he pushed off, away from gravity's artificial embrace, and out of the fifth-force field into the void. A couple of heads turned, which meant that whole bodies turned, as he jetted toward the platform of girders.

For an instant, feeling the MMU spitting tiny attitude corrections, Reice thought he was careening toward the silver sphere, out of control. All his chemistries spiked. The sphere was spinning rainbows, sprouting rings like a planet, sucking him close as if it were a gravity well.

He thought he saw it open up, and there, inside . . .

Somebody was squawking in his ear. "Hey, Reice, do you copy?"

He hadn't. But he knew the voice. And he could pick out the suit from which the voice emanated: Customs had given

Joe South a slot and some rank, but you couldn't make a modern peacekeeper out of a Relic.

The Relic pilot was determined to stay five hundred years out of date. His suit was something from a museum of space-flight; his ship, upgraded but visibly antique, was docked off the *Tick*'s bow.

"Copy what, Customs Leader? The bunch of you ladies sitting out there like you were on some picnic, waiting for me to come by and unwrap your sandwiches for you?"

Whenever there was trouble—real trouble—ConSec got called in. Whenever, lately, Reice got called in to trouble-shoot something significant, South was at the heart of it—or at least on-site.

South had been Reice's bad luck charm ever since Reice had been tapped to round up the Relic from Before Time Began and bring him safe and sound to Threshold.

"This sandwich we got," South's com shot back, "needs to get to Remson's plate without being crushed, dirtied, or dam-aged in any way. Got any ideas, since he's not letting us in there?"

Reice toggled his com onto a private, scrambled bandwidth. Even South's retrofitted electronics would match freqs and engage the requisite secrecy mode.

On that private channel Reice said, "I bet you've got your own idea, cowboy. Let's hear it." Reice's attitude jets puffed into braking mode and he used the key pad on his left wrist to finesse an elegant descent that would put him right beside Joe South, on the strutwork before the science module's door.

South was saying, "Yeah, I want to *ask* Keebler to let us in there. He's got three hostages, so he says, and the techs here confirm that. I want to promise him that nobody's going to hurt him, and offer him anything else I can think of. I got a real bad feeling about this, Reice."

Reice had gotten drunk with South, once or twice. They'd pulled off a coup or two together since they'd met—even if South's part had been more accident than intelligence.

Reice knew South was counting on Reice to remember the pluses, now. It was clear from the tone of his transmission. South was never going to understand Threshold society. If the ancient test pilot weren't so stubborn he'd have admitted it to himself by now and gone outsystem, where nobody cared so much about perfect performance or subtlety or the letter of the law.

But South was here, under the auspices of Riva Lowe's Customs Office and—somehow—on the Working Group attached to the sphere study, because Vince Remson, Threshold's Assistant Secretary, had taken a liking to the pilot.

So South had clout, in Threshold terms. Worse, he knew it. Worst, he didn't have the faintest idea how to wield that clout.

Reice warned himself to be patient before he said, "Look, South, you can say anything you want to Keebler, as long as ConSec isn't bound by what you say. My orders are to bring him out of there, free his hostages—alive, if possible—and bring him back to the Stalk."

On the Stalk—the administrative core of Threshold—heavier hitters than South or Reice would deal with Keebler.

Reice could now see, if he looked down, the top of South's helmet, and other heads, turned "up" to look at him as he descended.

South was saying, "I'm telling you, Reice, I got a bad feeling about spilling any blood out here. I'm real sure we don't want any casualties. No matter what it takes."

"Neither do I. What do you think this is, the twenty-first century?" The Relic pilot talked a lot about instincts, hunches, dreams, and feelings.

The poor sucker had been one of those guys who sponge-jumped into nowhere, with garbage for equipment, for God and country. When South had gotten free of relativity's grip, God was a moot point and country—in this case, the U.S.—was a political affiliation more than a place.

Worker bees like Reice and South never got to set foot on

the Earth, let alone in ancestral America. That privilege was reserved for the very privileged, the very blue-blooded, and the very, very rich. You couldn't even get into the Harvard School of Ecological Management without clout beyond measure; the yearly tuition was twice Reice's annual salary.

And South, who still dreamed of going "home to earth—to America" was telling Reice how to handle the Scavenger? South had as much chance of guessing right about Keebler as he did of getting back into Space Command. But, Reice reminded himself, South never quit trying.

Consolidated Space Command (U.S.) was about as likely to welcome an aboriginal test pilot into the ultra-high-security fold as Reice was to get Keebler out of the science module with no casualties.

Still . . .

Reice's feet hit the strutwork. His computer-assisted magnetic grapples kicked in, and he was standing as solidly as he would have been in his Threshold office.

"South, if you've got such a strong feeling that you don't want violence out here . . ." Reice began. He paused, and twisted from the hips to look at the Ball. From this close it loomed like a space habitat. He felt like an an ant faced with a whole peach. And he felt a strange longing, something like what the ant might feel. He could almost smell the desirability, the wonder, the sweetness, the unexplored pleasure of the Ball.

Reice turned back. The thing gave him the creeps. How the hell did Keebler tow something that size, anyway?

South stood up, and they were visor-to-visor. Then they were helmet-to-helmet: South wanted to talk without the constant record of the com systems. "We ought to talk him out, I'm telling you. If there's trouble here. . . . Well, we can't risk it," said the Relic.

"I don't want trouble either. Take it easy. We know all about your low-profile study and your classified parameters."

Maybe that wasn't exactly what South had meant, but this

was no time to talk about weird feelings. Reice wished he didn't share them.

This close to the Ball, Reice didn't want *any* trouble. It almost seemed as if the Ball would disapprove.

The sphere was a quiescent silver now. But Reice couldn't shake the feeling that it was more than an inert ball.

You didn't want it to catch you doing anything wrong. You felt like it was watching. You felt like it was learning. And then you remembered that it was a hollow ball with nothing inside it that read on any signature-reader that the Trust Territory of Threshold could bring to bear.

South's helmet clicked against his, demanding his attention. "Let me try now that you're here, okay?"

"To talk him out?" Reice needed to get in there. If he could find out whether or not the Scavenger was in full life-support, he could determine what options to employ. "How about you and me go in?"

"Unarmed?"

South didn't know a modern weapon from a coffee hottle.

"Sure," Reice lied. "Unarmed."

Reice let South tell his story, on general com, to the other men on the platform.

Then, when South was trying to make contact with the Scavenger, Reice said to the waiting support team, "Despite all that, here's what I want. If we get in there, and you get any signal that everybody's breathing the same life-support, chuck one of these in the system." He tossed a chemical flask grenade to one of the Customs cops.

It spun lazily on its trajectory, and the light reflected from the silvery sphere sparkled off it as the Customs cop caught it. "Then what?" the officer asked.

"Then we'll all take a nice nap and you guys can come in and sort things out."

South was listening to Keebler. This was Reice's best, last chance. "If that doesn't work, and I don't bring him out within one hour, I want you fellows to decouple this module and tow it back to Blue Mid. We'll quarantine it there and starve the bastard out." If Reice ended up a hostage himself, Keebler was going to pay for it with the rest of his natural life. Reice made sure of it, giving harsh, uninterpretable orders.

Maybe he was going to die here, or die in there, but he'd trust South's instinct, too: they'd get the science module as far from the silver sphere as they could, as quickly as they could, if Reice wasn't out in one hour.

He ported all the specs of his action plan to the *Blue Tick*, and back to HQ from there.

Now the plan was graven in stone. Reice was the commanding officer on-site. Nobody out here had the rank to argue with him. And the Scavenger's fate was sealed, one way or the other.

South was waiting to talk to him when Reice got off the secure channel: Reice could tell because a little diode was blinking an alert to him that he had queued message traffic waiting, and South's was the first call sign group in the queue.

"Keebler says okay, come in, just us two. He wants to talk about bad dreams. He's been having dreams about the Ball. I said I've been having them, too. No reason to lie."

The insect-eyed visor turned toward Reice was polarized, expressionless, but South's voice was thick.

"Let's go then. Or have you got cold feet, sonny?"

"If I'd wanted to go in there I wouldn't have called you, Reice. But I should have known you'd need company. Yeah, let's do it."

South bowed exaggeratedly, with the slow, graceful motions of a space-suited man in microgravity: Reice should go first.

Well, Reice had the weapons. And his best weapon had turned out to be South, who'd convinced Keebler to let them into the science module.

They'd already gotten farther than Reice had expected when they stepped into the lock and the outer doors closed. A red light told them that the lock was cycling. When a green

one replaced it, Reice reached out to push the button that
would open the inner lock and put them face-to-face with
Keebler.

Then he hesitated. He could hear South's slow, deep
breathing in his com. It was almost like the breathing of someone asleep. He said, "Here, take this. If you need to use it,
don't think. Just do what's obvious. Aim, and squeeze."
South muttered, "Shit," and took the microwave weapon.
The wedge-shaped weapon had an obvious business end. The
ramp sights were yellow. The trigger was where triggers
always were.

Reice punched the lockplate before South had a chance to
ask him about the weapon. The Relic pilot probably had never
seen one. HPM weapons were ConSec/UNE Peacekeeping
issue. You didn't get that kind of firepower when you worked
for Customs.

Reice didn't want South asking questions about what the
HPM gun did or didn't do. He wanted somebody pointing
something at Keebler, and he wanted that somebody behaving
like backup ought to behave. Maybe he should have brought
one of his own men in with them.

Too late for second thoughts.

The lock slid slowly back and Reice strained, clicking his
visor onto low-light magnification, then heat signature, then
through every other quick scan he could think of, trying to
determine whether or not Keebler was wearing a suit.

Keebler wasn't. The fool was standing right in the hatchway, helmetless. The crazy Scavenger's big, greasy face was
grinning at him, greenish teeth and all. Keebler held out a
grimy, hamlike hand and started to open his mouth.

Reice didn't wait another second. He palmed the calmative
gun and shot from the hip, right up into the Scavenger's
turkeylike neck, right below the jaw.

Keebler grunted, then staggered back, eyes wide. "Aw,
sonny, why'd ya have t' go 'n' do that fer? I been tryin' to
tell Southie here, that I figgered out what we gotta . . .
gotta . . ."

The Scavenger staggered back, one step at a time, as if he were trying to play a hopscotch game sketched out by giants.

". . . do . . ." Keebler finished, as he crumpled slowly to the deck.

"Watch him, South. Tie him up. That dose will only last so long with a crazy like that."

South was demanding to know what the hell Reice thought he was doing, and then what to tie Keebler up with.

Reice said, "Cable. Anything. Just do it." Reice had to find the hostages. His adrenaline was pumping. If this fool had hurt innocent people . . .

Reice began searching: opening doors, cabinets, looking for traces of blood, thinking about what it would be like if this science module was the scene of a massacre.

But it wasn't. The hostages were piled in a utility closet—alive—and there was some poly rope there, as well.

"Everybody okay?" Reice prompted hopefully. As he helped the two men and the pale-faced woman out, Reice grabbed the rope on the shelf above their heads.

He was hardly listening to the hostages, who were thanking him. He had to make sure that South secured the Scavenger.

"South?" No answer.

"South!" Reice nearly screamed into his com. But South wasn't answering.

Reice left the hostages and tore back through two doors, into the main section of the science module, with the rope over his shoulder and a foreboding he couldn't understand in his heart.

So what if Keebler and South had gotten into a tussle? So what if the Scavenger, or even the pilot, was dead? The hostages were safe. Reice could handle whatever he found.

But the repugnance, the horror of death, here, now, swept over him like a maelstrom.

He barely remembered to point his calmative gun, as he came bursting into the main module and skidded so hard that his magnetic boot soles screeched on the module's flooring.

South was huddled over Keebler. The crazy pilot had his

own helmet off. That was why Reice hadn't been able to reach him.

South was cradling Keebler's greasy, gray-haired head in his lap as if Keebler were a baby. Reice snarled, "You asshole, South! Tie that guy up! If he comes to fast, he'll grab you by the throat and we'll be back where we started."

The hostages were straggling in behind Reice, chattering, asking questions.

South looked up at Reice, and the pilot seemed nearly vacant-eyed. "You don't need to tie him up. He's out cold. . . ."

Reice pulled South off the Scavenger. "Crazy Relic." He tied Keebler securely, wrapping the poly rope around his space-suited form until Keebler's arms were pinioned to his sides and Reice had a long tether.

"Find his helmet at least, South."

South was trying to talk to the hostages. The female one was crying in his arms.

In the end Reice had to do all the real work himself: he found Keebler's helmet, enabled it, put it on Keebler's head, locked it, sealed it, ran the self-test mechanism from the exterior panel on the helmet flange. Then he found Keebler's gloves, put them on the limp hands, and mated the gloves to the suit system.

Finally Reice hoisted the Scavenger on his shoulder and headed for the lock, ignoring the hostages and the Relic pilot, South.

South could handle the hostages, take depositions. Reice had his prisoner and he was headed back to Threshold.

Keebler's unconscious form was an awkward burden. In the lock, Reice contacted his ship and filed a report. Then he filed another one, straight to Remson's office. When he got back there with this Scavenger he didn't want any problems about how he'd taken Keebler into custody.

If Remson had any questions that Reice or the running log of the event couldn't answer, then South would be around to answer those questions.

That was why Reice had taken South in with him in the first place.

Once the lock opened and Reice was out of the fifth-force generator's range, Keebler weighed nothing and Reice felt better. Maybe rescuing three hostages, saving the science station and perhaps a classified project, was all in a day's work, but it was a good day's work nonetheless.

CHAPTER 3

▽

Its Ugly Head

"You can't expect me not to demand an inquiry when my son and his bride-to-be are lost in space as a direct result of harassment by your ConSec Nazis, Secretary Croft," said the father of the missing Richard Cummings III. "I'm holding you, and your whole Secretariat, directly responsible." The executive stood up and paced the pale blue oval office until he came around to the chair in which Riva Lowe was sitting.

You could have heard a pin drop in the office of Threshold Secretary General Michael (Mickey) Croft. Riva Lowe was conscious of the stars moving in their courses, as if those she could see above her head through the skylight were actually spinning. But it was her head that was spinning.

Just keep moving, Cummings. Don't involve me in this. I'm here as Mickey's moral support, a neutral witness—I hope. Riva Lowe had worked too long and hard to get where she was in the Threshold bureaucracy to lose it all now, over a couple of runaways whose parents happened to be part of the spacegoing aristocracy.

But Cummings didn't move on. He was handsome and he was cultured and he was acutely aware of his power, even here in the Secretary General's office. He towered over Lowe as if she were receiving a dressing down in one of his corporate strongholds, not sitting in the sanctum of Threshold's highest official.

She wanted to tell Cummings that he had no authority here, but she knew it wasn't true. And you don't bait lions when you're an antelope. She met Richard Cummings's stare and held it, hoping she could will his attention away.

No luck.

"Well, Director Lowe," said the handsome heir to the North American Mining and Exploration Corporation's fortune, "don't you agree that a full investigation is in order? You're certainly one of the people we most need to talk to— since your Customs officials seem to have committed a number of the errors that may soon be deemed contributory negligence."

"Contributory to what?" she said icily. "Sir," she added, "I must tell you that Customs and the Secretariat acted in accordance with the law. And I hate to remind you that your son and . . . Ms. Forat . . . were breaking that law when they disappeared. So I don't see what any negligence on our part could have contributed to, that you'd find helpful." She had to protect her people. Her reputation. Her office . . .

Mickey Croft, Threshold's horse-faced chief executive, got out of his chair and said, "Richard, what is it you think happened that could possibly be laid at our doorstep?"

Croft had big ears, a lank, thin frame, a mobile mouth, and long-suffering eyes. He put that frame between Riva Lowe and Cummings, and looked fondly down at her.

"Riva's people helped save those kids' skins. Ms. Forat's father, the Imam, was intent on having both lovers executed, according to Medinan tradition. And you know it. So get off our backs, Dick, or we'll climb all over you and yours in return. Customs has been thinking of tightening up import/export regulations."

Thank you, Mickey.

Riva Lowe would never have dared threaten Richard Cummings, Jr. The NAMECorp honcho, aka Richard the Second, was on Threshold specifically to make Mickey Croft's life a living hell. As Customs Director, Riva was catching some of that hell, but she wasn't qualified to deal with Cummings the way Mickey was.

It took years of experience to know when to threaten and when to make good on threats, when to finesse and when to smooth feathers. Lowe's job didn't call for much diplomacy. She checked manifests. Sometimes she found problems. In the case of the Cummings boy, who'd been smuggling controlled life-forms and contraband life-forms as well, she'd only been doing her job. The way she was doing it now. She needed to get Mickey alone and tell him about Keebler and the hostage-taking out at the Ball. The last thing they needed was for Cummings's attention to be drawn to the Ball.

The silvery sphere had been right in the path of the Cummings ship that disappeared. They had log tapes of the event. The sphere had behaved strangely, then all of the intervening spacetime between the ship and the sphere had behaved strangely, and then the Cummings boy and his NAMECorp freighter were gone—along with the daughter of the Ayatollah Beni Forat, the girl who was the lover of this man's son.

So you didn't want Cummings nosing around when you didn't have any answers to the real questions. Questions like what happened out there, and how, and why.

If Richard Cummings, Jr., realized there was an ongoing investigation to determine what, if any, effect the mysterious sphere had had on the kids' disappearance, then not only Riva Lowe's career but Croft's as well might hang in the balance.

If TTT—Trust Territory of Threshold—authorities could be found negligent in their decision to park that sphere at Spacedock Seven, the consequences were unimaginable.

One thing Riva knew about Richard the Second was that the NAMECorp exec was an inveterate womanizer. Maybe she could distract him from the real problem.

And maybe she was doing just the wrong thing by drawing attention to herself, she thought, as she uncrossed her legs and stood up to face the chief executive officer of humanity's most powerful corporate entity.

But Cummings's attention was already clearly fixed on her. So what did she have to lose? "Mr. Cummings, we did exactly what was necessary to defuse a situation that threatened the lives of those children. We also showed leniency in dealing with serious Customs infractions. When you're done here, if you'd like to come to my office I'll be glad to go over their files with you."

Get Cummings out of here, so Mickey could take Remson's report. He had to know that the sphere was doing its coruscating act again. Know that Keebler had gone off the beam. Know that Reice was bringing Keebler in for observation.

That meant that South was coming in, too. Riva Lowe wasn't just sacrificing herself for the good of Threshold when she offered to babysit Cummings. Joe South made her increasingly uncomfortable. It wasn't the pilot's fault. But dealing with the man who ruled the Earth might be dangerous, but it beat trying to deal with a walking artifact from ancient times like South, who made her feel guilty and inadequate and . . .

Cummings had finished staring at her. He said, very slowly, as if he were noticing her for the first time, "Well, well, then let's do that, Ms. Lowe. After dinner, if you'll allow me. And if the Secretary wants to join us . . . ?"

"No, no," said Mickey, pulling on one large ear.

Riva knew that poker face hid admiration and relief. She straightened her shoulders as Croft said, "Director Lowe is right: she can give you the background you need. When you have it, I think you'll realize that if we work together to try finding those children, we'll be using our energies more effectively than finding fault, which solves nothing, especially in a matter like this."

So it was settled.

Off she went with the universe's most deadly lady-killer, swept up in a dizzying and offhanded display of wealth and power. First an aide met them at the door of Mickey's office and escorted them to a private tubeway car. Then the car dropped them at the Cummings Building, a glittering palace of opulence and overtly displayed power.

She could see the stars from the restaurant at the top of the Cummings Building, of course. Located at the most desirable location on Threshold, outside of the administrative sector, it was where the rich and famous ate and celebrated.

Riva Lowe wasn't dazzled. She was worried. She should be dealing with her problem: the Scavenger. The fact that South was coming in from Spacedock Seven shouldn't make her want to run for cover.

And Cummings wasn't a man one should deal with halfheartedly.

At their private table, in an alcove that seemed to be floating in space, Richard the Second was telling her, "You must see Earth. I think everyone involved in government should see it. The wildlife. The plant life. The magnificence of our heritage. It will bring tears to your eyes."

"I'd love to," she said automatically, trying to remember what he'd been saying that had led up to this. She didn't understand this man's subtlety, and was increasingly sure that he thought she knew where this was leading.

If it was leading to Earth, then somebody didn't understand what was happening. "People like myself," she said carefully, "don't expect to set foot on the Earth in our lifetime. Part of our responsibilities is keeping people from spoiling what's left of Earth, not keeping it for ourselves to spoil."

For the first time since that brusque exchange in Mickey's office, Cummings frowned. She knew he was a big-game hunter, covertly; but he hunted on his own earthly preserve. Overtly he was an ecologist, a preservationist, a savior of species.

"Some people need to see where their roots are. Don't argue with me when I say that I know you're one of those people. And when you go to Earth with me, you'll despoil nothing. I have a place there. I lead one of its protective enterprises. You know, I'm not accustomed to being argued with, Ms. Lowe."

Not "Director." All right, then . . . "Call me Riva. And I wasn't aware I was arguing. I'm not accustomed to being offered trips beyond price by men of extreme wealth. If I understand what you're suggesting, I couldn't possibly accept. It would look as if I took an outrageous gift."

"You mean it would look like bribery." The frown had smoothed. A look of amusement, which seemed out of place to her, had replaced it. Cummings had a full head of blond hair, fine features, and a square jaw in an ageless face that could as easily have been the result of microsurgery as of good breeding—if one hadn't seen his son, who so resembled him.

But he was urbane, and charming, and unpredictable. "I'll arrange it with Secretary Croft. We'll take a party of your peers, Customs people, the like. As a fact-finding expedition, nothing more. Propriety will be observed. What do you say?"

Say? The man was indefatigable. "I . . . If the Secretary General wishes such an expedition, I could hardly say no. But what I'd like is to satisfy you that there were no irregularities in our procedure where Dini Forat and your son, Cummings the Third, were concerned—beyond those courtesies extended from the Secretariat to your office, of course."

They'd bent the rules for this slick bastard. But he might yet ignore that and try to hang them all despite what they'd done—or because of it.

"I keep getting the feeling," said Cummings, cocking his head at her, "that there's something you people aren't telling me."

"And I keep getting the feeling," she said with her heart in her mouth, "that you're looking for someone to blame for the fact that your son is an ungovernable spoiled brat who decided to play Romeo and Juliet with a Medinan heiress. Wherever those two are, I doubt that we'll find them until and unless we stop quarreling among ourselves and join forces."

"Join forces?" Cummings reached out to take her hand amid the silver and crystal and linen of the restaurant table. "That might be the ticket, after all."

What had she gotten herself into? She had to kill at least another hour with this cocksman. Mickey and Remson needed

time to get Keebler into Threshold and the whole incident
under control.

So she said, "As soon as we're done eating, we'll go over
to my office and take a look at my files." That sounded provocative, as if she'd said "Look at my etchings." "Then you'll
see that I'm right."

"No hurry, Riva Lowe. No hurry at all."

But there was one. She could feel it in her bones. She
shouldn't be sitting here letting this lecher ogle her. She
should be down in her Blue Mid office right now, talking her
people through the damage control on the hostage-taking. Be
there when South got in, with whatever interim report he'd
brought with him.

South was her link to the Ball project, her man in the loop.

She grinned, thinking suddenly of what Joe South would
give to be in on Cummings's proposed trip to Earth.

Cummings thought she was grinning because of him and
started to relax, telling an expansive tale of NAMECorp
exploration among the stars.

Maybe Cummings could be reasoned with. Or maybe he
was purely trying to charm her socks off. But one way or the
other, she was stuck with him for the next few hours.

If she hadn't had this awful feeling that Keebler was going
to blow the lid off everything, she might even have been having a good time.

But she wasn't. She couldn't. That Ball was still out there.
And every time she looked at Cummings she could see his
son. The kid was lost somewhere, and she'd seen the
recording that South and Reice had made of the event.

If Cummings saw that recording he wouldn't be so friendly,
so accommodating. So she had to keep him from seeing it,
while proving to him he'd seen everything he needed to see.

And get him off Threshold before the Scavenger hired lawyers, or found out that Cummings was here and got to him
somehow.

You can't be romanced when you're terrified. Riva Lowe
told herself she should be thankful for small favors.

But when they left the restaurant to go to her office, she wasn't thankful for anything.

Cummings was grilling her unremittingly, and she wasn't sure she knew how to make him stop.

CHAPTER 4

$\triangledown$

To Fly Again

Following the ConSec cruiser *Blue Tick* back to Threshold, Joe South had his hands full keeping *STARBIRD* on Reice's tail.

And those hands were trembling. Reice's cruiser, with its cargo of hostage-taker and hostages, was not only breaking speed limits and safety regulations, it was bending the laws of physics themselves.

South was having trouble keeping up. He told himself his ship wasn't up to it; *STARBIRD* didn't have warning beacons and police flashers, but that wasn't it. *STARBIRD* had a new power plant, new astronics, everything that Joe South's limited Customs credit could retrofit into her. The ship probably could have handled the stresses without coming apart.

It was South who was in that kind of danger. Seeing the Scavenger tied up like that, nearly frothing at the mouth, had shaken the pilot to his core. South had been a prisoner of war in Africa once, centuries ago. He was having all the symptoms, now, of Delayed Stress Syndrome. His mouth was dry. He felt like somebody'd turned him inside-out, so that he had no skin to protect his raw nerves from grating against everything physical, mental, and emotional that came his way.

South was mourning his dead, a whole planet full of twenty-first-century people.

South hadn't felt this alone when he and *STARBIRD* had punched out of spongespace that first time, to behold an alien solar system, to be the first emissaries from Earth to the stars. And found . . . what? His mind rebelled, repelled from lavender skies and soft, sad eyes, and a planet he'd never landed on but remembered as if he had.

Joe South sat safe in his acceleration couch, trembling uncontrollably.

Birdy sensed how frightened he was. The ship's AI monitored his physiology through the suit he wore, and his physiology kit was clucking at him as it tried to balance his chemistries.

So there was the occasional prick at his wrist where the pharmakit cuff was, as the artificial intelligence that provided the man-machine interface between him and *STARBIRD* tried in vain to get Joe South, the person, to match Joe South, the acceptable spectrum of responses alloted to the ship's human pilot.

He lay back in his acceleration couch, visor up, and stared at his control suite. The retrofitted flight-deck electronics were outwardly unchanged, more familiar than his new, augmented heads-up display. But even the familiar flight deck around him wasn't helping. Not this time.

He hadn't had the shakes this bad since he'd had the first dreams of X-3: the dreams of someplace he'd never been. Dreams of aliens he'd never met.

His mouth tasted like a sneaker soaked in urine. He could barely croak when Reice called back to find out what was holding him up.

He told the voice in his com, "Common sense. You want to cowboy around in traffic, you're ConSec. If you hit something, the Threshold government pays the bills."

Reice's voice crackled back: "You ought to get a real job, South. You were a test pilot once. You ought to get a real ship and do some real piloting, not toodle around in that old heap. Or expect the rest of us to make allowances for everything you can't handle. I'm goin' on ahead. Catch up when you can."

"Yeah. Okay. See you in Blue Mid. South, out." What could you say? *STARBIRD* was South's personal property—his only personal property of any real value, so far as he was concerned. He and Birdy and the ship around them were all that was left alive of South's entire society. When he'd signed on with Customs, he'd leased the ship to the service through a complicated set of government regulations. But if it were totaled, the loss would be his. No amount of money would replace Birdy, or the physical hull of *STARBIRD* herself. Like South, the AI called "Birdy" and the ship that enabled it were relics of a vanished civilization.

STARBIRD had been an experimental wonder in her day. But she was five centuries out of date. Just like her pilot.

Reice accelerated away from South so fast that his sensoring packages couldn't do better than give him a receding dot trailing an acceleration plume. No way was South going to try accelerating like that in a traffic lane. His reactions weren't up to it, even if Birdy's were and *STARBIRD*'s power plant could take the stress.

He told Birdy to plot a discreet course back to Threshold, ignoring Reice. He'd dock at Blue South, the way his Customs credentials required, and take the tube up to Blue Mid. Keebler wasn't his collar. He wasn't a cop, like Reice.

He wasn't really anything, except a curiosity that had gotten lucky enough to draw the attention of some high-rollers in the Threshold government.

Sometimes he felt like an imposter, but never more than when he called Sol Base Blue Control for docking clearance.

Surrounded by *STARBIRD*'s tightly packed flight deck, artifactual evidence from his own time, the displacement he felt when he contacted Threshold, either visually or on audio, was always the worst.

"Sol Base Blue, Customs Special *STARBIRD*, requesting docking clearance."

The voice in his com was unconcerned, but attentive. The aftermarketeer who'd worked on *STARBIRD*'s retrofit had put a standard com system in South's heads-up. So when he flipped his visor down he could see the traffic controller's diagrammatic display, with his vectors highlighted in red, among all the other incoming traffic.

He muttered, "Declutter," as he'd learned to do, and the diagram simplified, showing just the relevant traffic, the interior slot he'd been alloted, the Customs' entryway, and Threshold itself.

Even in the diagram, the sight of Threshold's Trust Territory still took his breath away. The Terminal. The Stalk. A quarter of a million souls lived out here, between Mars and Jupiter, servicing the UNE and Threshold itself.

The habitat still looked to him like an old-style TV antenna with toys strung on its lateral struts. Threshold had tried its best to accommodate him, but it would never make him one of its own.

The matter-of-fact voice of the traffic controller told him that, every time he made contact.

Birdy locked on to the telecontroller, and South dumped his display mode. The rest was automatic, unless he wanted to interfere. Birdy had adapted to Threshold so much better than he had, because Threshold interfaced artificial intelligence more comfortably than intelligence like South's. Birdy might be dedicated to keeping Joe South alive and functioning, but the AI was so completely at home with Threshold systems that sometimes South got jealous.

Which just showed how crazy he'd gotten, out there alone on an interminable test flight with only Birdy for company. He'd begun to think the AI was a person.

It wasn't. He was alone out here. The last of his kind. Alone except for the Ball. And if he wasn't careful he'd end up like Keebler, trussed and dragged off, doped into submission, because he couldn't adjust to the way things had to be done out here.

Keebler, the greasy, dirty, crusty old Scavenger, was

becoming a symbol of all of Joe South's worst fears: losing his grip, losing control, losing his freedom, losing his mind.

For Keebler *was* losing his mind, if he hadn't lost it already—because of the silver sphere he'd towed in and parked out at Spacedock Seven.

South couldn't let that happen to him. He pulled the ConSec pilotry manual from its pocket and turned to the page he'd been studying. Once a test pilot, always one.

If he could pass the ConSec entrance exams, he could get in line to reapply to Space Command. Spacecom wouldn't have him yet; he didn't have the credentials. Yet.

But if he played his cards right he could earn them. He had friends in high places. Remson would help him. So would the Secretary General himself. But South had to be capable. He had to be competent on modern equipment. He had to be able to fly a state-of-the-art ship, not just a retrofitted hulk like *STARBIRD*.

Having thought that thought he looked around guiltily, as if the ship could hear. But not even Birdy could hear his thoughts. At least not with her current level of upgrade. Contemporary command-and-control electronics anticipated their pilots to a spooky degree. Contemporary MMUs took performance cues from neural firings, he'd been told. Nobody talked about what the current generation of experimental spacecraft could do—not with South, who wasn't cleared for those kinds of conversations.

But somewhere, somebody was testing something. Somebody always was. He wanted to find his way into whatever cadre that was and do what he'd been trained so expensively and laboriously to do.

Until then he had to keep making himself useful, accrue brownie points, collect skills. If he hadn't needed to do those things, he'd never have had anything to do with Keebler's capture.

If he couldn't stop shaking and get the Scavenger's plight out of his head—and the Ball with it—he wasn't going to help himself the way he needed to.

And he needed to.

By the time Birdy was parking in her slot, South was calmer. He racked his suit, slipped into Customs coveralls, and locked *STARBIRD* up tight. He was going to be late for his meeting on Keebler as it was.

A little later wouldn't hurt. Maybe he could miss it altogether. After all it was a ConSec meeting, and he was Customs staff. Any after-action report he gave should go through his own channels, through Lowe's office, be vetted by Remson, and then go back down to Reice's people.

He took a pager, enabled it, and clipped it onto his belt. Now Riva Lowe could find him wherever he went.

So he went where he wanted to go, not where he probably should have gone. He went down to the Loader Zone, where things weren't so damned squeaky clean, and where regulations weren't the only way to get anything done.

The smell of stale beer and vomit and grease and hot electronics soothed him. The chipped yellow-and-black enamel of the loading docks seemed almost as old as he felt. Neon shivered from bar windows. Bioengineered subspecies and extrasolar provisional workers gamed on street corners below streetlights strung on naked girders. Some people thought the Loader Zone was Threshold's armpit; South was sure it was Threshold's heart.

He didn't really realize he was on his way to see Sling, the aftermarketeer who'd done the retrofit on *STARBIRD*, until he found himself at Sling's door.

Nobody home, the inner lock's message-reader told him. He left his handprint and his name, then turned in the enclosed space to push the exit button and leave.

Behind him the inner lock opened. "Hey, Joe?"

Sling stood there, back-lit, twirling the end of his single long braid in his fingers. The shop behind was dimly lit, its contents a collection of hulking shapes in the semidarkness. "Comin' in?"

Sling swaggered into the dimness, hands in the pockets of his coveralls, not waiting to see if South followed.

Usually the shop was bright and all its clutter clearly delineated. Inside, when the door had squeaked shut, Sling sat on his desk made from an ancient spacecraft's wing flap and picked at a scratch on the old metal, watching South narrowly. Weird. Sling just kept staring at him.

South said, "You okay?" They had been friends. At least he'd thought so.

Sling said, "Compared to what? Want a beer?"

Blue beer. South almost said no. Blue beer had a tendency to blitz him before he knew it. But then, "Yeah, okay. Couldn't hurt, after the day I've had."

"Am I next?" said Sling, as he handed South the blue bottle. There were lots of drinks that didn't faze South the way that blue beer did, but Sling didn't drink any of them.

And guys like Sling didn't trust you if you didn't drink with them. "Are you next for what?"

"I heard they arrested Keebler. Am I next?" Sling had worked for Keebler, making a black box to order that Keebler thought might open the Ball. ConSec had confiscated the box, but by then Keebler was sure the box hadn't worked.

South wasn't sure the box hadn't worked. But he was pretty sure that Sling wouldn't be arrested for consorting with Keebler in an attempt to open the Ball. South hadn't gotten arrested. He'd just been recruited by the Alien Artifact Working Group.

And Sling had worked for South as well.

"So that's how come you're looking at me funny, how come the lights are off. First, I'm not a cop." They'd had this kind of discussion before. Paranoia was a way of life in the Loader Zone. Sure, Sling had made a black box that Keebler had thought might open the Ball. But nobody besides South had an inkling that the box might have worked—not even Keebler. "I'm just a Customs Agent who likes your work."

"So you've said." Sling crossed his arms.

"Second, if you were worried I'd bust you, why'd you let me in? This is no place to hide out."

"Hide in plain sight. I figured maybe we could cut a deal.

You didn't answer me: Am I next? You guys going to come haul me off?"

"Not my guys. And not if I can help it. I only wanted to talk to you about getting some training time on a patrol-type vehicle. I want to fly—"

"Damn it, South, don't talk to me about stuff like that. Where would I get access to a patrol-type vehicle? They ain't legal for civilians. Just give me a little break, okay? You say you're not going to bust me. You going to ask me to come in and testify?"

Information traveled faster down here than anywhere else on Threshold. If Sling knew that Keebler had been arrested, he surely knew that South was part of the Alien Artifact Working Group. "Nope. And if we were it would be as a friendly witness, way off the record. Promise."

"Gee, thanks. Does your promise hold for ConSec, since you don't work for them?"

South took a deep drink of the blue beer and said, "Nope. But that doesn't mean it's not worth something. And maybe I'll end up working for them, if that's the only way I can get in some time on milspec spacecraft."

South hadn't meant to say it. He was still thinking about it only obliquely. Sling, who had a horror of authority and its inertia, looked at South as though he'd announced he was planning to turn into a python and swallow Sling whole, here and now.

Of course Sling had never seen a python in his life, so maybe the aftermarketeer was looking at South some other way.

Sling said, "Remind me not to make friends with strangers from lost times—next time."

"Next time, I will. But this time, since I'm here, I want to talk to you about what my ship can really be expected to do, and whether there's anything else we can do to make her more capable, and how soon we can do it." Sling was only comfortable when he was working.

South sympathized. And anyway, even if he did apply to

ConSec and was accepted, *STARBIRD* needed constant upgrades. If he couldn't get his ship up to modern standards, he'd never get himself up to speed.

It all seemed clear to him, now that he'd drunk half the blue beer. He didn't know how much this was going to cost, but he did know that he had to be able to keep up with Reice, the next time.

If there was a next time. And there would be. That Ball was out there. It wouldn't go away. And South couldn't get away from it. He'd tried, ever since his flyby of an alien solar system, to do that.

There'd been lots of those silvery balls out where he'd been. Flying around his ship, swarming and gliding like bats or butterflies, flouting every law of physics, in space and in atmosphere. . . .

But he hadn't been in any alien atmosphere. He'd just flown by X-3. Not landed there. The landing was a figment of his imagination, a phantasmic artifact of putting a human mind/body system through a spongehole.

Silvery spheres in a lavender sky, swooping like seagulls. One of the damned things had followed him home. Might as well admit it—if not out loud, at least to himself.

Having admitted it, South's nearly compulsive need to acquire the fastest possible getaway spacecraft made perfect sense to him. After another blue beer, he'd probably even know how he was going to pay for all this additional retrofit he was sure he needed.

CHAPTER 5

$\triangledown$

Job Description

Riva Lowe hit the virtual-reality enabler of the helmet she was wearing and the recreation bay around her disappeared. The stationary bike she was straddling became the back of a horse. The curving outer wall of Rec Bay Red became an African veldt.

She felt reins in her hand and even the muscles of the dappled horse under her as it lunged forward, propelling itself with hindquarters and landing jarringly on its forefeet. Maybe she should have read the manual for Horseback Riding (with Jumping) more carefully before she'd started.

But she was angry, and she needed to throw her body into enough strenuous exercise and real challenge to work off her fury. Otherwise she was going to say the wrong thing or do the wrong thing, and real trouble would be the result.

How hard could this horseback riding be? Ancient people had done it every day, long before the birth of Christ. She'd read that in her orientation manual.

She smelled deeply oxygenated air filled with something that tickled her nose, as if she were strolling in the agronomy bays: grasses and pollen and . . . dust.

Her buttocks kept hitting the saddle hard. She gripped with

her knees and leaned forward, raising her butt a few inches.
As long as her knees held out, this clearly was the superior
position. Her hands on the reins grazed the smooth muscles
of the horse's neck and shoulders. Her thighs were beginning
to burn.

Good. Ahead she saw a silver glitter she didn't at first
understand. Then she recognized it as water, running free in
a channel. A lot of water. A wide channel. And in the distance, a cascade of water coming down from a sheer cliff.

So this was Earth. She'd better hope the simulator knew
what it was doing. She needed to be able to handle herself
on the ancestral planet if this proposed trip of Cummings's
became reality.

She had never thought it would. But she'd never had a day
like yesterday—or today.

First His Royal Highness, Richard the Second, tried bribing
her with the promise of a trip to Earth that Riva Lowe had
dutifully passed to higher authorities. (Was the sky on earth
really filled with rainbows and purple mountains topped by
conifers, as it was in one of her office paintings?) Then
Mickey Croft had decided that the trip was a great idea, not
a dangerous flirtation with compromise.

So she'd booked the simulator time. Never hurt to be
prepared.

Then the Scavenger had been brought in by ConSec,
trussed like a Christmas turkey. (Maybe she'd get to see a
real turkey when she went to earth; she thought they were
pink and hairless with square snouts, curly tails, and long
toenails.) When the Salvagers' Guild lawyers caught up with
Keebler, their client, the Scavenger was in the indisputable
custody of Threshold Secretariat under security lock, and
Remson was personally making sure that the Scavenger didn't
get so much as the one vidphone call to which the law entitled
every citizen.

Riva Lowe pulled on the reins and the simulated horse
slowed before she, and it, plunged into the simulated water.

The equine simulation was blowing hard through its nostrils, shaking its head and showering her with froth, and steam was rising from its shoulders.

She was sweating herself, and breathing nearly as hard. Her thighs ached and burned and felt as if they wouldn't take a command of any sort. They were trembling.

She muttered, "Simulation, end," and the horse was a stationary bike. The reins were rubber grips. Those grips were slick with her sweat. And her thighs were still weak and burning.

She flipped back her helmet visor, thinking she'd go take a shower.

Joe South was standing there, in a track suit with a virtual-reality helmet under his arm, watching her.

"What are you doing here?" She was embarrassed. She clearly was winded. Sweat had soaked her gym clothes. Worse, she felt guilty. It was the middle of the day.

"Needed to see you," South said, as if that made it perfectly fine that he'd chased her into Rec Red to gawk.

"Well, this isn't my office." She swung off the bike and couldn't quite suppress a grunt. "Even if it was, you haven't made an appointment." *I have a right to some privacy. Some recreation, damn you. Don't look at me like that.*

The pilot's eyes were still as wild as when she'd first encountered him. His body was still disturbingly animal in its presence, as if he inhabited it differently from the men of Threshold—as if he were somehow more inside it than a civilized person.

South said, "I need to talk to you, off the record." He shifted to a wider-legged stance, holding the helmet in front of his crotch so that technically he stood at ease, alert, demanding, and more like some predatory beast in the simulator's banks than an employee of hers.

"Because I tabled your request for transfer to ConSec?" she guessed. It truly had been a busy seventy-two hours. "If everyone who worked for me came to me personally to discuss every decision I make . . ." She started to walk away from him, toward the showers. He made her uncomfortable. Sometimes it seemed she could feel his emotions, his animus, his distress.

He followed doggedly. "Ma'am, there's got to be a way I can convince you. . . ."

"There's not." She stopped. Looked around. Nobody else within earshot, just empty simulator stations, unused bikes, and a few open racquet courts. "And you don't want to transfer out right now. We're preparing a mission to Earth, at the request of Cummings the Second. I need your expertise for that trip—you're the only one of us who remembers Earth at all. We won't know if something's not right there, or whether Cummings is pulling some kind of scam." She dropped her bomb crisply, then looked back at the pilot to see the effect of her words.

South seemed to be shivering all over. Then that stopped. His eyes narrowed and he stared even harder at her. Then he shook his fine head infinitesimally. "Okay," he said softly. "I give."

She thought, then, that maybe it was the way his head sat on that muscular neck that made him so different. Or perhaps it was the way he absorbed the shock with just the tiniest hint of amusement flickering around his mouth.

She didn't know, but suddenly her tired body wanted to find out what made this man so extraordinary. "South," she said, "walk with me." Toward the showers.

He fell in beside her, looking down and over one shoulder at her, waiting for her to speak.

"I . . . What did you think to gain, transferring to ConSec? Aren't you happy with us? We've spent a lot on that ship of yours, trying to help you acclimate. You can't just decide to transfer out, without a reason."

"I was a test pilot, remember? I want to fly test craft. I need to requalify. I can't do that in my ship—in STAR-BIRD." He shrugged. "Tell me about this mission to Earth."

South always wanted a mission. "You still haven't given up on getting back into Space Command, have you? I keep telling you, things aren't what you remember."

"I'm finding that out. Thanks for putting me on the Earth roster."

Something made Riva Lowe trip over her own feet. He caught her arm before she fell. Their helmets clanked together. Warmth ran up her arm. His eyes seemed huge.

She shook him off, stepped back. "Commander South, you're clearly qualified for this junket. I'm going, and I want you as my advisor." There, she'd said it. She had a right to say it, but it sounded . . . personal.

Oh, dear.

South was waiting for her to say something else. So she said, "I want you to agree to drop the ConSec matter for now—at least until we've finished working the Ball problem. You can't hop from service to service while you're on a project like that one. Understand?"

"For now."

Infuriating man. "If what you want, eventually, is SpaceCom, then you'll need some special help." She moved forward, and he followed.

"What kind?"

He just couldn't understand the subtleties of deal-making here. She shouldn't get angry. She fabricated something he could understand: "Special counseling. A physical and psychological evaluation specialist—a therapist." A fitness report on South was just what she needed. "The fitness requirements for a test pilot, obviously, are higher than for the sort of job you have now." *Idiot, just do what I tell you. We'll get you where you want to go.*

"Therapy?" he nearly growled. He stopped, shook his head, and then said, "Yeah, I guess I need it."

Strange man. Strange reactions. She said, "Wait for me, and I'll take you to see someone about it right now. We'll call from my place."

Having offered South her personal assistance, she was more

surprised than angry when he said, "I can't, now. But leave
the name of the therapist with my ship's AI. I gotta see somebody like that, sooner or later. I'm so tired of trying to make
sense out of things on my own."

*Name? Somebody? Did he understand what she was offer-
ing?* South's voice was thick, and she reached out to comfort
him somehow. He tossed his head and stepped back.

Rebuffed, stiff and awkward, feeling clumsy, she said,
"Fine. You'll find our therapy very thorough." She couldn't
believe the pilot was rejecting a chance to come home with
her.

But she damned well wasn't going to ask him again.

"Anything that'll help," he said, and waved at her. "Gotta
go. My report'll be waiting for you."

She watched him move through the simulator bay and wondered what the hell she'd done wrong.

It wasn't often that she invited a subordinate to her home
in the middle of the day. It wasn't often she bent the rules
for anyone.

Talking to South was like talking to some creature from
another world. She told herself it didn't matter. He was useful
on the Ball project, and now on the Earth junket if it came
off, precisely because he was so different.

She didn't need to complicate her life.

But there wasn't another soul on Threshold who moved like
that, or looked at her like that, or had seen or done the things
that Joe South had seen and done.

He was a peculiarly invaluable asset right now, when they
had an alien artifact in their midst and Richard the Second
breathing down their necks.

She was damned if she was going to lose South to ConSec,
or SpaceCom, or even to Mickey Croft's Secretariat.

She'd made that clear to Remson. Now all she had to do
was make it clear to the man who made her body remember
that they were both descended from animals, both made of
flesh and blood.

You didn't think much about animal heritage up here. Perhaps that was what South brought with him: a sense of racial continuity, of physical being, of humanness.

Whatever that sphere was out at Spacedock Seven, there wasn't anything human about it at all.

South's classified reports of a long-forgotten exploratory mission talked about spheres and aliens. Nobody had missed the significance of the similarity between the sphere out at Spacedock Seven and the things South had described.

But then the pilot was clearly crazy, or had been, from sponge travel via primitive technologies. Everyone was agreed on that.

Maybe therapy was what South really needed. To ever qualify for ConSpaceCom, or to take a test pilot's exam, he had to have a clean bill of health. What Riva Lowe needed she wasn't going to get today, not from South. Not a real understanding of what it was like to be looking at her world through his eyes. Or what it would be like to be intimate with such a person.

So she settled for a shower instead. Some things couldn't be simulated. When you had the simulator access that Riva Lowe did, you learned that. She'd modeled Joe South once in the General Secretary's psychometric modeler, but the model hadn't been any more informative than the real South.

South, whatever else he was, was real.

Whether his reports of X-3 were real or not, she and South would have plenty of time to find out.

If the Earth trip came off, at least Cummings the Second would be distracted from asking too many embarrassing questions about the sphere.

Those questions had to be avoided. At any cost. Until the Threshold government knew the answers. Until Cummings's missing son and his girlfriend were found. Until the correlation among Joe South's reports, the Scavenger's demented musings, and that damnable Ball out at Spacedock Seven could be assessed.

Somehow, in the face of incontrovertible evidence of an alien civilization, Riva Lowe wanted more than anything else to make a physical liaison with South, a living piece of humanity's path.

Maybe she needed therapy herself. But she wasn't going to get it. There was barely time for her shower before her next scheduled meeting to discuss the continued detention of the Scavenger.

From what she'd heard, the Scavenger had gone raving mad.

All of which, she supposed, meant that, by contrast, the rest of them were sane. Even Joe South.

CHAPTER 6

$\triangledown$

Premonition

In the psych ward observation cell, there was no way to hurt yourself. Micah Keebler knew for certain. He'd run full-tilt against the padded door. He'd bounced back, repelled from the dusky pink quilting as if by an anti-fifth-force generator.

Then he'd tried strangling himself in his bedding, but they'd thought of that, too. Keebler didn't want to hurt himself. He wanted to make somebody come in here. He wanted to demand his rights. He wanted to talk to somebody.

Anybody. He had a right to an attorney. He had a right to due counsel. He had the rights of a member of the Salvagers' Guild. He paid a goddamned fortune in dues every year to make sure he had those rights.

And now that he needed them, what did he get? Nothing, that was what. Keebler climbed onto his bunk and threw himself off it, trying to hit the floor as if it were the surface of a pool—headfirst.

If he hurt himself, they couldn't keep him in here.

But Keebler couldn't help protecting his head with his arms. And the floor was only two feet lower than the bed. So he couldn't hurt himself that way.

He decided he'd smother himself under his blanket, but

46

that didn't work either: the blanket had holes in it, little honeycomb holes, because it was never too hot and never too
cold in a space habitat. You had blankets because people
don't like to sleep without a covering. The covering on his body was carefully designed to be useless to someone intent on suicide: it was a johnny with head
and arm holes, made of slippery stuff that gave but wouldn't
knot. And worst of all it was pink, too.

"G'damn 'em all," Keebler muttered to himself, and
stalked over to the farthest wall from the door to try a running
start. He'd just keep running at that door until somebody
came.

They were watching him, you could be sure. Watching his
every move. Recording him, too. Whatever he did, whatever
he said. So he didn't say much out loud that they could edit
however they wanted and use against him later. He didn't
want to say anything without a live witness there, a human,
to make sure that what he said got heard the way he meant
it.

Keebler hated bureaucracies with an all-consuming passion.
You didn't become a beachcomber on the shores of eternity
if you liked company. Keebler had combed many a beach,
and fished many a white hole. But he'd never fished a hole
like the white hole that had spat out the silver sphere. In
theory—well, in one theory—everything that ever was, is, or
will be ought to come out of a white hole eventually. But that
didn't mean it had to come in a recognizable form.

Keebler had been fishing this particularly rich hole for two
years before he woke up one morning and there was the
sphere, glimmering in the white hole's light.

Hot damn, what a moment that was. Keebler had fished
some rare elements out of this hole in the past—some palla-
dium, some real interesting blue diamonds the size of basket-
balls, even an itsy-bitsy pellet of super-dense material that he
sold to a collector who wanted to feed his obstreperous relatives to it—or at least threaten to.

But nothing like the sphere.

Keebler remembered it as if it were yesterday. The sphere had gleamed at him, welcomed him, spun before him. . . .

Suddenly the pale blue eyes of the Scavenger widened. His large-pored skin, ruddy and wrinkled from years of exposure to transient radiation, began to sweat. His hands, gnarled and strong, began to shake.

He balled his fists. He jammed shut his eyes. Behind his closed lids he saw memories he'd never remembered before. He saw the sphere, opening wide. He saw the inside of it.

He saw—

Blackness.

The Scavenger dropped to the floor, limp as a dead man. His eyes rolled up in his head. His mind, behind his eyes, shied away from what he'd remembered.

Sad-eyed aliens, whispering to him. A way to tow the sphere to Threshold; a need to tow the sphere to civilization. Not his need.

Their need.

He forgot. He remembered. He forgot again. And remembered again.

The old man's heart beat slowly, then double-time. His hands opened and closed. His mouth moved, articulating growls of fear and misery.

He swam slowly toward consciousness, as if he were deep under the sea. He could see a shimmery light, like the surface of an ocean far above. And in the light hands beckoned.

Those hands weren't human hands.

The Scavenger dove again, to the deeps of unconsciousness. Forget whispered voices. Forget deep, dark eyes with no white. Forget bringing the sphere to civilization's heart.

Mankind had never encountered a superior intelligence, anywhere among its three hundred colonies spread throughout the stars. Mankind had never even encountered the relics of a spacefaring civilization.

The sphere wasn't anything threatening. The sphere was going to make Keebler rich and famous.

He'd been holding that thought for so long. He'd articulated it a hundred times. The litany was like a rope by which, hand over hand, he pulled himself from the depths of his soul toward consciousness.

Toward the light. Toward realization. Toward memory. Toward understanding. Toward revelation.

Keebler's eyes snapped open. His tongue wet his cracked, scaly lips. He jumped bolt upright and ran to the padded door of his cell, screaming, "The aliens are coming! The aliens are coming!"

Nobody came. For far too long, nobody came to his cell.

So Keebler just kept beating the door with his fists and screaming, "The aliens are coming! Let me out. I gotta get out of here! I gotta get to the Ball! The aliens are coming! Don't you understand?"

But of course they didn't. How could they? He hadn't, and he'd been the one who'd found the sphere and towed it in, from the edges of the universe to humanity's home system.

"The aliens are coming!" Keebler screamed until he was hoarse, and then whispered, and then sobbed, as he sank to the padded floor by the padded door of his padded cell, images of sad-eyed aliens dancing in his head.

CHAPTER 7

▽

Trapdoor

Back out at Spacedock Seven, Reice glared at the Ball glimmering on the science station's real-time monitors as if he could will it away.

But a second glare proved it was still there. If it weren't for the Ball, Reice wouldn't be stuck out here overseeing an evidence search.

He had four officers scouring every bit of the science station for proof of what any fool damn well knew had happened here.

Keebler had taken three hostages and held off all comers until Reice and South had talked their way in here. That was goddamned history. But was that good enough for Mickey Croft, the Secretary General, or for Remson, his mother-hen assistant?

Hell, no.

Now five ConSec officers were scouring every surface on the science station for fingerprints, downloading every log for relevant voice and data entries, and generally acting like a bunch of anal-retentive cleaning women.

Waste of the Trust Territory's time and money, if anybody asked Reice.

"Be goddamned careful with that dump to supplementary!" he snarled at one of his techs, who was backing up a real-time log's time-slated entries and now had to stop to change storage cards. "If a second of the transcript is missing, Kee-bler's lawyers will accuse us of editing the record."

The beleaguered tech muttered, "Don't you think I know that?"

Reice took a half step toward the technician. "What?"

The fellow said, "Yes, sir. We're getting every bit."

Reice let it go. These days, he was letting lots of things go. If this had been any other criminal act, you could have dumped the data to Threshold ConSec Control remotely. You wouldn't have to send humans out here to port the data onto copycards by hand.

But this wasn't any other criminal. This was the Man Who Found The Sphere. The Sphere was bringing normal life on Threshold and its surrounds to a halt, as if it were spewing some sticky substance in which more and more of them were inextricably stuck.

It loomed in the real-time viewscreen, fat and smug and shiny. There was nothing inimical about the Ball, nothing threatening, nothing intimidating.

It was beautiful. Peaceful, even. Perfect and smooth and seamless and warm against the dark of night, as if it were a product of nature, of natural evolution, of the ordering of more and more complex systems. . . .

But it wasn't. There was nothing natural about it.

It was metallic. But it wasn't any metal or alloy or compos-ite anyone had ever spectroanalyzed before. It was hollow inside. At least, so far as crateology scanners could determine. It was neutral to sensoring packages that measured electronic emanations or radiation in any bandwidth. But whenever it wanted to, it coruscated through displays of color that made the inside of your mind itch.

Reice really was beginning to hate the Ball.

He was beginning to think that the Ball hated him back.

The four techs were grumbling at each other, as cranky as Reice felt. They were all nervous, out here with that thing. It got to you. You started wondering what it was.

You wondered who made it, because you were sure the Ball wasn't a living thing.

Then you wondered why you were sure it wasn't a living thing. Lots of living things were spherical, weren't they?

Then you wondered if it was some kind of intelligence. You got the sense that it knew you were there. That it was watching you. That it was spying on you. That it was judging your performance.

Then you really started to sweat.

Keebler had towed this thing in from the edge of nowhere, with just regular electromagnetic grapples. But the thing wasn't responsive to magnetic fields—anymore.

If it ever had been.

One of the techs swore feelingly.

Reice clanked over to the man hunching over one of the station's consoles. This science station was government spec, built by the lowest bidder, and its comfort zone was minimal: the fifth-force generators in here had glitches. They failed intermittently, and you found yourself floating in microgravity.

Nobody had been able to figure out why, so far. The fifth-force generators had been failing for short intervals ever since the science station was bolted onto the scaffolding around the Ball. It only bothered you when, as now, your computer-assisted magnetic boot soles kicked in to compensate for the missing gravity.

Everything loose in here was now weightless.

Including the tech who'd been bitching at his console. The tech swore again.

"What?" Reice demanded.

"Just before we lost the grav, I had a spike." The tech swiveled in his chair, holding on to the bumper with one hand. "All my data was gone for a second—wiped, even the operating system, according to the error code—then it all came back."

Impossible.

"Systems failure? Self-correcting? More likely you screwed something up, or a backup rebooted when the power fluctuated." The power would have fluctuated when the fifth-force generator failed.

Wouldn't it?

The tech stamped with his boot to make its magnetics kick in, then let go of the bumper. He stood up, nose-to-nose with Reice, and said, "I don't make those kinds of mistakes." His voice was challenging, harsh. His pale face was quivering, as if the whole station were vibrating very fast.

"Back off, sergeant," Reice said, with a quick look at the man's ID patch. His own voice was harsh. Too harsh.

Everybody else stopped what they were doing and looked at Reice and the sergeant, nose-to-nose.

Reice purposefully turned his back on the angry man, snarling, "You all done, girls? Everybody finished and ready to go home? Because if you aren't, there's no reason for you to be standing around gawking."

And that wasn't like him. He was cooler than that.

The other three techs exchanged glances and went back to work, muttering.

Reice forced himself to move away from the sergeant behind him without looking back, as if he were certain he'd settled the dispute and that order was prevailing here. He wasn't. Every muscle in his back was crawling, as if he expected the sergeant to jump on him from behind any minute.

They'd been at this too long, was all. It was spooky out here, was all. It was that damned Ball, that was what it was.

Reice knew it, but couldn't have proved it if his life had depended on it.

He walked over to the MMU bay and got his helmet and gloves from the rack. Without a backward look he said, "I'll be outside, examining the exterior for any unusual evidence. You've got another hour here before we leave. Make sure that there's nothing left undone when that hour's up."

And he clamped his helmet down over his head, half turning it viciously to seal off anything anyone might have said.

Any retort. Any wisecrack. What the hell was happening to
discipline up here? What was happening to Reice's leadership
abilities, that he was worried about controlling four lower-
echelon types who made their living inside yellow-tape barri-
ers that said CONSEC INVESTIGATION—DO NOT CROSS?

This team should have been running perfectly. They worked
together all the time. Yet they were an hour behind schedule,
and Reice knew it. And they were all as prickly as he was.

What was the goddamned problem, anyhow?

He mated his gloves in the lock while it cycled. *Sloppy
procedure. Dangerous.* If the lock depressurized before the
suit and gloves were sealed, Reice would be sorry.

He beat the red light by a couple of heartbeats, and the
lock slid open. At first he could see only the stars, and the
steady light that was Threshold in the distance.

You could always find home. It was comforting. He pulled
the joystick pad of his MMU down into his palm and tested
it before he stepped off onto the scaffolding. No use taking
a single unnecessary chance.

Belatedly, he went through the rest of his security procedures: checking his life-support, his coms, making sure he had
a link to the *Blue Tick* and to his men, still inside.

*What the hell was I thinking of, storming out here without
running standard systems checks?*

He was really losing his grip. He stepped out of the lock
so that it could close and slid a step, free-flying, before his
computer-assisted boot soles found the right intensity and his
trajectory brought him close enough that his soles and the
scaffolding made contact.

Sloppy. He knew better than to walk in space the way he
walked in gravity. He knew better than to come bounding out
of a fifth-force well, as if he didn't expect microgravity on the
far side.

His stomach flipped, and settled when he was firmly standing on the strutwork. He had his MMU. He could have jetted back, safe and sound, from any error.

He started to rub his eyes and hit himself in the faceplate. *Damn, I'm disoriented.* He ought to go back to the *Tick* and wait, carefully and quietly, for the rest of his team to come aboard.

Before he hurt himself. Before he screwed up where somebody else could see.

Reice headed carefully along the scaffolding toward the *Blue Tick*, watching his feet. Then, when he was almost to his ship's air lock, he looked up, toward the Ball.

It loomed behind the station as if it were a planet, beyond a ship in orbit.

Pink. Blue. Lavender. Gold. Ripples ran over the sphere, tides of color. Once. Twice. Three times.

It seemed to spark. Sparks flew. Little sparks that grew. Grew large. Grew in substance. Grew in number.

Reice's mouth opened wide. Inside his helmet he could hear his deep, raspy breathing.

This was the damnedest hallucination yet.

Or was it?

Reice said, "Reice to *Blue Tick*. Patch me to Remson's office. And to ConSec HQ, simultaneously. Secure lines."

As he waited for the com patch to be completed, he kept blinking his eyes.

But the sparks he'd seen didn't go away. They didn't get any smaller. In fact they were getting larger. And they weren't just sparks anymore.

The sparks that had seemed to come out of the Ball hadn't come out of the Ball—couldn't have, Reice reasoned dully, with the part of his mind struggling to hold itself aloof from the chemical tide of fear sweeping through his body. His pharmakit was struggling to normalize his reactions, and his mouth alternately tasted of peppermint, eggs, iron, and copper as his suit tried to bring his blood chemistries to within normal limits by injecting drugs into him via his wrist cuff.

Maybe the fear would go away. Maybe his suit-management systems could keep him from peeing himself, but nothing was going to make those sparks go away.

They weren't sparks anymore. They were ships.

One. Two. Three alien ships. Not spheres. Teardrops.

The sparks he'd seen were some sort of exhaust plumes, because the ships were braking.

They were coming around the sphere and parking.

Reice looked up.

The huge belly of one of those ships was going to park right over him. The three ships were taking up positions around the Ball.

And they were like no ships Reice had ever seen. Nobody human had ships of that design. No UNE ships had coruscating hulls. No UNE ships could have maneuvered the way these had.

They had seemed to come out of the sphere, but of course they hadn't. They'd come around it. They must have.

Reice said, "Emergency. Emergency alert." Very flat. Very crisp. *God, let me not be crazy.* "ConSec Lieutenant Reice, EVA from *Blue Tick*, reporting three alien spacecraft at the Ball site. Repeat: three alien spacecraft of unusual design. Parking here. I'm going into my ship if I can, to await further orders. I'll leave this channel open."

Could anybody hear him? He couldn't tell. He tap-scrolled through his com parameters, afraid to voice-command his heads-up.

Everything seemed okay. But Reice needed to be assured that his transmission had been received. Or at least that what he thought he saw was real. He moved very slowly toward the lock of his spacecraft.

No need to let them know they'd scared him. No need to spook them, whoever they were. No need to have them think he was running for cover or looking to make some aggressive move.

As he reached his ship's hull and slapped its lock open, he

tried to contact the team in the science station: "Anybody read me in there?"

Silence.

Oh, shit. If his coms were jammed, then was it by accident or on purpose? An aggressive act by the huge ship over his head? Or just some weird glitch at the worst possible moment?

Had he overloaded his own systems somehow, looking for self-tests and long-distance comlinks on open channels while he was trying to contact the science station?

He dumped the long-distance link and tried again: "Anybody home in there? If you read me, get out here. Now. Repeat, evacuate science station. Return to spacecraft. Departure imminent."

He wasn't sure if departure was imminent, but he wanted it to be. He wanted somebody to tell him to get the hell out of here.

So he tried to get somebody to tell him that, not waiting for an answer from the science station.

"ConSec, this is Reice. We need reinforcements out here, somebody to watch what's happening out here. I want to come in with my data. Or I want to dump it now. Please indicate if you copy."

He wasn't going to beg.

He was inside the *Blue Tick*. The lock closed behind him, shutting out the suddenly hostile space around him.

In his mind's eye he could still see that huge, teardrop-shaped ship, gliding over the *Blue Tick*. He wanted to go to the bathroom.

The inner lock opened. His ship looked fine. Nothing appeared to be malfunctioning. Her lights were on. Her electronics were reading the way they should. His flight deck showed no sign of attempted—or successful—jamming.

Without taking off his helmet he dropped into his command seat and tried to contact ConSec again, this time using the ship's system.

And a voice said, "What's going on out there, Reice? Haven't you heard a thing we've said?"

Reice nearly babbled with relief. He said, "Get me Remson in Mickey Croft's office, ConSec Control. There's three ships out here that aren't like anything I've ever seen before. And I don't think anybody else has, either."

CHAPTER 8

$\triangledown$

On Your Watch

Mickey Croft, Threshold's Secretary General, couldn't believe his luck: He had Richard Cummings, Jr., on his ass, demanding an investigation into the disappearance of his son and heir; he had the mysterious Ball parked at Spacedock Seven, which clearly had something to do with the disappearance of Cummings's NAMECorp freighter, his son, and his son's Muslim girlfriend. And to top it off, now he was about to become the first contact ambassador to a whole new race.

And not just any race. A race that brought an armada with it when it stopped by to say hello.

Well, it was Monday, so what could you expect?

Croft unwound his long, lanky frame from his chair at the Secretary General's desk and walked over to his window. He was a privileged person. He could glimpse the sea of stars outside, if he looked out and up. The stars twinkling there didn't look very different, considering that Reice's news had caused those stars to shift in their courses.

The human race had never made contact with an alien spacefaring race before. If "spacefaring" in this case meant "superior," Croft hadn't the faintest idea how humankind was going to handle the news.

Croft left the window and began to pace around his desk.

He'd worn a track in his carpet over the years. If he could have, he'd have left this office now. He'd be on his way out there, to the Ball site, to see the ships. But he couldn't just pick up and leave. He had to prepare. He had other responsibilities.

But he had none so pressing. Croft hit his desk com and said, "Get me Remson, Mr. Dodd. Get me Riva Lowe. I need them both as soon as possible."

He didn't wait for young, fat-faced Dodd to acknowledge his orders.

Throughout its adventures among the stars, nothing had occurred to shake humanity's image of itself as God's most evolved and beloved creation. Everywhere humanity had gone the species it had found had been less evolved, less artifactual, less mechanically inclined. If man had crushed any brilliant civilizations of nonartifactual Einsteins the size of bacteria underfoot, he'd never noticed.

Some of UNE's member states still purported to long for a contact with another "intelligent" race—with a race from whom it could learn, or at least with whom it could share the study of the universe's wonders.

What the hell was Croft going to do about Cummings, in the midst of all of this?

He stopped before a holographic view of Earth's Grand Canyon and stared into the canyon's depths. Richard Cummings wanted to take Riva Lowe and a few others, including Croft himself, to Earth. This magnanimous gesture was part bribe, part show of power. A few minutes ago Croft's participation would have been inappropriate.

Now, it might be necessary. The last thing Croft needed was Cummings, Jr., trying to cut some trade deal with this alien culture before Croft had a chance to ascertain who, and what, humanity was about to deal with.

Mickey Croft had never wanted to be the man who put mankind's professed longing for company to the test. UNE held uneasy sway over its member states. The Cummings boy and the Medinan girl, Dini Forat, had discovered that when they'd fallen in love and found themselves sentenced to death by Muslim law.

If Reice was right, and those three ships now confirmed to be out there really were alien ships, the UNE was in for one hell of a shock.

"Riva Lowe on the line, sir," said Dodd's voice from Croft's desktop com.

Croft nearly lunged to take the call. "Riva, tell Cummings you'll be glad to accompany him. Get going as soon as you possibly can. Don't take no for an answer."

"Ah . . ." The tiny face of Riva Lowe blinked up from his desk communicator in surprise. "I see. I understand, sir. Shall I take South with us then, as we discussed?"

"South?" For a moment Croft couldn't imagine what South, North, East, or West had to do with getting Cummings out of Threshold and back to Earth, where he'd be sheltered from news and too far away to interfere. Then he remembered the Relic pilot. "Lord, Riva, I don't know. Do as you wish, where he's concerned."

The little face frowned at him. Riva Lowe's slightly Oriental eyes gleamed with their most inscrutable look. She said, "What I wish is to take South out to the Ball site. I want him to see what's there. I haven't had time to update you, Mickey, but the Scavenger predicted all this. . . ."

"Don't get specific, even on this line. Fine. Do as you wish. You're saying you think the Artifact Task Force members may be uniquely qualified, I know. But I've got to get Cummings away before he hears."

"Too late for that. However, I think he'll go to Earth anyhow. If you'll trust me, Mickey, I'm sure I can help."

A fine woman. Too smart, but a fine woman. "I can use all the help I can get, Riva. As Customs Director, I realize you should be on hand for . . . whatever this turns out to be."

The little face grinned. "Yes, sir. I certainly should. So I'll get Mr. Cummings thinking about packing and itineraries, and make sure he can't go where he's not wanted. Then I'll see you out there—at the site."

"Fine. I'll be looking forward to it." Croft gave Riva Lowe his most professionally warm smile and switched off.

"At the site." Already, this extraordinary occurrence had taken on its inevitable cloak of bureaucratic understatement.

"At the site." At the site of mankind's first historic meeting with an alien spacefaring culture.

Croft tried to think of what he'd say. Without realizing it he'd begun to pace again, and he paced until Remson came quietly into his office without knocking.

Vince Remson was a big, Slavic man with jutting features and a nimble intelligence. He was, despite various titles, chief advisor to Croft and in charge of Secretariat security.

"So, Vince, what do you think?"

"I think we're almost ready to take a trip out to the science station, Mickey." Remson flashed white teeth. He was as alert as a hunting dog, and clearly on the scent.

"I don't know that I'm qualified for this, Vince," Croft said, when he'd stopped pacing and turned to face the other man.

"Nobody is, sir," Remson said softly.

Somehow that simple truth made Croft feel much better, much stronger, much more competent.

"So we'll be blazing a trail together, eh?" Remson was the closest thing that Croft had to a confidant. In the Secretary General's position, even a single friend was rare.

But Croft had gotten here not entirely on his inherited money or his excellent education or his carefully cultivated manners or his inherent charisma. He had gotten here, as much as anything, by luck.

In his younger days Mickey Croft had been fond of saying that it didn't matter how good you were, if you weren't lucky.

Croft's luck was about to be tested as it had never been tested before.

The Secretary General of Threshold looked at his assistant and said, "Vince, if they're unfriendly, I'm not going to invite them into Threshold. I just want you to know."

"And if they insist on coming anyway?" said Remson, with a raised, pale eyebrow.

"Then we will do our best to protect ourselves. So you should call up SpaceCom—whatever reserves you can without causing a panic or tipping our hand."

Remson's pale eyes closed and then fixed steadily on Croft once more. "Mickey, let's assume that we can handle this. Whatever it is. I'm not saying I've been preparing for an alien invasion all my life, but I am saying that three ships hardly constitute an armed incursion. They're not encircling Threshold, after all. They parked out there at Spacedock Seven. I'd like to interpret that as an attempt on their part to obey the local customs and be polite."

"I wonder how much they know about us," Croft mused, half to himself.

"We can't very well bring a translator fluent in an unknown language. I can set up a language-analysis program on your ship, but that's it. So let's hope they know something. Enough that a first historic contact won't be one in which you go down in the history books as saying, 'Me, Croft. You, little green guy, what do you call yourself?' "

Croft smiled wanly. "You think perhaps they're prepared for us?"

"That Ball's been there a while. I reran Reice's reports. He thought they came out of the Ball, at first. Then he said they came out from behind it. They're surely not parking there by happenstance. We have Spacedocks One through Six, as well. So either the Ball is theirs, and they'd like it back, or—"

"Or," Croft interrupted, "they commonly send their spheres out first as greeting cards. Is that what you're getting at?"

"Calling cards, maybe. But yes, that's the way I read it. Of course, I could be wrong. I've been wrong before."

"When was that, Vince? Refresh me. I forget when you last indulged in the sin of human error."

Remson flushed. "I let the Forat girl and the Cummings boy get away."

"That's not over yet," Mickey promised his assistant, and then said, "I wonder what I should take with me. I mean, one wants a briefcase, at least, so that one appears prepared. But what shall I put in it?"

"Pictures," Remson quipped, and the two of them started trying in earnest to decide just what sort of artifacts would be appropriate when you were going out to greet so unexpected a flotilla of guests.

Hours later, aboard the UNE flagship, the *George Washington*, and accompanied by an honor guard of armed cruisers that Remson had insisted were there only as part of the space-borne pomp and circumstance, Croft was increasingly nervous about his level of preparedness for this meeting.

He kept trying to envision what he'd say when he met who-ever was inside the teardrop-shaped ships with the magnificent coruscating hulls.

Reice had sent back video from the *Blue Tick* and Remson had put it through every possible analysis. Not all of Remson's work, nor all of Threshold's computing power or human brainpower, had been able to shed any light on the possible encounter to come.

ConSec Lieutenant Reice had been ordered not to contact the ships directly, or do anything more than send back a con-stant feed of reports.

So Mickey didn't know, as he paced around his stateroom, paneled with simulated rosewood, what he would say or what he would do when he stood face-to-face with the aliens.

Would they be short, green, and have tentacles instead of arms? If they were, how did one shake hands? Was a particu-lar tentacle the greeting tentacle?

If they were ovoid, red, and ten-eyed, how could he look them straight in the eye?

If they had no heads and hence no faces, how could he be sure that his facial expressions were being properly read and understood?

If they were big worms with no front end, how could he be sure he didn't offend by talking to the wrong end?

If they were giant croissants floating in huge tanks of liquid, how could he make himself understood at all?

Perhaps they were gaseous. Perhaps they were energy creatures, providing physical craft only because humans would need physical evidence and a physical focal point, a nexus at which to direct dialogue.

But no, they wouldn't be. Would they? One only created a spacecraft out of hard material if one needed a hard enclosure for life-support and was capable of manipulating hard substances. Assuming, of course, that whatever was in the teardrops had created them, not moved into them after they were vacated by some other species, the way hermit crabs moved into seashells.

But even hermit crabs had protective skeletons.

So they would have some sort of skeleton. They would have some requirement for ships in which to travel, for enclosing life-support. They would have come up from the primordial slime, along their own evolutionary chain, and learned to make artifacts and manipulate physics.

Otherwise there would be no ships out there. The ships were proof of a common heritage—the heritage of the toolmaker.

Having found this point of contact, this clear correspondence of nature, Croft finally sank down on his stateroom couch.

Reason is the only thing a person can count upon in a crisis, yet it is one of the most difficult and elusive weapons to bring to bear when emotions run high.

Between now and the moment when he first stepped out onto the scaffolding of the science station, hand outstretched in a time-honored gesture of friendship, Mickey Croft must be sure that reason, and not emotion, guided his actions.

For the sake of humanity, he must be sure of that.

CHAPTER 9

▽

Hot Date

South, sitting on his bunk in *STARBIRD*, looked blankly at the machine wedged into the narrow space between his galley and the head. He didn't know why, but he'd assumed the "therapist" would be human.

The AIP/PDE (Artifically Intelligent Preprogrammed/ Pilotry Digital Evaluation) Therapist before him was about as far from that as you could get. Birdy must think this was really funny. South's AI was monitoring everything that went on back here, where, along with sleeping quarters, head, and galley, there was a redundant astrogation console.

The digital therapist had South flying *STARBIRD* around in circles while it monitored his reactions to various stimuli, including simulated control and power failures it was tossing into his aft control suite. Meanwhile, up front, Birdy had the real data and was making sure that *STARBIRD* went exactly where she was supposed to go.

This hardwired simulation of a therapist was giving South a headache, as well as a hard time. It seemed to want to know what he'd do if he was sure he had only moments to live—as if that were some kind of extraordinary state. South, who'd been in that state throughout his lengthy test flight to and from X-3, hadn't yet decided if living in Threshold's continuum was better than making a suicide run for parts unknown.

So no wonder the digital therapist couldn't get physiology readings from South that varied one hell of a lot from his baseline.

The machine was a cube with a belt of meters across it and a monitor above the meters. It had stereo speakers on each side of the monitor, and on top of that was a goose-necked videocam that followed him whenever he moved. When the therapist chose, it could be a real pain in the ass.

As a matter of fact, maybe that was all it could choose to be.

Right now it wanted to know about alien life forms. How he felt about them, how he reacted to the thought of close proximity to them, and how he would deal with one that threatened him.

He considered reaching over and punching it in the speaker grille, but that was no way to get into Consolidated Space Command, the Threshold version of U.S. Space Command. Maybe it was trying to prepare him for this trip to Earth that Riva Lowe was using to blackmail South into submission.

He said, "Aliens, huh? Well, if you're talkin' about the cute little fuzzy kind, well, you can sleep with 'em, or on 'em. If you're talkin' about the big, ugly, scaly kind, you can fry 'em, or broil 'em, but of course the best is to microwave 'em. And then there's the purely arrogant, more-human-than-thou kind, with citizenship and rights under law: those I'd treat as if they weren't any more alien than the rest of Threshold's population."

The therapist burped. Or maybe it hiccuped. Then it said, "How would you behave if you encountered an uncataloged alien life-form in need of aid?"

The thing had no sense of humor. "I'd do my best to help it, as long as it wasn't dangerous or inimical, and then I'd try to see that it got cataloged, studied, and whatever else the law recommends." He hadn't really been ready for this test.

He hadn't read all he should of the "alien encounter" handbook. When Riva Lowe had said "physical and psychological therapy" he'd thought she meant some nice lady who'd help him deal with his dreams, or reach peak physical condition circa the day before his experimental flyby.

He hadn't thought she meant that some machine would come aboard to analyze his physiological reactions to stimuli and, from that, determine if South was level enough to be considered for a job as a test pilot or a pilot of a heavy-weapons patrol spacecraft.

But that was what this machine was doing. Threshold didn't want any crazies flying birds with destructive hardware under discretionary control. He should have realized it. He hadn't. He wasn't used to thinking like a twenty-fifth-century citizen.

South was afraid he was failing and the machine knew it.

It burbled, "Commander South, you're doing fine. Let us continue with a scenario in which you find yourself interviewing a member of a bioengineered race who claims to have had his civil rights violated by members of a human colony."

Fuck. I'm not up to this.

South shot to his feet, hitting the therapist in the meters with his knees. All the meters redlined and the machine said in a fluttery voice: "Please resume your seat. Session is not over."

The hell it wasn't.

But South sat back down. Patience clearly was a desirable trait in today's test pilots. He said, "Look, have you got the right program? I thought you were here to get me ready to go to Earth with Riva Lowe's party."

It wasn't a question, but the videocam ratcheted on its stalk to face him. The therapist's voice said, "Earth is a big place, with open skies and very few conveniences. Does rusticity bother you?"

"Hell, no."

"Do you suffer from agoraphobia?"

"Agorawhat?"

"Fear of open spaces."

He suffered from a dislike of enclosed spaces, if anything. He said, "I used to race bikes in the desert, okay?"

"Do you suffer from a fear of open spaces?"

You had to give this therapist direct answers. He wished he'd asked Lowe what she meant before he'd said yes. "No."

"Do you—"

The therapist stopped in mid-query. Its videocam face gyrated wildly. Its meters peaked, then all fell to the left, inactive. It turned itself off.

The rest of the lights in his bunk went down, too.

"Birdy?" South could hear his own fear. This was probably another one of the therapist's spot tests. But he couldn't hear his life-support system. You got used to the soft whirring. The sudden absence of the sound usually made by air blowing through the duct above his head was deafening.

The lights came back on. The therapist's metering band pinned and zeroed, like a bunch of saluting soldiers.

Beyond the therapist, on the control monitor in his redundant system, South's message light was blinking.

The digital therapist resumed as if there'd been no interruption: "Do you have any fear of the unknown?"

But the question sounded strange.

"Of course. Everybody does. Human nature. But I like it more than I fear it. It excites me. I'm the explorer type." What did he have to do to convince this thing he was for real, pull out his Dan'l Boon coonskin cap?

The therapist was implacable. "In the event that you were part of a contact party meeting uncataloged aliens, how would you recommend that party initiate dialogue?"

"Do I look like a diplomat to you?"

"Please answer the question, Commander South."

"In a minute. I got a message light blinking."

The therapist started blinking itself: a green standby light came on under its monitor.

"Birdy," he asked his AI, "what's the message?"

And then he couldn't believe his ears.

"Replay, Birdy," he said, forgetting the digital therapist entirely.

But the therapist hadn't forgotten him. As Riva Lowe's words rang in South's ears for the second time, the therapist's meters shivered and its video camera zoomed in on him with a hum that made him want to smack its intrusive lens out of his face and off its mounting.

Riva Lowe's voice was far too calm and reassuring, considering the content of the message: "Commander South, this is Director Lowe. We have three unidentified alien ships at Spacedock Seven. They seem to be of the same manufacture as the sphere. Please call me at your earliest convenience. We'd like your input on this matter." And she gave call signs.

South brushed unseeingly past the digital therapist, bumping its extended videocam with his shoulder, on the way to his flight deck.

Screw the infernal thing. The Threshold brass had known all about this alien contact—known before he had. Otherwise, how come all the "What if you met an alien" questions? They'd worked up some kind of method of vetting his fitness through that damned machine, and he hadn't had an inkling until they'd wanted him to.

Until they'd decided he wouldn't start frothing at the mouth if they told him what was happening out there.

He was so angry he could feel his pulse in his eyeballs. And if he hadn't passed the digital therapist's tests, then what? Would they have shut him off? Fired him from the Ball project? Or just kept him tooling around in circles out here, with only Birdy and the digital therapist for company, until the aliens were gone or until everybody knew what was going on out there at Spacedock Seven, because something had happened out there so explosive that not even the Threshold bureaucracy could keep it quiet?

When he reached his flight deck he threw himself into his command couch and said, "Birdy, Riva Lowe; if she's not at the message call signs, then find her."

Birdy was good at Threshold comlinks. Better than he was. He didn't even try to keep up with the search the AI made. "Just flash her location on screen, coordinates and all, when you find her. I want to see what's going on wherever she is."

He considered putting his helmet on his head so that, when he got her on his com, all she'd see was the polarized screen of his visor—from outside.

But he didn't. He sat with it between his knees and waited, watching his flight deck search near space for the director and the ship she was traveling in.

But traveling wasn't what she was doing, according to Birdy.

His main astrogation monitor put up a split screen of Spacedock Seven in near real-time and a grid showing the science station, the Ball, and all nearby ships, parked and in traffic lanes. Each ship had beneath it a name, a designator, and a status report.

Riva Lowe was on the Secretary General's flagship, the *George Washington*, and the *Washington* was parked, with an escort flotilla, near the Ball.

Between the *Washington* and the Ball were nine armed TTT vessels of varying displacement, including Reice's cruiser, *Blue Tick*.

It was a damned Sunday picnic out there.

Except that about forty-two feet, six inches northeast of the ball were three teardrop shapes that Birdy couldn't identify, which meant that no Threshold AI could identify them either.

The three teardrops on his schematic were hovering over identifying designators, just like the TTT ships; only these designators said UFO-1; UFO-2; UFO-3.

Some days it just didn't pay to get out of your bunk.

When Riva Lowe answered Birdy's page, she said, "South, I've been waiting for you to call."

He nearly snarled at the tiny face displayed on his flight-deck com screen: "I bet. Waiting until that digital babysitter of yours approved me as psychologically ready to get the big news."

"Commander South, this is no time for recriminations."

"What's it time for?"

"It's time for you to get out here, unless you have some pertinent objection. According to your psych evaluation you're capable of continuing your duties as part of our Alien Artifact Working Group, despite recent developments."

"Or maybe because of them," he muttered. At least he wasn't crazy. He could tell anybody his dreams now, and nobody would think he was crazy.

"What did you say?"

"Never mind." He could even talk about his memories to somebody besides psychiatrists and intelligence officers—if he wanted to. But seeing those ships, he wasn't sure he wanted to. Still, she had a right to know. She was his director, after all. "The ships I . . . saw . . . weren't that shape. They were like the Ball," he told her. "So I'm no expert on those . . . whatever they are."

"And you think we are? Do you want a piece of this or don't you, Commander?"

He'd never get used to being called "commander." He said, "Yeah. Why not? When do you want me out there?"

"As soon as you can."

"I'll drop off this digital pain-in-the-arse and be out by, say, twenty-two hundred hours, if that's soon enough."

"Bring the psych-evaluator with you. We might need it. And I don't want to wait too long. Maybe you'll have an idea or two we can use."

"Anything you say." The helmet between South's knees slipped because his knees weren't gripping it hard enough. He reached over to roll it up into his lap. It felt comforting, there under his arm. He could put it on and declutter the whole universe into whatever number of data streams he felt ready to handle. But he didn't. "They . . . they didn't . . . ask for me, did they?"

Christ, that sounded dumb. Still, if he didn't ask he'd be worried all the way out there.

At least Lowe didn't smile or laugh. She said, "No, they

haven't asked for anybody—or anything. Maybe there's nobody in those . . . shapes. We're assuming they're vehicles because they look to us like vehicles. For all we know the sphere was pregnant and reproduced while Reice watched."

"Reice. ConSec Lieutenant Reice?"

"He took the log of their . . . arrival. We haven't had any contact with any purported intelligence that may be in or directing them. They just . . . parked."

South's eyes kept straying to his near real-time display. Teardrops of color, parked near the Ball. "I hope you don't think I have the magic formula, or a key to those things in my pocket," he sighed. "Cause I don't. Just some weird feelings and a few half-remembered impressions."

They had his impressions, his dreams, his memories, his whole flyby transcript. He couldn't pretend they didn't. But he didn't want to go out there. And he couldn't tell her that.

She said, "We know. But Keebler predicted this, and you've had many of the same reactions to the Ball that he had."

"Predicted it? When?"

"When he came to, in custody. While we had him under observation."

"Had?"

"We released him. Had to. Salvagers' Guild sent lawyers. We couldn't hold him longer without formal charges. If we'd pressed charges they would have raised holy hell publicly, immediately, and brought our confiscation of the Ball into question." Lowe shrugged. "Unfortunately, where the Ball is concerned, we're allergic to lawyers. So you're our expert on close encounters. Just get out here, South, will you? I can make it a direct order."

"I didn't realize you hadn't," he said softly. "I'm on my way. South, out."

Once he got off-line with her he tried to get Birdy to connect him to Croft. So Keebler was free. Somehow the news eased a weight South hadn't realized was so heavy on his shoulders. *Poor crazy bastard.*

Crazy like a fox. Keebler had just jousted the Threshold windmill and walked away, victorious, after terrorizing innocent civilians. South knew the old guy. This wasn't the end of Keebler's attempts to regain ownership of the Ball. Riva Lowe was underestimating Keebler.

But then Lowe hadn't taken Keebler out to the Ball, the way South had. She'd ordered South to do it, to keep them both out of the way. South had an impulse to tell Mickey Croft, the Secretary General, about what had happened with the black box that Sling had made for Keebler. He'd never felt the need to do it before.

South had pacewalked with that black box, right up to the Ball, the way Keebler had told him. And the Ball had opened up for South. Keebler hadn't seen it happen. South hadn't told anybody—because at the time he wasn't sure it had really happened.

He'd been afraid nobody would believe him. He'd had no proof, no record of the Ball's opening up for the black box that way. But they'd believe him now. Maybe the Secretary General should know that the Ball had done that, before anybody went out to meet with anybody—or anything.

But South couldn't get to Croft. He didn't have the clout. He did get to Remson, and the pale blond man listened without a word to South telling him that Keebler had found a way to get into the Ball. "But Keebler doesn't know it. I didn't tell him. I didn't tell anybody. I . . . couldn't."

"Don't be so sure Keebler doesn't know it, South. And don't worry about it. Maybe we should ask Keebler to come out here too."

"Christ, that crazy old coot? He'll blow this thing sky—"

"Don't worry, I said. We'll see if we can recreate the phenomenon, once you're on-site." Remson had a predator's smile, and he shined it at South like a beacon.

South couldn't have said no to Remson if Remson had asked South to go up to the Ball and let himself in.

But Remson wasn't asking that.

Not yet, at least.

Remson just wanted South to act like nothing was wrong and go out there and be a good boy and follow orders. Okay. He could do that. He had the digital therapist with him, and the digital therapist had pronounced South fit for this duty.

It bothered the hell out of South that they'd used the digital therapist to vet him for this mission, but what could you do? He was living in a different culture, with different rules.

They'd waited for that damned machine to decide if South could be trusted, before they risked bringing him on board. So they weren't taking any risks, not with those three giant, polychromatic teardrops hovering over the science station like Armageddon. They sure weren't going to risk having Keebler shoot off his big mouth.

He had to trust that Remson knew what he was doing.

He had to trust that the digital therapist was right, too: it thought South, Joseph, Commander, TTT Customs, was capable of performing the duties about to be asked of him.

So he must be capable.

He wanted to believe that. He really did. But all the bad dreams in the universe had suddenly come to life on his monitors and he wasn't believing in much else, right now, except the foreboding that made him so clumsy he could barely fit his helmet on his head.

When he got his suit sealed he said to Birdy, from behind the safety of his visor, "Okay, let's go to the party, Birdy."

He hoped it wasn't going to be a surprise party. South hated surprises.

Especially when the joke might be on the whole human race.

CHAPTER 10

▽

Crazy Old Coot

Vince Remson commandeered one of the work stations in the flagship's middeck and set about finding Keebler.

Or trying to find Keebler. Not all Remson's clout or all his ingenuity could turn up the Scavenger. After an hour of running up electronic blind alleys and dead-end streets, he sat back in his chair and slid it sideways along its track until he sat before the in-ship secure communications grid. The flagship was huge. The system in front of him wasn't simple. Nothing about this venture was simple, he was beginning to think.

Remson had his finger on the touch-sensitive screen that would connect him to Mickey's stateroom, but then he thought better of it.

He slid back the way he'd come, pulled his headset back up over his ears, and talked into the throatpad mike: "Dodd, do we have anything on a black box that Keebler and South took on the first Ball EVA?"

Dodd's search came up negative.

Remson got off-line and stared blankly at the console in front of him. He had that slightly crawly, slightly unsettled feeling that always overcame him when he'd discovered an error. The feeling would go away when he knew just what kind of error, but now it was still a feeling of something unspecifiable being wrong.

Vince hated that feeling more than any other.

How the hell was he going to find the Scavenger from here, if the Scavenger didn't want to be found? And was he right to be spending so much time on this, when they were parked starboard of the biggest potential problem ever to confront the Trust Territory?

He got up and left the com deck. This was a big ship. It was, in fact, a floating city. You could walk down its corridors with your arms spread wide and not graze the walls on either side. You could do almost anything here that you could do on Threshold—except find Keebler.

Damn, was it really that important?

Remson scratched his right arm, then his left. The feeling of irritation got no better. Rationally, if he was going to worry about anything peripheral, he should be worrying about NAMECorp's CEO, Richard Cummings, Jr.

But what the Relic pilot had said kept haunting him. Why hadn't they uncovered this matter of the black box previously? Or had they, and underestimated the value of the information?

He turned in the corridor and retraced his steps.

At the same com console, he called up the entire Ball file and searched for black box entries. He found seven, by different investigating authorities, including Reice.

So they'd just underestimated it. Now Remson might be overestimating it. But he trusted his gut. They'd underestimated it because South hadn't bothered to tell any of the investigators, including Reice, that he'd thought the box had worked.

Of course nobody at the time—or later—had been putting much stock in what the Relic pilot had to say. That was changing now.

Vince Remson glared at the screen and blanked it. He mustn't overreact now, simply because he was sure they'd underreacted in the past.

He tapped three keys, and his work station isolated itself from the others around it with a privacy field that looked as if it were made of silver gravel floating in midair. Couldn't be too careful.

In his cylindrical privacy field, Remson contacted his office on Threshold. "I want you to find the Scavenger. I don't care what it takes. Cut a deal with his lawyers, if you have to. He may have a black box built for him by an aftermarketeer named Sling, from the Loader Zone. I don't have more detail. If the Scavenger has the box, get it from him. If he doesn't, get the aftermarketeer to make another one, exact duplicate. And get it out here, fast. You can bring the Scavenger out if he's got the box, but I want the box. I don't want you to confiscate the Scavenger's property to get hold of it, though. Is that clear?"

Remson's staff was well trained. They'd do the best they could.

He hoped it would be good enough.

Remson dumped the privacy field and wiped all record of his transmission back to Threshold. There were times when security was the only rule. *What if South was right?*

What difference did it really make?

Vince Remson still had that itchy feeling as he headed for Mickey's stateroom. Croft ought to know about this.

But when he got there Croft was hunched over his desk, his head on one arm, free hand over his eyes, in the middle of a voice-only conversation with Cummings, Jr. It wasn't going well, from Mickey's body language.

Remson tiptoed out again. If Richard the Second had been a reasonable man, you might have asked him to donate his skills and resources to this effort. But Cummings wasn't a reasonable man. Nor a trustworthy one.

Vince Remson wouldn't have had Mickey's job for all the world.

He wandered around the decks until he found the observation lounge. It was crowded with off-duty folk. Normally most of these crewmen would have been at the bar, Remson knew, from other missions aboard the *Washington*.

But not this time.

Nearly two dozen people were standing around the observation port, a twenty-foot window onto real-time space.

And in that window, framed by the solidity of the ship's hull, was the Ball.

The Ball looked as if it were rising over the science station, the way the moon was rising over a mountaintop in one of Vince's Earth holographs. Beside the Ball, one of the teardrops was facing them head-on. In the foreground, you could see the curving underbelly of another. The third was out of sight.

A few people sipped beers. Most were just staring. Nobody was talking. Lute music from some forgotten century played in the background, lonely and languid, from an age when every impulse of the human mind had been worth noticing.

It had been a long time since mankind's shared consciousness was placid enough to produce such music. Listening to ancient music always made Remson wonder about the circumstances in which it had been created, the setting for which it had been appropriate.

This music sounded as if it should be played in a canopied boat gliding down a calm river toward a group of noble friends picnicking under a pavilion, with retainers standing by to attend to their whims.

It didn't belong in the same universe with an imminent invasion from the depths of space. It was music from a time when man was newly preeminent, and proud of it, when his battle with nature on Earth was just beginning to go well. It was music from a time when the control of hunger and cold and heat and pestilence was a triumph still out of reach, when any sound made was a sound that wafted up to heaven and God's ears.

In those days people had thought that beyond the clouds was a realm of angels and cherubs and spirits and glory man could not know in his physical form. All of Vince Remson's life had been spent in a culture which knew for sure that preeminent power was a matter of physics, that man was either God's instrument in the cosmos or the finest expression of the ordering principle of the universe.

By our power, we had been validated. By our triumph over all the forces of nature, we had become supreme. We were unchallenged in the universe.

Until now.

Vince Remson found himself standing just behind a lieutenant in a crisp uniform. The lieutenant felt Remson's gaze and looked over his shoulder.

"Sir. Nice to see you. We were just . . . looking."

"Me, too," Remson said. Now people were looking at him. The mood was broken. The sense of being one with this group of wondering souls, half-filled with apprehension and half with hope, evaporated.

The lieutenant was busy making sure Remson understood that no one here was idling away time meant to be spent otherwise.

"Everybody's taken to coming up here, to acclimate themselves to the situation."

"And what do you think the situation is, Lieutenant?" Remson asked.

The officer squared his shoulders. "Sir, I think we have a great opportunity here, but we've got to be on our guard. We're prepared for any eventuality, of course."

You couldn't argue with the pragmatic understatement on the man's lips or the hard, ready gleam in his eye.

Remson said softly, "I'm sure the Secretary General will be glad to hear that the morale of the ship is high," and extricated himself. He was making them uncomfortable. The lieutenant would retell the story of his encounter with the Assistant Secretary General for the rest of his days, inane as Remson's words had been.

Remson found himself scratching his arms as he left the

observation lounge. Whatever was wrong, he hadn't solved it yet.

Otherwise he wouldn't feel as if all the hairs on his arms were waving in a nonexistent breeze.

He hoped the lieutenant was right. He hoped they were ready for this encounter with the teardrop-shaped ships from some far-off place. The ships clearly were ready for them.

CHAPTER 11

$\triangledown$

Skinning the Cat

Keebler slunk through the Loader Zone as if he were a fugitive. Nobody was chasing him through the cargo bays and bars and whorehouses of Threshold's underbelly, but somebody might be following him.

Keebler passed two camel-lipped Epsilonian whores with beads woven into the hair on their humped backs. "Maybe later, honey," he said to the one who swished her hips at him and made kissing noises. No use insulting anyone.

The Loader Zone was the only place on Threshold where a man could at least hope to lose himself. There were no false ceilings here, just bare struts hung with lights. So you could see where the surveillance cameras were, and they were only where somebody had paid to put them.

Down in the Zone, every nation had an interest in keeping things off the record. You could work here, if you were a subhuman or a bioengineered species, without the sort of red tape you needed to work up where the ceilings had holographic skies on them and everybody paid a services tax that kept out the riffraff.

The riffraff down here paid a head tax for temporary work cards that kept ConSec off their necks. Maybe you couldn't get everything in the Loader Zone, but you could breathe down here. You could get into a street fight and not end up in psych-evaluation. You could sign on to crew a ship to almost anywhere.

But Keebler was only half thinking of shipping out while he still could. He was free and he was angry, and he was going to teach these Threshold bureaucrats a thing or two.

Maybe even a thing or three. His lawyers had put the fear of litigation into those smug bastards up there. And that was just the beginning.

Keebler stopped in three bars before he found the one he wanted—the one with the aftermarketeer in it.

This bar was homey enough to have been at any good trading station, outsystem. You could get any legal want satisfied here, and a whole lot of wants that weren't exactly legal.

Keebler wanted his black box back. "Now, sonny, b'fore I decide y' tried to steal m' property . . ."

The aftermarketeer named Sling didn't turn to face Keebler. He looked up into the mirror behind the bar and shook his head so that his single earring gleamed. "What is with you guys? I don't want anything to do with you, Keebler, not anymore. Not since I found out you come complete with Con-Sec lieutenants and Customs jocks. You and South are a matched set of fools, and I'm allergic to fools."

Keebler nearly grabbed the kid and spun him on his stool. But cunning prevailed.

Keebler hopped up onto the stool beside Sling and said, "If y' weren't so damn talented, sonny, nobody'd be houndin' ye. Y' should chuck this line o' work, sonny, and come outsystem wit' me, where your cree-ay-tivity'll be 'preciated."

"Yeah?" Sling was working on a pyramid of beer glasses. He looked over at Keebler and shook his head. "There ain't enough money in the universe to get me to go across the street with you, you daffy old Scavenger."

"That's 'crazy old coot' t' you, sonny. Wanna bet?"

Sling liked to bet.

"Bet what?" said the aftermarketeer.

"Wanna bet that box ye made me did more than folks were

tellin' us it did? Wanna bet that iffen you and me went out to that Ball, say t'night, we'd see somethin' worth a fortune? Somethin' that'll make you and me the richest and famousest men in the whole universe?"

"What are we bettin'?" Sling wanted to know.

"My ship against yers."

Keebler's ship was still in quarantine, but Sling didn't need to know that. Anyway, Keebler's lawyers were going to get the ship back for him. Get everything back for him. This Threshold bureaucracy had gone too far, finally, and Keebler, according to his lawyers, was about to become richer than his wildest dreams by the mechanism of a lawsuit against the Trust Territory. Famous just came with the turf.

Sling slowly sipped his blue beer. "Lemme get this straight: You'll bet me your ship against mine that, if we go out to Spacedock Seven, it'll make me rich and famous, just like you, right?"

"That's it, sonny. God's own truth. If I win, you win. If I lose, you win. So what you got to lose?"

"What's the catch?"

"I need my black box, sonny."

"That goddamn black box is going to be the death of me. We took it apart one night. . . ."

Keebler knew better than to ask who. "Put it back t'gether, sonny. Right now. Or there's no bet."

"No problem," Sling said, sitting back. "You're sure there's nothing illegal here now, old man?"

"We'll take your ship out there," Keebler offered slyly. "How could there be anythin' wrong with that? You 'n' me, just cruisin' out toward the sponge lanes, with that ol' black box that couldn't be illegal or somebody'd have taken it away from ye by now, right?"

"I dunno . . ."

"Let me tell y' about m' ship, sonny," Keebler wheedled.

He knew he'd won. Sling was drunk enough, and Keebler had made the bet rich enough. He wanted to go see what was out there so bad he could taste it. He needed to go. He had told Sling the truth, as far as he went.

Sling might end up rich and famous. Stranger things had happened. Those aliens out there were Keebler's aliens, the way he saw it. The tranquilizers they'd given him in the psychiatric ward had made him see that there was nothing to be afraid of.

He'd been on a vector with these aliens his whole life. They'd come here to see *him*, not any of these Threshold fools. Keebler just needed to keep his mind focused on the real truths of this l'il ol' mystery.

As he saw them, those truths were these:

The Ball was a gift from the aliens.

The aliens had put it into his mind that if he towed the Ball to Threshold, he'd be rich and famous.

The aliens had never hurt him.

The aliens wouldn't hurt him.

The aliens had never lied to him.

The aliens wouldn't lie to him.

The aliens had been guiding him to this moment.

They wanted to meet him.

They'd helped him figure out what kind of box to have Sling make.

Therefore, the box would work.

Either South had lied to him, or the box just hadn't been ready to work.

The box would work.

Keebler would go out there and the aliens would greet him, in front of everybody, with open arms.

He'd be their chosen liaison with all the trading planets of the United Nations of Earth.

Rich and famous was what he was going to be.

He'd be the man that gave humankind its chance to meet a superior civilization.

No bunch of bureaucrats was going to steal his thunder.

And they were trying. They'd taken his spacecraft away. They'd tried to take his freedom away.

They wanted all the glory for themselves.

But Keebler was too canny for them.

As he lurched out of the bar beside the aftermarketeer, to pick up the black box before they shipped out for Spacedock Seven, Keebler was sure he'd outfoxed the lot of them.

When you had a superior civilization on your side, you were bound to find a way to win out in the end.

Sling kept asking Keebler, "Are you sure there isn't somethin' else you got to tell me, old man?"

And Keebler kept assuring Sling, "You know all you need to know, sonny. The mysteries o' the universe are out there waitin' fer us. You and me's gonna be the most famous team o' explorers to ever suck a mother's teat."

You just had to keep Sling well enough oiled with blue beer, and then the kid was downright reasonable.

Maybe Keebler would take Sling with him when he went off as envoy to the race from beyond the white hole.

One thing about a superior civilization was that they were going to want a superior-type human to be their guide to mankind's itchy-fingered, sneaky ways.

And Micah Keebler was going to be that guide. If he could get out there in time. If he could remember that the aliens weren't here to hurt anybody.

They were here to make Keebler—and now his sidekick, Sling—rich and famous beyond the kid's wildest dreams.

Keebler vaguely regretted that it was Sling and not the other kid, South, who was going to be with him on this historic journey.

But Sling was the one with the black box.

When Sling put the black box on his bench and ran it through a self-test, Keebler knew that everything was going to be just fine.

The box beeped and gave them a green light, and Keebler said, "Well, come on, sonny. Hurry up. Fame and fortune is awaitin'."

And Sling said, "Take it easy, old man. I'm comin'. I can't wait to win this bet."

But it was Keebler who was going to win. A little voice in his head kept telling him that in no uncertain terms.

All the riches of the stars and all the fame in the universe were about to be his. Finally.

Funny how he hadn't remembered that the aliens had been talking to him all along.

But when they reached Sling's ship and got clearance for takeoff, Keebler stopped wondering about how come the aliens hadn't made themselves clear from the beginning.

He was lucky he'd been chosen. Lucky he'd been fishing that hole when he was. Luckiest man alive.

And if his hands were shaking a little when he fastened his crash harness in the seat next to Sling's, at least the kid didn't notice.

You had to be willing to risk a little to become rich and famous. To become as rich and famous as Keebler was going to be, you had to be willing to risk a lot.

As Sling's ship shot out of its slip toward Spacedock Seven, Keebler told himself that he wasn't afraid.

Not anymore.

CHAPTER 12

$$\triangledown$$

Meet a Monster from Outer Space

Mickey Croft's head was spinning as he prepared to step aboard the alien craft—if "craft" was the word—sent to collect him.

The craft was a sphere, translucent as a soap bubble. From where Croft stood waiting, alone in the open air lock of the USS *George Washington*, the bubble was clearly empty.

The soap-bubble craft, perhaps thirty feet in diameter, glimmered with rainbows of softly colored swirls as it wafted toward the lock. Not drifted, as one would expect in space. Nor speeded, purposefully, as if on a dire mission. Wafted, as if being driven by a breath, by a zephyr. The only breath out there beyond the air lock was the breath of God.

Croft struggled to suppress the impulse to put up his gloved hands before his helmeted head to forfend the coming of the bubble.

He failed. His hands went up. He couldn't see it anymore. Ergo, so far as his senses were concerned, it wasn't there.

Then, ashamed of himself, he had to put down his hands and look again. He had to. Eyes squeezed shut, he forced his hands away from his face. Duty was calling, loudly enough to make his ears ring. He was a diplomat, wasn't he? UNE Secretary General, wasn't he?

He had to look at the bubble. Consider it. Evaluate it. And stride boldly forth to treat with whoever had sent it, the way he was expected to do. The way he was paid to do. He had to, didn't he?

Somebody had to confront the beings who'd sent the bubble, that was certain. And Mickey Croft had been cashing this check for his entire adult life. All the experience of a lifetime's diplomacy ought to have prepared him for this moment.

He forced his watering eyes open. There was the bubble-craft. Closer.

Close enough that he could see his distorted reflection sliding along its surface. The Mickey Croft reflected there looked as stretched and twisted as he felt.

The craft itself looked for all the world like a giant soap bubble that was about to bump into the *Washington*'s hull.

How the hell could anybody expect him to just walk into that thing?

But everybody did. His staff. Every single privy soul.

Maybe the bubble-craft wouldn't hold him. Maybe it would burst on contact when it met the *Washington*'s hull.

Then Mickey Croft would be safe. Temporarily. But then he'd never have a chance to see if he could just walk into the bubble-craft, the way he thought he could. He kept envisioning himself inside, standing there, without falling through into space.

The image made sense, made all the sense in the world somehow. Despite reason. He began to sweat in his suit. The suit's physiological monitoring package hummed busily, trying to cool him. He wasn't even sure where he'd gotten the idea that the bubble was a craft. But of course it was. They'd sent it for him.

They'd sent it.

So the bubble-craft wouldn't pop when it hit the *Washington*'s hull. It wouldn't disappear when he tried to step aboard—step inside. Would it?

"Mickey, are you all right?" came Remson's soft voice in his ears. It was nice to have something to listen to inside his helmet, beside his own shallow breathing and the humming of his suit's cooling system. But it wasn't nice to remember that Remson would be monitoring not only events visible in the air lock but Croft's physiopackage as well.

No secrets from his assistant, not this time. Not even how uncertain were his private reactions to this encounter with the unknown.

Mankind had no privacy anymore. You couldn't even sweat in one of these Manned Manuvering Unit space suits without everybody knowing it. Life seemed to be a contradictory set of sacrifices: You were separated from your fellows by technology that precluded the necessity of face-to-face contact or physical proximity; you were intruded upon constantly by intimate communications and the ability of everyone who needed you to get to you—and *at* you—no matter how far away you were from them.

At this moment Vince Remson was only a few yards away, behind the sealed inner air lock. But it might as well have been a light-year.

The alien message had come when the aliens had decided the time was right to send it. The contact team aboard the *Washington* hadn't precipitated it in any way. They hadn't sent a message. They hadn't blinked Morse code. They hadn't thrown a pebble at the hull of the nearest craft or sent smoke signals or a telerobotic snooper. They hadn't even bathed the alien craft in sensoring radiation. They weren't ready to do any of those yet.

They'd just been . . . watching.

Waiting, supposedly, for Joe South to arrive. Riva Lowe was sure South's presence would be helpful.

Maybe it still would, but not to Mickey Croft.

The alien ship had lased a matter-of-fact message on a UNE

hailing frequency: "SENDING GREETINGS. WISH REPRESENTA-
TIVE HUMAN. WE WILL TRANSPORT. FIRST MEETING, THESE
COORDINATES. WE WILL RETURN HUMAN AFTER ONE HOUR'S
MEETING. HUMAN SHOULD BE RANKING. ALL PROTOCOLS
OBSERVED."

They'd sent it in English, and then in Farsi, as if they talked
to UNE ships all the time.

Vince had volunteered to go.

Mickey Croft couldn't allow that, although he'd wanted to.
Farsi?

Everybody in Mickey's suite had looked around blankly.
Only Vince had said, "Maybe they found the Cummings boy
and the Forat girl—English and Farsi, after all."

There were more than ninety separate languages and five
times that many related dialects spoken among the United
Nations of Earth.

Croft had always known, in his heart, that he was destined
for something more than caretaking on his shift. Steering
humanity's boat was a weighty responsibility, but discharging
those responsibilities had been, until now, pedestrian.

This was . . . something else again.

Now the bubble was so fascinating, he couldn't take his
eyes from it. It seemed to undulate as it came closer. He'd
loved soap bubbles when he was a kid. He shouldn't be afraid.
But for a moment, as the leading edge of the bubble bumped
the open air lock, he was afraid.

He was afraid the bubble would pop.

Then he was afraid it wouldn't.

It didn't. It squeezed inward, without breaking, as if it were
reaching for him. He stepped back.

Remson's voice in his ears rang again: "Mickey, talk to me,
damn it! What's happening out there?"

Remson. He'd forgotten all about Remson.

Croft tried to speak. His voice was a croak. He tried again:
"Vince, the bubble's made contact with the hull and some of
it's in here. It's . . . coming toward me."

"It's okay, Mickey. I'm sure it's okay. If you don't want to get into it, we'll understand. There's still time for me to come out there."

"No."

Get into it. How do you do that?

The bubble hadn't popped when it contacted the hull. It was now an oval, questing bulge, with purple and green and gold oily swirls on its transparent, curved surface.

And that surface was coming toward him.

The bubble was filling the air lock. It was almost touching him.

He took a step backward, then another.

Vince said, "Remember, you've got your MMU jets."

As if Croft could—or would—try to escape the thing by using jetpack assist.

He realized dimly, dully, that all this was being recorded for posterity, through the surveillance capability of the air lock monitors.

So he wasn't going to quail before the bubble, or cower visibly, for the record, at the historic moment of making contact with the alien craft.

He wasn't.

He closed his eyes and took a bold step forward, thankful beyond words that he was safe inside a space suit. He was in a controlled environment. He wouldn't feel anything, unless the inside of the bubble was filled with some unimaginable acid or unsurvivable heat that would overwhelm his suit's capabilities. . . .

He opened his eyes. He was inside the bubble. Even his feet seemed to be inside the bubble. He hadn't felt a thing.

He asked for a status report, and his visor display told him that his suit was reading no abnormal stresses or exterior conditions. According to his suit, the space inside the bubble was indistinguishable from the space outside the bubble.

Except that Mickey Croft was being wafted out of the air lock at what seemed to him a frightening speed.

He said, "Vince?"

He got no response in his com.

"Vince?"

Remson didn't answer. The bubble was bearing him away from the UNE flagship now. It seemed to be headed toward the teardrop hovering over the science station.

Very fast.

Yet the only sensation of movement that Croft experienced was precipitated by observing the rate at which the *Washington* was receding and the teardrop above growing large.

He didn't ever seem to bump the membrane of the bubble. Croft wasn't conscious of any g-force, or of being thrown back toward the bubble's skin. He simply hovered in the exact middle of the bubble, as if he were floating in empty space. Except that his feet felt as if they were firmly planted.

He talked, for the sake of his recording log, and also in case Remson could hear him, even though Croft couldn't hear Remson. "I'm being swept up toward UFO-1 at considerable speed. There's no sensation of movement. There's no sensation of being in microgravity. The bubble's as transparent from inside as it seemed from without. My sense is I can move around in here if I wish."

He tried it. He could walk forward, as if he were standing on a level surface, for a while. Then he came to a point beyond which he couldn't proceed. If the bubble had an invisible cube within it, and Croft were within that cube, he would have met this sort of resistance when he reached one of the cube's walls. And yet he couldn't find a ninety-degree angle as he palmed along the barrier. Neither could he touch the clearly visible interior surface of the membrane surrounding him. His hands stopped, as if he'd encountered glass well before that point.

An ancient named Escher had etched geometries reminiscent of the one in which Croft now found himself. He said, "I can't touch the interior of the membrane. I can now see a circular dark spot in the underside of UFO-1. We seem to be headed for it."

He wished he knew if anyone could hear him. The aliens had promised that they'd return him after this meeting, hadn't they?

Somehow he couldn't convince himself that it was worth the effort it took to keep describing his approach to the teardrop shape above him.

That shape was now the size of a Threshold habitat module, anyway. He felt as if he were being swallowed by the biggest whale that ever lived as the bubble bore him "up" into the dark spot.

As the bubble shot into darkness, Croft felt a sudden gust of wind. He was cold all over. Every hair on his body rose and fell. Then he was warm, and in a bright place full of more swirling colors.

The geometry here made his eyes ache. Was it a cavern? A well? Were there stalactites? Stalagmites? Or were they curtains and stairs?

Colors performed arabesques and turned impossible angles. The bubble in which he floated continued to rise.

He thought he was rising in some sort of tube. It seemed that he was looking at cross sections of levels. An elevator? A lift of some kind?

He saw a stratum that appeared to be the home of a tidal sea, phosphorescent and full of froth and seaweed.

He saw a level that seemed to be all pillars and holes, a honeycomb made by drunken bees.

He saw a stratum that might have been a silicon world of chips and thousand-stranded, colored wire, going on forever.

And then he saw nothing at all.

The bubble continued to rise through a brown darkness and then, perceptibly, stopped.

It was as if the bubble had reached a surface through which it could not pass, like a balloon bumping against the ceiling at some child's party.

Croft heard a loud, rasping noise, and recognized it as his breathing. He tried to stop panting. His pharmakit should have been taking care of all this.

But pant he did. He was afraid to ask for a physiology scan. Surely he wasn't dead. And he wasn't blind. He could see the lights of his visor display. And beyond, he could just distinguish the whorls of color on the membrane of the bubble.

Then he could make out something else. The darkness was not black, but brown; maroon, the color of venal blood; then midnight blue; then deeply purple.

And in it he saw a bright speck of light. The light jittered. It bobbled. It seemed to be growing bigger.

Maybe it was growing closer. Maybe it was coming from very far away.

Croft said, "I see a light. A spark. White." The sound of his own voice surprised him, it was so loud. Harsh. Somehow importunate. As if he were in a cathedral at night.

As if he were disturbing a meditation. As if he were chattering at the knee of God.

Still he continued to speak, for the record, because it was his job to assume that there would *be* a record, and that what he perceived here would be of some import, once he got back to his own people.

His own people. He started gasping again, and this time a little red warning light on his visor told him that his suit was having trouble keeping his body's reactions within acceptable limits.

Yet he wasn't frightened. Not yet. Or not now. The light kept coming, or growing, whichever it was doing. There was a second, and a third.

The lights spun like huge sparks, like pinwheels, like fireworks. Then they steadied.

They stopped spewing sparkly bits of tail and became round. The bright round spots became three bright ovals. And the ovals became three humanoid forms, walking in bright suits of light, toward him.

Croft's red light was still on. He cautioned himself that he might be hallucinating. Hyperventilating. Dying.

You saw all sorts of visions when you were dying.

You saw ancestral mythic images of godhead, pink clouds and white lights, didn't you?

He said hoarsely, "I'm punching myself in the stomach to see if I can feel it."

He grunted when his fist hit his midsection—from the concussion that ran up his arm, not from any pain in his stomach.

His suit dutifully recorded the impact.

He couldn't be dead. Those weren't mythic images of godhead, coming toward him.

The lights were making slow, measured progress. He was almost certain that one light was in front, two behind. They were tall and very bright. They reminded Croft of churchmen, religious figures in long, gorgeous robes with huge conical hats.

Now where had he seen that image?

"I'm having a feeling of . . . holiness, but I don't know why. The lights are dimming as they're coming closer. Three figures are approaching me, and now they have discernible arms and feet, if not legs. They have heads, as well. This species seems to be walking upright, basically bipedal, or else it has a way of approximating a two-legged gait. If they're two-legged, they're wearing long robes or skirts."

And so they were, he soon saw. The lights about the creatures dimmed as they came on, and Croft was able to make out that one carried a staff and the other two carried basket-shaped censers.

Someone, he thought, had made quite a study of the human race—or else was damned similar in heritage.

The darkness around him, he realized, was receding. He could see shapes through a thick mist, as if dawn were beginning.

But this was not a place, this was the inside of a spacefaring craft.

He said, "It's getting lighter. I can see geometric shapes, the sort of things you'd expect to be dwellings in a habitat. The three are nearly here now. And I think—"

The bubble around Croft burst with a distinct bump. He

was standing on something different. And the three aliens were right in front of him.

He couldn't imagine how they'd crossed the remaining distance so fast.

He was looking into slitted eyes, within a conically shaped helmet with a clear faceplate. He saw a harelip with fur around it, and a bottom lip. The lips were moving.

And in his ears he heard, "Welcome, human. Greeting you."

The alien was using Croft's com system, somehow, to communicate.

Mickey Croft held out his hand and said, "On behalf of the United Nations of Earth, welcome, strangers. I'm Michael Croft, Secretary General of the Trust Territory of Threshold."

The alien shook its staff at him and stepped back.

Behind it was a second alien. This one had a more complicated suit of colors and a helmet with a sealed faceplate, like the first. Mickey was sure that these beings were wearing life-support.

The second being said, "Welcome, human. Greeting you. Fear not our hospitality."

Mickey said, hand still outstretched, "We're hoping to begin a long, fruitful, friendly relationship."

The second being shook its basket at him and stepped back.

Then Croft got a good look at the third one. This one was taking off its helmet. It had huge, sad eyes and a wonderful smile, a thin neck, and hands with too many fingers.

It took his hand in its and it said, "We will have many happy talks, Michaelcroft. I am the Council's Interstitial Interpreter. I will speak for the others to you, and for you, to them. We have been looking forward to this meeting for a long time."

Croft hoped he hadn't offended protocol by offering his hand to the other two aliens.

This one said, "Come, take off your breathing things and we can talk in good air, with good ears hearing."

Croft hesitated. He couldn't keep a record without his helmet. But clearly he was expected to do as his host suggested. The two who'd preceded the interpreter were taking off their helmets and walking away. His host indicated that Croft should follow. Beyond the two furthermost aliens a vista like a landscape seemed to stretch out forever.

Croft had to remind himself that he was inside a finite, teardrop-shaped craft of unremarkable size. Or was he?

The alien had its hands in its sleeves, and those sleeves were like clouds blowing in a gentle wind.

He fell in beside the alien, wondering why he wanted to cry every time he met those sad eyes. And why he couldn't see anything more fascinating among all the wonders around him than that wide mouth smiling at him, as if he'd been away on a long journey and was just now coming home.

Around them, as he walked beside the interpreter, behind the two slit-eyed aliens, everything turned lavender and gold. Overhead, a flight of fireflies began to dance in circles around a globe that looked very much like ancestral Earth.

CHAPTER 13

$$\triangledown$$

A Cop Is a Cop

Reice's one-man patrol cruiser, the *Blue Tick*, was parked in a 135 × 142 nautical-mile orbit around the three teardrop-shaped alien ships and the Ball at Spacedock Seven, working security the way he was paid to do.

You'd think the high-and-mighty Vince Remson, the Secretary General's XO, could have found something more significant for Reice to do.

After all, Reice was the initial reporting officer on the First Encounter with Alien Life, wasn't he?

Didn't matter. Nothing ever changed.

"Reice, put together a standoff force. Commandeer however much support from ConSpaceCom you need. My authority," Remson had ordered.

Yessir, yessir, three bags full.

What else did you say?

Reice got every damned dirty, boring, risky job in the universe. There was nothing new about that.

There was no use pointing out to Remson that Reice had called in the historic message, had been the first on-site, and therefore ought to be doing more than sitting around in his cruiser presiding over jurisdictional debating teams made up of ConSpaceCom officers from various nations who wanted their piece of the pie—and Reice's hide—on this mission.

If you could call it a mission. The real-time view out Reice's forward monitor reminded him more of a traffic jam caused by gawkers at an accident than a security cordon. Everybody with the clout to arrange it was out here in a division flagship or a private yacht.

Coordinating a bunch of protocol-conscious heavyweights was nothing new to Reice. He belayed every attempt to muscle him and went strictly by the book.

But there was no entry in the book for "Initial Encounter with Real-Live Aliens From A (Probably) Superior Culture."

And there was plenty new about coordinating an "honor guard" trying to surround three teardrop-shaped alien vessels of unknown provenance and manufacture.

Plenty.

The vessels weren't cooperating, although they weren't failing to cooperate either. They were parked exactly where they'd chosen to come to rest, around the damnable Ball.

The twenty-five ConSec and Space Command ships armed to the teeth that were standing off at a "safe" distance didn't seem to bother the visitors. That was something, anyway.

All you needed was one of those alien craft spitting a peppermint-striped ray that disintegrated the Chinese Space-Com flagship, *Ancestral Cloud*, or the *Imam*, or the *Diego Garcia*.

Reice licked his lips at the thought of aggression from the mysterious teardrop craft. According to Remson, Croft was "safe" inside UFO-1 and that was all anybody knew.

UFOs 1, 2, and 3 were politely ignoring all of ConSec's displayed might, as if Reice's security contingent really was the honor guard it was trying fitfully to resemble. Even the big guns of ConSpaceCom's "peacekeeping" vessels didn't seem to faze the aliens.

These aliens knew what they were doing. They'd sent a weird-ass dinghy to pick up Croft, despite Reice's objections to Vince Remson himself that you didn't give up a hostage when you didn't know how you'd go about getting that hostage back.

Not when the hostage was your Secretary General.

But nobody had listened to Reice's warnings. Not that he'd expected to be listened to. He stretched out his legs on the bumper of his console and flexed the long muscles in his thighs, which were aching with suppressed tension.

Official complaints were meant to be ignored, Reice knew. You logged them so you were on record if you turned out to be correct. Standard procedure for a screw-up in the making, right?

Right. But this was no standard screw-up in the making, here. This was genuine history, parked out there before his very eyes. Reice had never been very good at history.

It was boring. It was, more than anything, over with. Dead as yesterday's dinner.

Reice could only hope that Mickey Croft didn't get that dead. Vince Remson was way out on a limb this time.

Reice got up from the *Blue Tick*'s console and slapped at his auxiliary monitor bank. No use pretending that he wasn't worried. It was his job to worry.

It was bad enough pretending that he hadn't been slighted. After all, he'd been the first to encounter the alien craft, hadn't he?

It still rankled that he wasn't over there on the *Washington* with the brass, consulting, rather than out here with his finger on a trigger nobody was going to want him to squeeze.

Reice knew all about standoff. You displayed your power, because you couldn't be allowed to use it. If those aliens sent back Mickey Croft all ground up, arranged into a patty, and lying on a bun with lettuce and tomato, nobody was going to let Reice and his ConSec contingent open fire.

Not when you didn't know what those teardrops could do to Threshold. The Trust Territory of Threshold was sitting back there, with two hundred fifty thousand arguably innocent souls on her, going about their daily business. And nobody knew enough about these alien teardrops to be able to guess whether they were armed. Or if they were, whether the Trust Territory of Threshold was in range of whatever kind of weapons those teardrops might be sporting.

It was just one of those situations that couldn't be quantified. The element of surprise, of the unknown, was always the most dangerous. You couldn't tell how much was underreaction, how much was overreaction.

Whenever Reice saw something new and unexpected, it was unwelcome. Like the image nosing into the viewscans on his supplemental monitoring screen.

Reice hated the unexpected.

He ported the view to his forward console, flopped down in his command chair, and slapped his com channel open. He could have voice-commanded the *Blue Tick*, but right now Reice didn't trust the identifiability of his own voice.

"What the hell makes you think you're invited to this party, ULD-1001?" he demanded, his fingers flying as he punched up a traffic report to further identify the interloper. Nobody got out here who wasn't cleared to be out here. Those were standing orders.

So what had happened? Who'd screwed up?

The comlink was scratchy: "ULD-1001 to ConSec Spacedock Control. I'm cleared for this, take a look. My invitation's in order. Sir."

The flip voice sounded familiar. The traffic schematic showed Reice the interloper's destination: the *Washington*. And of course nobody'd bothered to inform Reice, because if he'd been doing his normal job he wouldn't have been monitoring traffic approaching from the Stalk to begin with.

But still . . .

"Who's this?" Reice demanded. "Who'm I talking to?" That voice was too familiar.

ULD-1001 answered with a different voice: "This is Micah Keebler, Spacedock Command. I got me a pers'n'l invite to this-here party, courtesy o' the Secretary Gen'ral hisself. You got some problem wit' that?"

"Checking," said Reice levelly, with all the control at his command.

Keebler. Here? Now? Was this somebody's idea of a joke? Reice's mind raced. If he identified himself, was it going to cause a flap on the comlink? Keebler probably didn't know Reice was the ConSec authority calling.

He toggled to another channel and spat at traffic control: "What the hell you doin', Jerry? Picking your teeth? I should have been informed that we were expecting a volatile visitor— a goddamned criminal visitor. Put an escort on that ULD-1001, and have four ConSec guards accompany Mr. Keebler everywhere he goes on the flagship—even to the head."

Then he got back to ULD-1001. This time, the respondent whose voice he heard was the first man he'd spoken to.

And Sling identified himself in a quavery voice, saying, "Look, sir, we don't want any trouble. I was asked to bring my passenger out here, and a piece of equipment or two. Commander South knows we're coming. It's all duly cleared. I really don't think we've done anything out of the ordinary. Anyway, Keebler and I made a bet: I bring us out here, to Spacedock Seven, and if that doesn't make me as rich and famous as Keebler himself, I win his ship. So you can't inter—"

"Your bet's off, called on account of ConSec, hotshot. And don't tell me what I can and can't do. You got a record, kid, of doing things out of the ordinary. And nothing like that's going to happen out here. Not now. Because I'll stay on your ass and see to it. That's a promise." Gordon Sling was an aftermarketeer, somebody who made his living in the gray areas of the law. Reice was tempted to push his advantage, because he was angry and because, at heart, he was a cop.

Cops are cops. But this wasn't a police situation. Not yet.

The nervous aftermarketeer stammered out his various permits and clearances, while Reice imagined the young operator twisting nervously on his pigtail.

Reice could deny all prior permits and keep Sling's ship

from entering a ConSec-controlled area. He was tempted to do that, for fun. For instinct's sake. And because he hated like hell to have somebody—anybody—invoke Joe South's name like the Relic was some sort of trusted authority.

But then Keebler would find out that it was Reice who was hassling him, and Keebler had lawyers. It had been made clear to Reice just how determined the Secretary General's office was to avoid tangling with Keebler's lawyers, who were still contesting the confiscation of the Ball by Customs.

Keebler's voice came over the horn: "Ye can't stop me from visitin' the area of m' property. Fer an inspection. I know m' rights!"

Reice sighed. "Cleared for entry, ULD-1001. But you get your ass over to the mother ship, and you don't go anywhere else. You do your inspection eyes-only. Or we'll blow you out of existence. Got that? And no bets. No games. This is your single heads-up: Any deviation from course will result in punitive action without further warning."

"Got it, ConSec Control," Sling said breathlessly, with a grunt at the end and a muffled sign-off, as if he were struggling to keep Keebler from grabbing the com mike.

Reice shut down his com channel and reconsidered the protocol problems he'd almost started. Irritation was sheeting over him as if he'd stepped into a charged field; his whole body was slightly itchy. He scratched at his chest.

Damned South. "Commander" South, these days. South was always where he didn't belong.

In Reice's face. And Reice, especially now, didn't need the grief.

He tried getting South on the horn, but the *Washington*'s comlinks were all busy. He found himself on interminable hold.

And that gave Reice time to cool down. He was antsy, that was all. He and South were trying to get along these days, and marginally succeeding.

It was the three teardrops from the ends of creation that were making Reice so twitchy this time.

And the fact that Croft was aboard UFO-1 wasn't helping.

But whoever had thought up the bright idea of inviting the Scavenger out to Spacedock Seven ought to be spanked. The fool was dangerous. A hostage-taker. A certifiable crazy.

Keebler was the very certifiable crazy who'd brought the Ball to Trust Territory in the first place.

For all Reice knew, the Scavenger was going to go down in history as a modern-day Pandora—as the man who brought the seeds of humankind's eradication into its midst. As the guy who decided to haul the Trojan Horse inside the walls.

Reice's hands began to sweat. He should have shot Keebler when he'd had the chance. Should have killed him stone-dead. There'd been enough pretext. Then none of this would be happening.

Well, some of it would. But at least the man who had started all the trouble would have been punished.

Reice had gone into ConSec because he liked to punish evildoers. Right now, for his money, Micah Keebler was looking like the greatest evildoer in history.

Of course, to believe that the aliens' purpose was unfriendly you had to see things Reice's way.

And sometimes the brass could never be convinced to see things Reice's way.

But that didn't mean you couldn't keep trying. Or even, if things went from bad to worse, manage to personally see that justice was done.

Reice decided, there and then, that if Mickey Croft didn't come out of that UFO-1 safe and sound, he was going to blow Keebler to smithereens.

He might have done it anyway, right then, if Keebler's ship hadn't been so close to the diplomatic flagship *George Washington*.

He ran the targeting lock-on sequence, just to be sure that Sling's ULD-1001 *was* too close for comfort.

When he'd proved that to himself, Reice settled down to wait for an opportunity to trash the ship that Keebler had rode in on.

It was the least that Reice could do for history. As for the purportedly innocent aftermarketeer who might die along with the Scavenger, Reice knew in his heart that Sling had committed untold crimes, which an overworked Threshold policing apparatus simply hadn't been able to pin on the proper perpetrator.

Finally, as he concocted a way to destroy Keebler's ship when it debarked from its berth at the *Washington*'s side, Reice began to feel better.

The unendurable sense of waiting for an alien shoe to drop left him—to be replaced by a sensual, almost sexual, excitation that came over Reice only when he was stalking prey.

And Keebler—the hostage-taker, the junk collector, the dizzy beachcomber who'd found the Ball at some benighted white hole and dragged it in here—was clearly the right prey to soothe Reice's jangled nerves.

Who the hell did Keebler think he was, anyhow? Look at this mess. Around Reice, in his monitors, ships sparkled in hovering profusion.

Keebler and his damned aliens had brought the whole of Threshold's normal life to an abrupt halt.

Everybody who was anybody was out here. At home, on the Stalk, the rank and file of the United Nations of Earth were all holding their collective breath.

That fool Keebler might have signed mankind's death warrant.

If he hadn't, Keebler had at the very least changed things irrevocably.

Nothing would ever be the same. Could ever resume its familiar shape. Mankind's fate had been permanently changed, from the moment Reice first saw that huge teardrop. Maybe from before that—maybe from when the damned Ball had first been towed in to Spacedock Seven.

With a jerky motion and a curse, Reice wiped all his monitors. He didn't want to look at anything right now. He reached above his head and told the *Tick* to alert him when Keebler's ship left the safety of the flagship vessel's side.

Then, for a reason he didn't understand, he called over there on a voice-only channel, and asked for Commander South.

It took a little while. Then South said, "Yeah, Reice? What's up?"

"I called to ask you that."

Reice could almost see the Relic test pilot's deeply circled eyes narrow as South's careful voice said, "Waiting to find out what Mickey wants us to do next, is all. Everything's well within normal limits here."

The Relic was learning the language of bureaucracy. Reice should have expected it. "Commander" South of Customs was Riva Lowe's protégé, the Titanium Lady's personal pet.

"Same here," Reice assured him. "But I was wondering how come you folks asked the Scavenger and that aftermarketeer out here, after what happened at the Spacedock. . . ."

There was a silence on the other end of the line. Reice hadn't asked a direct question and South, a military type, wasn't going to volunteer an opinion.

Reice kept quiet, too. The verbal game of chicken on the comlink made the silence on the line deafening.

Finally South broke and spoke, very slowly, with long pauses between his carefully chosen words: "We're hoping to . . . control . . . this . . . situation, that's all. It wasn't my idea. And Keebler was bound to get as close as he could. So they told him where to report."

"They?" *On whose damned authority, anyhow?*

"The SecGen's office isn't leaving anything to chance," said South, as if reading Reice's mind.

"Which is what you're doing there, I expect," said Reice, pushing for information way beyond what he had any right to demand.

South knew what Reice was doing, and why, and his discomfort was clear as the Relic pilot said, "Look, thanks for your concern. I really think we can handle whatever comes up. If we can't, it's good to know you're out there keeping tabs on things. South, out."

South, out: an ancient convention; a habit from the misty past. The comlink went dead, and took with it every iota of good feeling that Reice had been able to squeeze out of his determination to murder the Scavenger.

The Relic was telling Reice that things weren't any better than Reice had thought. Maybe things were worse, if South was telling Reice that South was glad to have him around.

A cold spot began forming in Reice's stomach, eating it up and reaching outward to engulf his chest and groin, sending icy tendrils through his arms, his legs, his face. South was scared.

He knew the Relic too well not to have gotten the message.

And now, shorn of busywork and sitting alone in a ship, shut away from all outside stimuli, Reice was scared, too.

For the first time the utter and complete enormity of being visited by a possibly superior race swept over him.

He felt as if he were drowning, asphyxiating.

Reice croaked an override and all of his monitors came to life in response to the verbalized command. There were the stars, twinkling comfortingly. There was all the might of ConSec and ConSpaceCom, ranged around the visitors.

But there too, in his monitors, was the Ball, silent and smug and gleaming from the midst of the scaffolding that anxious, curious men had built around it.

Around the Ball were the three alien, teardrop-shaped ships.

And then there were *two* teardrop-shaped ships.

UFO-1 disappeared.

Blinked out of existence.

And all hell broke loose on the coms.

Reice leaned so far over his console he seemed to be hugging it. He was talking as fast as he could on four channels in close succession, screaming, "Hold your fire!" and "Signature scans!" and "Clear this channel, damn you!" and whatever else needed to be said to restore order and clear the com jam.

Reice had to keep anybody from shooting or jumping to conclusions while he tried with all his might to get through to

Vince Remson on the *George Washington*, to find out what Remson wanted to do now.

Somebody had better tell him, and the people under him, what to do. And fast.

Otherwise, somebody was going to do something—just because something clearly had to be done.

"Remson, where the hell are you?" Reice muttered to himself, still crouched over his console, when all attempts to raise the SecGen's XO had failed.

On his monitors, proof was there in infrared, in electro-optical, and in ultraviolet that UFO-1 was gone.

Two of the teardrops still remained.

Two targets.

What the fuck?

Reice started handing off targeting data and apportioning tactical fire positions to his ConSec ships.

For all Reice knew, Remson wasn't in any shape to give orders. Maybe Remson had been abducted too, right out of the *Washington*, from under their very noses.

Nobody knew what these alien ships could do.

But they were beginning to find out.

And Reice didn't want to regret finding out a whole hell of a lot more than humankind could survive.

He was just beginning to get a little flak from the Con-SpaceCom contingent when two things happened:

Remson returned his call.

And UFO-1 popped back into being, exactly at the spot where it had first appeared and then disappeared.

Vince Remson was saying in a hoarse and carefully articulated voice, "Hold your fire, Reice. Is that clear? Hold your fire."

And Reice was saying, "Yes, sir. Clear, sir. Holding fire, sir," because he had no time to argue.

He had to get off-line with Remson before he could execute Remson's orders. He had to make sure nobody took a potshot at UFO-2 or UFO-3. Or at the frigging Ball.

And he needed to do that as fast as possible. Not only

because somebody, in these circumstances, might shoot—
because they were nervous, or because instinct was sometimes
overwhelming, or because the need to act was so strong when
facing the unknown. But also because, until he made sure
that everyone was safely back to standby, he couldn't go to
the head and retch.

Which was what he wanted to do. Needed to do.

Those aliens had just made it painfully clear that they were
toying with all the muscle that TTT could muster. The entire
display that the Trust Territory had deployed here, all its
shiny firepower and dissuasive might—all of these were
merely being tolerated by the aliens, who could wink out of
this spacetime whenever they chose.

Without a warning. Without a trace. And without the consolidated forces of Trust Territory being able to do a damned
thing about it.

And those aliens had Mickey Croft in their clutches. The
SecGen was clearly beyond the protection of the UNE, of
ConSec, of ConSpaceCom—of humanity.

Reice had never been so frightened, or so demoralized, in
his entire life.

CHAPTER 14

$\bigtriangledown$

Minding the Store

Back on Threshold, in the Simulations Bay, the sky was blue. The trees were green. The water had wrinkles on its surface that moved lazily before her eyes.

Riva Lowe laid out a checkered tablecloth and put a wicker basket on the grass, feeling ridiculous, ludicrous even, in a plaid skirt and a blouse trimmed with lace.

Opposite her, Richard the Second, CEO of NAMECorp and bereaved father of the missing Cummings III, wore a lumberjack shirt and a pair of faded blue trousers with rivets at the pocket corners. And boots.

"I feel like I'm in an old movie," she admitted to Cummings. "All that's missing are violins." But she couldn't admit to Cummings that she was going through all these infinitely silly motions with him only in hopes of keeping secret the fact that there was an alien armada parked within striking distance of Threshold.

Cummings looked as if he hadn't a care in the world. His handsome, broad head dipped slightly. His face, when it turned to her, had a vid-show smile on it.

"You look as if you were born to it," he said softly.

Born to what? Earth? She'd never seen Earth in her life. Never expected to see it. Never expected even to be in so expensive a simulation, learning to adapt to it. Or did he mean that she was born to the game of deception?

If he meant that, he might be right. But since she didn't know which he did mean, Riva was suddenly more concerned than she had been. If Richard the Second found out she was trying to distract him she would lose her trip to Earth, of course: her outrageous, unexpected, fantastically elite junket; her once-in-a-lifetime chance to see the ancestral planet.

But worse than that, she reminded herself forcibly, she would have made a powerful enemy. So she must find a way to prepare for the inevitable moment when Cummings, Jr., did find out she'd been keeping him busy while Mickey and his staff tried to deal with the aliens without causing a panic.

How did you do that?

Cummings was one of the largest stockholders in Trust Territory. His interspatial holdings were greater than those of many national conglomerates. He was a power beyond measure. If he became displeased with her, her career would be over. She'd end up serving drinks in the Loader Zone—if she was lucky.

Or deported to a terraforming world, more likely, where she'd die with silicates in her lungs and aluminum in her brain.

Richard Cummings the Second sat down cross-legged on the synthetic grass and patted it. "Sit. Let's have this picnic and pretend we have all the time in the world." He frowned. "Of course on Earth there'd be bugs."

"Bugs?"

"Insects. Bees, ants, mosquitoes that bite. Worms."

"Mosquitoes that bite," she said dumbly, doing as he asked. How had he sat so gracefully, folding into a squat without having to rearrange all his limbs?

Her bare legs flashed as she tried to emulate him in the unwieldy skirt.

Why would women have worn skirts, anyhow? But she

knew the answer to that: to make them quickly accessible to the mating instincts of men.

She was momentarily repelled by the thought, by herself, and by the man across from her, all power and patience.

He didn't seem to know about UFOs 1–3. He didn't seem to be worried. So maybe she was doing the impossible, which, unfortunately, seemed to be her job right now. She ached to tell Cummings the truth and be out of here.

He'd find out, eventually. So why not now? They might need her out there. Remson had convinced her that she was most needed here, dealing with Richard the Second. It hadn't seemed fair, even then.

But Vince Remson was calling the shots. So she was here. And South was out there. Even Keebler was out there.

And she was here. A twinge of resentment made her mutter.

Cummings said, "Here, let me help you." *Inane man.* He'd thought she hadn't known how to open the basket, perhaps. Or how to get out the champagne glasses and the paté and all the other delicacies that his staff had packed for them.

If this was a seduction, Richard the Second might, for the first time in his life, fail at something.

A look into the quiet blue eyes of the man made her know that the thought of failure hadn't crossed his mind.

So she said, "The matter of your son is one we want you to know we've been doing our utmost to resolve." *You failed at that, hotshot. At raising a son with more sense than to take off for parts unknown with his Juliet, in a ridiculous display of coming-of-age misjudgment.*

Cummings didn't wince, but he didn't nod his regal head either. He brought his level stare to bear on her and said, "My people feel that something extraordinary has happened to those two children. We've analyzed the disappearance of their ship and our technologists have come to more definite conclusions than yours."

So maybe this wasn't pure seduction. And maybe the trip to Earth was going to disappear from her wish list, if not from her future, at any moment.

But Riva Lowe was a professional. She didn't duck challenges, even when they came from men more influential than some presidents or kings. She said: "We don't speculate. We have theories, but theories don't qualify as anything more than speculation at this time. I hope you're not suggesting that we're dragging our heels on this investigation."

"I'm suggesting that you're holding back information, yes. And I'm telling you that it's a waste of time: I always find out what I need to know."

Suddenly, she didn't want to have a confrontation. She didn't want to have a picnic, either.

Cummings was popping the cork on the champagne bottle, which made an explosive sound.

Startled, she flinched. Froth poured out of the bottle. Cummings, chuckling, caught some in his fingers and licked them.

She found the gesture insultingly suggestive and overtly provocative. So she reached into her purse and toggled her office pager.

It would call her with an attempt to dump her messages in a few moments.

And then she'd be out of here, away from the NAMECorp CEO before she made some terrible mistake.

Mickey Croft had been wrong. She couldn't handle Richard the Second. Remson had been wrong, too. She wasn't up to the task of distracting this man sufficiently that he would keep his nose out of the alien encounter.

Cummings was handing her a glass, saying, "Let's change the subject. There's no reason for us to argue over bureaucracies and red tape. When we get to Earth, you'll realize how minimal these simulations are. And how extraordinary an experience it is to walk the homeworld ground. But until—"

Her beeper obediently demanded her attention. She didn't need to pretend to be flustered. She fumbled for it, nearly dropping the glass full of champagne, the surface of which was launching a flotilla of bubbles into the air.

"I've got to go check these. I'll be right back."

"And of course, you can't do that with me at hand. Shall I stay here then, until you return?"

She should have realized he wouldn't let her go this easily. But she hadn't. She felt outclassed. He knew how powerful he was.

What was going to happen when he was forced to learn that, as far as she was concerned, no one was powerful enough to lay a hand on her? She didn't consider the occasional discreet affair to be part of her job. She never had. She never would.

And Cummings wasn't the sort of man to take no for an answer.

Determinedly, she stood up and said, "Fine. I'll be back as soon as I can."

"Within the hour, surely," he said, to make certain she knew that he was expecting to be tended by her, to have his picnic, to have his way.

"Of course," she said, but the tone of it made him raise an eyebrow. Turning her back she walked swiftly to the simulator exit, between two brick columns.

One more step and she would be safe from Richard the Second. . . .

As her stride took her between the apparent piles of brick, the hairs on the nape of her neck rose and fell and the brick disappeared, to be replaced by the Virtual-Reality Bay with its gray-and-green panels.

She'd never been so glad to get out of someplace in her life.

She turned around, to be sure Cummings hadn't followed. The simulator entrance was clearly marked IN USE, and unremarkable.

With a sigh, she sat down along the wall and flipped her wallet communicator open. She did have three messages marked URGENT.

Two were from Vince Remson. *Two?*

When she'd listened to both of them she knew that Mickey had gone aboard the alien craft and that it had disappeared, then reappeared.

The third message was from South. When she replayed it, her hands were shaking.

The little screen on her fliptop displayed a miniature South with tortured eyes, saying, "I dunno what's happening here. The Scavenger and Sling are out here. Mickey's still out of contact. I'm going out to the Ball with the black box, the way we planned. If you don't get to me before I leave, Reice'll have a fix on me. I got to tell you . . . thanks for all you've done."

The little face disappeared.

Riva Lowe leaned her head back against the wall. She was suddenly very sad.

What did that idiot South think he was going to accomplish? And why wasn't she angry at him?

Couldn't he think clearly enough to realize that what had happened to Mickey and to UFO-1 dictated that no prior courses of action should be pursued?

But of course, he wouldn't understand that. She wished she'd been there.

She wished she was out there now.

And then she began to get angry. She should have been there. She was so wrapped up with this Cummings thing, and the foolish trip to Earth that would invest her with massive profile and clout by association, that she'd lost track of her real best interest.

Vince Remson would find a way to coopt South and use him for Secretariat purposes, while she was otherwise engaged.

It was just like Vince. Turf battles were his stock in trade.

She flipped on her pocket privacy field and stared at the comforting enclosure of silvery static.

From here she could call anyone, do anything she wanted, without worrying about who might overhear.

South wasn't available, she was told. Just that. The staffer she spoke to wasn't shaken when she tried to pull rank.

Okay, she'd expected that.

The staffer told her, "I'll be glad to give you the Assistant Secretary's extension. I'm sure that you'll be able to secure the progress report you wish by calling that office."

Kiss my ass, she thought, and said she'd try that later.

Then she called Reice.

Good old Reice had a longtime crush on her. Normally, there was nothing Reice wouldn't do for her.

But not today, of course. Today wasn't a normal day.

Reice was harried, and his miniaturized head was framed in a mosaic of signature-scanning monitors, all blazing with readouts.

"Progress report? God, Riva, we might be about to go to war here. UFO-1 disappeared. Then it reappeared. We're under a 'Hold Fire' order from Remson. It's quiet as a grave over there, and UNE Peacekeeping wants to fire one across their bow just to make sure somebody's inside. For all we know those are three empty hulks out there—now."

Reice was trying to choose his words carefully, and that made his excitation even more distressing.

"I want a progress report from South then, since you're too busy. Can you arrange that for me?"

"He's out there at the Ball, with his crazy buddies and an escort. You want to call him, here's what you do."

Once Reice had given her the right freq and call signs for this military emergency she told him that, if he spoke to South before she did, she expected Reice to pass on to South her order that South return immediately to Threshold and see her in her office.

Never mind that she couldn't possibly be expected to be in her office whenever the Relic pilot would arrive.

She didn't even know why she was giving such an order.

When at last she got patched through to South and tried

to give the order directly, she could only receive him on audio.

"I'm kinda busy," he interrupted in a whispery tone, before she could finish her demand that he return. "How about I call you back when the fun's over?"

"What are you doing out there?" she demanded.

"Classified," he said in a voice that might have been chuckling. "My therapist is here, though. So don't worry. We'll be home soon."

"You'll come back right—"

The circuit went dead.

She sat there, staring at the fliptop screen on her lap. His therapist? Then she realized he meant the psych-evaluator, a pilot-specialized AIP-T, or Artificially Intelligent Preprogrammed Therapist. This one was supposed to be evaluating South's fitness for a pilot's exam. So what use was it going to be in this sort of crisis? What was going *on* out there?

She was going to need some therapy herself, when this was over. South, the Scavenger, and the aftermarketeer all out at the Ball? With less going on than the visit of alien spaceships, she would have been disturbed by that news.

Now, it didn't seem any more unusual than anything else.

She shut down the privacy field and the flowing silver tube disappeared. The Virtual-Reality Bay beyond looked normal.

Maybe she was overreacting. Sure she was.

Nothing for it but to put her things away, smooth down her skirt, and go back in there to face Cummings and his picnic. After all, she had her job to do.

Today her job was Cummings, Jr. Vince Remson had made that clear. You did your job, everyday, and you didn't ask too many questions.

And this was just another day, minding the store here on Threshold. Sure it was.

Just because Mickey was in the hands of aliens, and South was out there with a crazy man and a black market electronics jock trying to open up the Ball, didn't mean she had to be there.

She wanted to be there so badly that she nearly told Richard the Second what the trouble was when he asked.

But she couldn't do that. She had to play her part, at least until she got rid of Cummings for the night.

Then, if she happened to need to consult with South, her Customs man on the scene, personally, who could argue with that?

CHAPTER 15

$\triangledown$

Flashbacks

Aboard *STARBIRD*, Joe South was sweating in his climate-controlled suit, despite his AI's attempts to cool him. "Birdy," he said to the ship around him through his open helmet, "what do you think?"

The voice of the artificially intelligent copilot interface didn't answer him.

Of course Birdy didn't "think," in the human sense of the term. But Birdy and he were the lone survivors of the experimental flyby of X-3, five hundred years in humanity's past.

Now that he had maneuvered *STARBIRD* nose-to-nose with the mysterious Ball that seemed to have followed him back to the home system across time and space, he needed to know that Birdy was reading this situation the way he was.

And he was feeling that something urgently relevant to the Ball and to the teardrop ships around it lay in his lost knowledge of those forgotten events, hidden from humanity by a curtain of relativity and from South's memory by a protective trick of his mind or a reaction to experimental spongespace travel.

Or he thought he knew that. His flight deck was his security blanket. Birdy whirred and purred around him, tending to his every need the way she always had, through *STARBIRD*'s multispectral capability to keep him alive and well. The space-craft he loved, and had fought to secure as his own, knew damned well that something strange was happening.

Birdy could interface with his life-support system, tweak the suit he wore to help keep his body at maximum efficiency. The cuff on his wrist and his pharmakit would combine to bring him back to a functional baseline if his chemistries spiked too far. But Birdy was giving him plenty of latitude this time. He was on an emotional roller coaster, here in his doubly safe cocoon of ship and suit, and the AI wasn't doing anything to brake the ride.

So maybe Birdy was scared, too. Or maybe the way he was feeling didn't indicate anything like parity with Birdy's artificial intelligence. Maybe Birdy felt fine. Maybe the AI didn't share South's overwhelming angst. Loneliness. Melancholia. Disassociation. All of those could be pure fear reactions that seemed familiar because South had seen aliens in his dreams and lavender skies and ringed planetary vistas he couldn't understand during his test flight.

Birdy hadn't been able to stop the dreams, or hallucinations, or the visitation—if that was what they were—that had plagued him throughout the spongespace test flight and after. *STARBIRD* had taken South where South and U.S. Space Command had dictated, and shown him what he wanted to see. The experimental spacecraft had made measurements and collected data and brought him back alive.

Five hundred years after he'd left. To a world of strangers, where *STARBIRD* was an antique and South was a Relic. He'd busted his ass to prove himself capable in contemporary terms and to get *STARBIRD* the retrofits she needed if she wasn't to end up as a museum piece or the butt of infinitely cruel jokes.

And now here was the Ball. And the teardrop-shaped Leviathans From Outer Space. Now everybody out at Spacedock Seven was seeing things they couldn't understand. The terrible sense of familiarity that was making South sweat was probably nothing compared to what the local government was feeling.

All the reactions he was fighting might be nothing more than a flashback to a similar circumstance.

But it felt like more. It felt . . . connected.

If his sense of familiarity was really an artifact of connectedness, maybe he could remember what he needed to know. The automated "psychotherapist" that he'd brought along and stashed beside his bunk thought he could.

Maybe he was better qualified than the locals, for once, to evaluate a situation. Maybe he had, finally, some experience that could come in handy. Or maybe the therapist was wrong. After all, the therapist might be state-of-the-art, but it hadn't been on the X-3 flyby the way Birdy had.

Memories could help South only if he could access them. Knowledge was useful only if he could find it. If he could just remember what he thought he knew—what itched in the back of his brain where he couldn't seem to scratch—then maybe he could do some good out here.

Otherwise, he wasn't going to be any more help than crazy old Keebler or Sling. Maybe less.

They weren't scared shitless of the Ball the way he was.

His suit hummed and began pinging. Birdy wanted him to put down his visor, close the system so that its climate-control would have a shot at bringing his body temperature down.

He said, "Come on, Birdy, talk to me. Evaluate the Ball data." He should have remembered that Birdy didn't like to answer the question "What do you think?"

The AI was still pretending to observe the parameters of its manufacture.

But South knew better.

This time, in response to the right question, Birdy spoke. In her automated voice, which had been his only link to sanity and humanity for so long on that interminable journey—and afterward.

The ship's AI said: "Captain, systems checks complete and all systems nominal. Proceeding with caution to specified coordinates." And Birdy clucked protectively.

Birdy never let on that her AI components had grown into a benign intelligence that cared for him in any way someone not intimate with the consciousness of *STARBIRD* could discern.

STARBIRD and the man/machine interface that South called "Birdy" were the only artifacts of any civilization that South didn't find alien, now that he was living in his culture's future.

So what's to sweat, really? "Gimme the Ball, all available scans," he said through his yet-open faceplate—he didn't want to shut himself away from the flight deck. Not just yet.

Birdy hummed and . . .

There it was. The Ball. A dozen Balls. Or a dozen views of the Ball, with its scaffold-nest that men had built around it, and the science station where so recently Keebler had gone berserk.

The Ball was quiescent, silver. It seemed to South that it was asleep.

He'd barely managed to control himself the last time, so close to it. And now Birdy was nosing *STARBIRD*'s hull right up alongside the sphere. Just the way he'd asked.

He watched the sphere grow and grow until he had to get Birdy to do tricks so that he could still see all of it, and not just a curve of enveloping size that blocked out everything, all the stars, all of time and space.

He could hear his hoarse breathing. His lips were dry. Birdy tweaked him in the wrist and he felt a little better.

In his ears, he heard the "Close Helmet" signal.

This time, he obeyed. His faceplate gave him a redundant heads-up display of the main monitor and an approach grid. He knew where he was. He knew where Sling and Keebler, in Sling's ship, were.

He kept telling himself he was safe. His pulse rate was climbing. He knew how to evaluate the data streams he was getting. Simply because he wasn't looking at real-time displays didn't mean he couldn't evaluate that data as real-time data.

Leave me alone. Get away from me. Don't open up. Don't change color. Don't even threaten to do anything strange. Go away. I don't want to know. . . .

He caught himself. That was the problem, the one his digital therapist had pinpointed: He didn't want to know.

He still didn't. He remembered the Ball opening. But nobody else did. He'd seen inside it, but he couldn't evaluate what he'd seen. There weren't places like that inside finite spheres of that size.

There wasn't a place in there. It wasn't a door to somewhere. It was a ship. He knew that. He didn't know how he knew that, except that he remembered that there were ships like that.

He didn't want to know how he remembered that there were ships like that.

There were sad-eyed aliens with big, mobile mouths who had ships like that; ships that cavorted under lavender skies and darted among rainbow rings of glorious hue—and he didn't want to know that either.

He wanted to go home—back to Earth.

He still hadn't managed that.

You don't get what you want, just because you want it. Life forces you onward, toward death, through trial and toward understanding, by way of . . . what?

Not by way of aliens.

There was no need for aliens in Joe South's life. Everyone around him was an alien. He couldn't understand humans, let alone aliens. He couldn't be comfortable with the alien beings who looked just like him. So what was he doing here, looking for more trouble?

Volunteering for trouble.

For risk.

Out here trying to force a confrontation with the one danger he wasn't qualified to face.

So that he could remember, the way his therapist said he would if he faced his fears.

Well, here were his fears, all housed in a silvery ball a

hundred meters in diameter that had ignored every other attempt to penetrate it but had opened its eye and winked seductively at South.

Come on in, big boy, it had taunted him. *You know my secret. Here I am. Come get me. Get in. We'll go fly the universal skies. You know what to do.*

A test pilot wants to push the envelope, go where nobody's gone, do what can only theoretically be done. Throw his life up into the air and see if God still loves him.

Well, he wasn't sure that God was out there, anymore. And he wasn't sure if the universe needed him to challenge it.

Yet here he was, and he had a collection of circuitry by his bunk that was telling him he was doing the right thing.

He snapped up his helmet, and the smell of Birdy at work invaded his suit, giving him a sense of reality.

"Birdy," he croaked, "patch me through to Keebler on ULD-1001."

He didn't want any time to think. He needed to act.

Or at least, something inside was impelling him to act.

Birdy cleared a com line and started hailing ULD-1001. Vince Remson wanted Keebler kept busy again. Remson didn't expect "any miracles, Commander South. Let's just make sure we know where these two are and what they're doing. If you have any luck with that black box, we'll consider ourselves blessed."

Remson was grasping at straws. Hoping the black box would prove effective in some way with one of these artifacts, but afraid to try anything that might be perceived as aggression against the teardrops.

So he wanted South to try the black box on the Ball. Like the last time. But this time, keep a better record. And keep Keebler from pulling any more stunts.

This government was paralyzed. It couldn't handle more than one crisis of this size at a time. Now that the Secretary General was out of contact they were obsessed over there on the *Washington*. Every move they could make had negative consequences, except not moving.

So they were sitting there in a painful, exaggerated stasis, trying not to breathe until Mickey Croft miraculously reappeared and told them what to do.

South looked at the scans Birdy was showing him and abruptly got up from his command chair.

He'd brought that therapist along. Doing so had caused a lot of trouble. Now he was going to see what it could do.

STARBIRD wasn't roomy inside. Behind the flight deck was a narrow corridor leading to his bunk, with its redundant command-and-control capabilities. The digital therapist looked like an old-time industrial vacuum cleaner. He'd secured it the best he could but there wasn't much room, so it blocked the way to the head.

He reached down and flipped it on. It whirred and said to him, "Ready, Commander South, to continue your session?"

Did the damned thing know he'd turned it off?

Probably not, he decided. His suit whirred again and tried to stabilize the biochemical spike that went through him as he said, "Did I ever tell you about the kids who disappeared in a spongehole that opened up real near here?"

"No," purred the therapist, blinking one red light at him as if it were winking an eye seductively. "Please do."

"Well, see, I was wondering if the disappearance of the kids had anything to do with the appearance of the teardrops, or with the Ball here," he told it.

But his suit got so freaked at the way his body was reacting to his attempt to verbalize those questions that it shot him full of tranqs.

He sat down, abruptly, flat on his butt, shaking his head to clear it.

He wasn't sure if the therapist answered him, at first.

He thought he heard something. He was dizzy and high as a geostationary orbit. Then the suit realized it had overestimated his reactions, and his wrist cuff pricked him three times more.

He merely sat there and breathed until the pharmakit brought him back to sobriety.

Then he said to the therapist, "What was that?"

"What do you think?" it said.

"I think that maybe I need to go out there and find out," he said harshly.

"Why do you think that?" it wanted to know.

It truly did resemble an old-time vacuum cleaner, the canister kind with a nozzle clipped on the top.

He said, "I think that because maybe I remember something being inside the Ball, and because the Ball seems to have started all this."

"Why do you think that?"

"I dunno. Birdy's better at this than you, you know."

"Why do you think that?"

"Because she has more responses than 'Why do you think that,' is why."

"How can you be sure that's the case?" it asked him.

"Got me. Maybe I'll take you out to the Ball and you can ask *it* dumb questions, okay? I can use the company."

"Whatever seems to help is appropriate," it said.

"Good." The therapist kept a running log, South knew. It was small. It was innocuous. No intelligence could possibly perceive it as threatening. It bore no resemblance to a weapon. And anyway, he wanted to see if he could make *it* sweat a little. "It's settled. You'll EVA with me, and then if Birdy and I are both destroyed by the Ball, or sucked into it, maybe you'll be left behind. After all, you're not the sort of thing a search for intelligent life would turn up, are you?"

"Why do you think that?" asked the therapist in its soft voice.

He'd forgotten that it had to respond to a direct question.

He stood up, and saw that his MESSAGE CUE light was blinking.

"Birdy, you could have patched them through," he told the AI disapprovingly as he flopped onto his bunk and hit the com activation button.

His bunk came alive with redundant command-and-control functions. If the forward flight deck were destroyed and the ship's integrity breached, a clear partition would come down between the bunk and the forward section. He could putatively survive and navigate his way back to safety from here.

Sure thing.

He'd spent plenty of time holed up in here on the trip back from X-3. Lying here, he remembered everything he'd felt then, and wished he'd gone forward.

Well, he was a whole hell of a lot better off than he'd been when he'd jumped out of sponge and found himself facing Threshold. He hadn't realized how far he'd come until this moment.

The old reactions were still there: the anger, the fear, the rest. But he was better than he had been. Lots better.

And Keebler was demanding to know, "What is it ye want, sonny? Are ye tryin' t' tell me they pulled the plug on our li'l mission? Cause if ye are, ye c'n fergit it. Me and Sling is goin' out there with our box, and this time, Southie, ye ain't pullin' no bait and switch on us. Hear?"

"I hear you, Keebler. Keep your pants on. I just want an update. We've got to coordinate our EVAs. You guys should be parking by now."

"We're right behind you," said Sling's voice. "We'll be up alongside in . . . three minutes, fifteen seconds. That quick enough for you?"

South could have had video, but he didn't want it. He lay back on his bunk and slapped his faceplate down. "That's soon enough, friend. I'll be right here, waiting."

He toggled off. Then he had Birdy bring up a full scan of the Ball on his heads-up and lay there, rubbing his arms through his suit, face-to-face with the Ball.

Or face-to-face with one of his own nightmares.

He kept waiting for the Ball to start doing its rainbow display. When it did, this time, he'd be ready.

He'd promised himself that much.

And now that he was here he wasn't going to back down, or turn tail and run.

Mickey Croft was facing these aliens, somewhere. If worse

came to worst and South got lost somehow, separated from everything, even from Birdy, maybe he'd find Croft there waiting for him.

In his dreams, his parents and everything he loved had been right there with those sad-eyed aliens, under their majestic, coruscating skies.

But he didn't want to lose touch with Birdy. He didn't want to go out there. He didn't want to get sucked into his past, where everything was so much harder than it was now; where he was less in control; where the unknown was inimical, and he couldn't trust anything outside his suit.

He really didn't.

So if worse came to worst, he'd throw Keebler into the maw of the Ball if it opened. Keebler could be his sacrifice to the god of the Ball. He grinned at that thought, and his face was stiff.

Birdy and he and *STARBIRD* had come this far. No matter how hard his tattered psyche was taking this, he couldn't turn back now.

Once a test pilot, always a test pilot.

He was going to get out there on a tether, fire up that black box of Sling's, and see if the same thing he remembered happened again.

And this time, he'd have witnesses: Sling, Keebler, Birdy— and his therapist.

The Ball that hovered before his face on his heads-up display didn't seem to give a damn. Or at least it wasn't doing its color dance.

Yet.

CHAPTER 16

$\triangledown$

Promenade

Mickey Croft shook the hand of the Council's Interstitial Interpreter and looked longingly into its huge, sad eyes. "You'll follow?" he said, and was vaguely aware that he sounded like a child seeking reassurance.

"We will follow, Mickeycroft, as agreed," said the Interpreter, with a bob of his conical head.

With that the mist around Croft's perceptions cleared a bit, as the honor guard of slit-eyed beings manifested to lead him back to the bubble.

Or another bubble. He kept looking over his shoulder, into the swirling pink and gold and green mists that surrounded the Interstitial Interpreter.

Every time Croft looked back the way he'd come the Interpreter would wave the light ball in his hand, as if he were standing on a bluff waving a lantern while one of Croft's ancestors pulled out to sea from a rocky shore.

This feeling of leaving home was so intense that Croft's throat closed up and ached.

And ached. And ached more. Then his ears started aching and he looked around again.

Now he couldn't see the Interpreter any longer, only a

small, bright light in the strange geometry of the ship's farther recesses.

But ahead, on either side, were two honor guardsmen—perhaps the same two. Long skirts. Conical hats. Slitted eyes, and a way of sliding authoritatively through the eye-teasing space around him that kept Croft from breaking down in great, wracking sobs.

He was a child again, leaving home for private school. He was walking the lunar regolith on his tenth birthday, because he'd had to have his puppy put to sleep. He was wandering through Threshold's lower reaches, because his mother had died and there wasn't anyplace to go that her memories didn't linger. He was being made Secretary General today, but his fiancée of twelve years had finally told him she couldn't marry him: there was no one alive in the whole world who cared about him.

Nevertheless, even then, there had been everyone. As now, there was everyone. Around him were ceilings that didn't lie flat, or curve in a way that a human eye could follow. There were pulsating expanses reminiscent of walls that met and twisted and breathed so that he could almost hear them sighing. Everything was lit from within with soft colors, some of which he could recognize as colors only because they made his eyes tingle when he looked at them.

Sometimes he thought he could feel the photons exciting his optic nerves. Sometimes he could taste the colors he saw. Sometimes he could almost see the feet of the two honor guards moving slightly ahead of him.

Sometimes he could sense the skirts they wore, as if those skirts were dragging at his own knees, brushing his own ankles.

And sometimes he seemed to be dropping through the solid floor, which was not solid at all. Then he would see layers and strata of curls and twists and curves and five-sided squares with an edge in infinity, all of which enclosed him and supported him and were in their turn supported by undulating, multicolored wraiths of stalactites and stalagmites, and snakes that were made up of colored spots that never touched but all billowed together in rhythmic being, as the seconds of time and the instants of time touched them and blew them and then blew on.

He was in an infinitely divided space which was at the same time unique and undivided, moving through the interstitial elements of eternity and an infinite space having no boundary conditions whatsoever.

He knew that his physiology wasn't capable of translating what he was experiencing into knowable parameters, because his host had made that clear to him.

But Croft hadn't needed to be told. His body knew what was happening to it. It was existing in another sphere. All of its functions were happening simultaneously and yet being held in abeyance.

Solid was liquid; liquid was gaseous; gaseous was elastic; elastic was rigid.

And yet his bones didn't melt. His heart didn't get confused about whether it had just beat or was about to beat. His thoughts proceeded in a good imitation of sequentiality, from subject to verb; from impulse to articulation; from stimulus to response.

So he could communicate. So he had communicated. So he would continue to communicate with these beings of immeasurably more evolved nature.

They had promised him that much, in no uncertain terms.

Otherwise, despite the people in his care, he might not have been able to bring himself to leave the vista within their vehicle. In here was infinite yet finite space and time, compressed so differently that Mickey Croft was living forever, each second he existed here.

He was content, yet ambitious. He was indescribably sad, yet unutterably content. He had complete volition, yet he was acting in harmony with a process greater than himself. He had no wants, but great desire. He could reach out and touch any surface here, and turn it into a part of himself, a portion of his experience. And that interaction would enrich and alter both the Mickey Croft that did the initiating and the subject that experienced his will.

It was so hard to leave this place of man's desiring, which had always been in his heart but which his imagination had failed to dream, that he nearly could not bring himself to step into the bubble that appeared before him, between his honor guard of two.

But the bubble did not come abruptly to bear him into exile. It came gently, slowly, with great warmth and palpable pleasure in manifesting. It was coming into being to bear him from this place out, to the rigid spacetime of his native universe. It was doing so with eagerness and a fine sense of adventure.

On either side the honor guard bowed their heads. The conical hats were the last he saw of them.

Then his flesh met the surface tension of the bubble and the guardians spun out of being, as if they had become tired of their current forms and preferred to be a billion fireflies ready to mate.

They sparkled away and left him alone, inside the bubble.

Again the floor under him was rigid, but invisible. Every surface he palmed as he made his way along the walls was a geometrically flat surface, but none led back to any other, and yet all converged to circumscribe his fate.

Around him the strata of the interstitial spacetime faded, and suddenly there were stars. At first these were not any stars he recognized. These were young stars, veiled in glorious, opalescent gases. These were infrared stars spreading out embracing arms to one another across a prickly space full of color.

When the color faded, the universe was shades of black and purple and blue and green. But Croft never again would look at those dark tones and fool himself that the space between the stars was black, or empty, or devoid of teeming life.

He sat down where he was when the sky turned black-and-white, and he found that tears were racing down his cheeks.

All the strength had gone out of him. He couldn't think of a single reason to go on, cast back here into the empty world of biological time.

And then he could. The Interstitial Interpreter was coming. He was bringing his ships. Bringing them to Threshold. He'd promised Croft he would.

As Croft began to reconstruct the fragmented memories of a visit that had not occurred in sequential time, he realized that the bubble was bearing him inexorably back toward the as-yet open air lock of the *Washington*.

Now he must articulate something to those who depended on him. Now he must find a way to describe a meeting held in a place that was neither a room nor a landscape, and an understanding whose parameters had been described not by words but by the rights of sentient beings who shared life.

How was he going to begin to explain?

The ship toward which the bubble bore him was the UNE's pride. It seemed flat, ugly, squat, and primitive. He wondered whatever had possessed him to come out here in such a poor craft.

Then he remembered that humanity had reached this level of culture, and none higher. And he remembered his body, which was bound by its physical constraints and its biological limits to a certain group of spacetimes, and no other.

So far.

Croft knew he must find a way to prepare his people for meeting the Interstitial Interpreter, because they wouldn't have the benefit of a trip into the Council's domain.

They called themselves only that, and they were wise beyond Croft's ability to weigh.

All of mankind could not go where Croft had gone. Not yet. Not for a long time, perhaps. So he must be an emissary for the inexpressible connectedness of being that he had experienced, and for the brave souls among that Council who would venture into Croft's spacetime to deal with beings like himself on their own turf.

Croft tried to imagine what it would be like to be one of

those aliens and to commit to spend finite time in a world dominated by a forward-moving arrow of experience.

Their new guests would be limited, during their stay, to moving only from the past to the future. They could travel in space only up and down, forward and back, and side to side. Their geometric choruses would be reduced to nursery rhymes.

Could they think in this linear spacetime?

Croft had thought, after a fashion, in their multilinear one. The Interstitial Interpreter had been trained for his job, had chosen it, as Croft had chosen his.

Mickey must find a way to prepare a welcome, to instruct his own people.

Most of all he must stop mourning for what he had just lost, which was something that no man could experience and ever forget.

He had been in a harmonic resonance—at one with, but separate and distinct from, and interacting with, another race.

He must say, "Remson, I want you to treat these . . . guests of ours with utmost courtesy. Be sensitive to their need for contemplation. Be attentive to their appreciation of solid and fluid states of matter. Walk softly, for they will be on hard floors that screech against their bones like chalk on a blackboard. Try to soothe them with roundness, for squares and angles are hard-edged and combative."

But when the bubble squeezed him inside the air lock and withdrew, what Croft actually said was: "Vince, come meet me. Alone." And the sound of it was so harsh, so filled with lines and angles and squares, that he was suddenly embarrassed for himself and for the whole human race.

Remson's voice echoed inside Croft's helmet: "Mickey, I've been trying to get through to you for hours! Are you all right?"

"Yes, Vince. All right."

"Then get out of the damned air lock hatchway, so we can close the outer door. We were about to start cutting our way in to get you."

Only then did Croft realize he'd been standing in the air lock itself, arms and legs braced against the opening, staring back toward the teardrops.

While he was there, the outer lock couldn't close. The inner one couldn't open. And he hadn't heard a thing if, as Remson said, they'd been trying to get to him for hours.

He stepped back. His arms and legs felt rubbery. Cut their way in? Croft realized what an undertaking that would have been: moving in a secondary air lock to protect the life-support inside; cutting through a safety system meant to withstand the forces of high acceleration and even kinetic attack. . . .

"Vince, is everything all right?"

"You tell me, Mickey. Those ships are moving toward us. We're ready to fire on signal."

"No!"

"Okay," said Remson. "No, then. You want to tell me something about your trip?"

"I have so much to tell you. . . ."

"Start with how come those ships are moving. Then try why you're certain we don't want to at least fire a warning shot or two. Then how about what, if anything, you learned concerning their intentions."

"Vince, I told you: It's all right. They're sending this delegation to Threshold. The three ships will follow this one back. Don't worry. We'll receive them as honored guests—the most honored guests mankind has ever had the pleasure to receive."

"Yes, sir," said Remson. "If you say so, sir. I'm right here on the other side of the lock, with some medical help. . . ."

"I don't need help. Tell me you'll make sure that all the ConSec and ConSpaceCom forces stay here, by the Ball."

The air lock light turned green. It must have been red before. Mickey hadn't noticed.

Vince Remson and three other suited figures came pouring into the little lock.

"Fine," Remson's voice said. "Look, Mickey, let's go."

Remson was tugging on his hand. Others had hold of his shoulders, his waist.

He shook them off irritably. "I can walk. I'm fine." He remembered how to put command into his voice. He pretended not to be dazed, not to be empowered with a new sense of purpose.

He would be the Michael Croft of their memories, Secretary General of the United Nations of Earth, the way they needed him to be.

When they met the Interstitial Interpreter and the honor guard, they would know the true import of this visit.

Now he must prevent them from making a terrible mistake.

They must trust him, trust his judgment.

"Vince, my office. Make sure none of those ships move from their current stations. I want a continual watch on the Ball. Call ahead and prepare Threshold. We're about to have one hell of a diplomatic reception."

As they stepped out of the lock, Croft palmed back the faceplate on his helmet.

Remson's helmet was already off. So were those of the medical team behind him.

Everyone was looking at him anxiously. Their faces were drawn and concerned, full of worry and fear.

"I'm sorry I couldn't talk to you as the meetings progressed," he told them. "We made substantial progress," he assured them. "And I *am* fine," he demurred, when the head of the medical team wanted to whisk him away for a physical.

Only Vince was not fooled. When they walked alone toward Mickey's office, Remson said: "What's really going on?"

"I told you. I'll tell you more. Now we've got to make sure that only our ship, as an honor guard, leads their three ships to Threshold. It's their custom."

"I'm having a little trouble with that." Vince Remson's pale eyes were fixed steadily on him. There were beads of perspiration on his forehead.

"I can't believe that such a simple order can be trouble-some, Vince," said Croft as they got into the lift.

Remson lit the indicator to take them to Croft's quarters. "ConSpaceCom isn't sure that your authority extends that far."

"How far is that?" Croft asked mildly, in a soft voice that made Remson duck his head as if he expected to be struck.

"Far enough to deploy ConSpaceCom forces."

"I think, if you'll check, you'll see that in extraordinary circumstances such as these I can function as Commander in Chief."

"You need to invoke that? Circumstances warrant it?" Remson had never, in Croft's experience, looked so dubious. "If we leave all our security forces out here, what's left to defend Threshold, if these three ships pull something, is a pitiful force."

"Not only do these ships stay here, but I am insisting that not just aggressive action but anything perceived as defensive action be expressly forbidden for the duration of the visitors' stay on Threshold. Is that clear?"

"Nope," said Remson, crossing his big arms over his pres-sure-suited chest. In one hand he still held his helmet.

Croft took the helmet from Remson's unresisting fingers and played with its faceplate. "Then let's make it clearer. No matter what happens at the Ball site, no one is to fire a weapon of any kind. Everyone is to maintain a watchful posi-tion, and not leave the Ball area without my personal and explicit permission."

"Why?"

"Vince, do as I say. You'll understand in due time. As for ConSec and ConSpaceCom, their duty is to follow our orders, not ask for explanations before they decide if they concur. Are you telling me you've had a mutiny while I've been away?"

Remson's eyes dropped. "No, sir. I . . . I'll see to it."

The lift stopped. The door opened. "Then let's get to it," Croft said, and led the way out.

"It's just that . . ." came Remson's voice from behind him.
Croft kept going.

Remson caught up, saying, "Mickey, the ConSpaceCom
brass is sure the home system's about to be invaded."

"And if it is? Or has been? What could we do about it?"
Croft stopped. Remson stopped too, staring disbelievingly.

Croft let what he'd said sink in and then clapped his assistant on the back. "We've got so much to do, Vince. I don't
know where to begin."

"The beginning, sir, will be fine with me," said Remson,
as he toggled through his helmet's comlinks, still holding it in
his hands, to establish a line to ConSpaceCom forces.

And since Croft knew that that was exactly where they
should begin, now that command was reestablished, he began
to feel better. With all human endeavor one started at the
beginning, proceeded to the end, and then stopped.

He'd forgotten that, having spent so long in a spacetime
where beginnings and endings were arbitrary and thoughts did
not proceed in a linear fashion.

At least no one had shot up the Interstitial Interpreter's
party.

Not yet, that is.

But Croft knew that Remson was going to have his work
cut out for him, making Mickey's orders stick this time.

Funny, he hadn't expected the threat of violence. But then
violence against such a superior force was unthinkable.

Of course no one else realized that yet, either.

But they would, soon enough.

The Interstitial Interpreter, his three ships, the honor
guard, and more were coming to Threshold. One way or the
other.

So they might as well come smoothly, with as much pomp
and circumstance as Mickey Croft could muster.

Humanity's future and its fate, its hopes and dreams, were
at stake.

CHAPTER 17

$\triangledown$

Guard Duty

The ConSec patrol cruiser *Blue Tick* orbited the Ball slowly. Behind it, the deployed vessels of the Consolidated Security Force waltzed in perfect formation around Spacedock Seven and the artifact parked there.

Reice's ship was the comet's head and the rest of the force made up its tail.

He felt about as useful as a comet. Pulled and pushed by powers beyond his ability to control, he was on a fixed course that nothing he could do or say would alter. Until it was too late.

The teardrop ships were gone now—on their way to Threshold with Mickey Croft's blessing and full UNE honors.

Out at Spacedock Seven, only the initial threat of the Ball remained to justify the commitment of Threshold's defensive might so far from home.

Inside the *Blue Tick*, Reice sat moodily in a darkened cockpit dotted with colored running lights and undulating graphic displays.

Blue. Green. Yellow. Orange. Red. Pretty colored lights in the dark. Lights that cascaded down the control suite and danced on the face of Reice's wrist chronometer. Lights with haloes around them because Reice's eyes were so tired. Lights that danced in place and shifted with the orbiting security force as it circled the Ball.

The Ball lit up sometimes. Reice knew it. He'd seen it.

The only people who didn't perceive the Ball as a threat were the Threshold brass. The ones who'd never been close to the Ball. The ones who didn't understand that the appearance of colors on the Ball and weird occurrences were somehow linked.

Reice had chased the Cummings kid and his girlfriend out here and seen them disappear. The cosmos had opened its mouth and swallowed them whole.

Right about here. At the very coordinates through which *Blue Tick* was now passing. Reice braced himself, in case a spongehole opened up and sucked his ship through into some other space and time—or into no space and time whatever.

He'd cordoned off this area once. He'd known what he was doing.

There was some spacetime anomaly out here. Some gate to another dimension—or worse. That was how the teardrops did their appearing and disappearing act, he had a hunch.

But a hunch didn't play with the powers that ran Threshold. And you couldn't tell your superiors they were acting like fools.

They probably knew that anyhow.

So here he was, promenading over arguably the most dangerous spacetime around, with the rest of Threshold's firepower spread out behind him. If that hole opened up under him, his ship and the rest of them were going to tumble over the brink into the abyss like a bunch of lemmings over a cliff.

And then what was Trust Territory going to do if it needed a little good old-fashioned human destructive power?

Not a damn thing, was what. If Reice and his security force were eradicated, Threshold would be all but unarmed. Incapable of defending itself from the teardrops or from anything else that might threaten it.

But did the brass care about that?

Evidently not.

"Reice, stay out there with the Ball," the ConSec line offi-cer mimicked his orders savagely. "Reice, keep anybody from shooting anybody, even if you have to destroy one of our own ships to keep it from firing on the enemy."

He made a sour face at the sound of his falsetto bouncing off the monitor glass in *Blue Tick*'s cockpit. Nobody could hear him out here, except his ship's black box. And he could take care of anything unfortunate left on his flight recorder, if he needed to—when he needed to.

"Reice," he continued, in a high-pitched imitation of Riva Lowe, "make sure Commander South doesn't do anything stupid."

He broke off and shook his head, as if she were still giving him orders from her nice cushy berth back on the habitat.

"How the hell am I supposed to do that?" he asked aloud.

The *Blue Tick* didn't answer.

Reice didn't like AI chatter. His ship's voice-response was encoded to deliver only emergency information, not chatter.

Normally he didn't need anybody to talk to out here. But it wasn't going to be easy keeping everybody parked out here from doing anything stupid, especially when the alien craft looked so . . . threatening . . . so alien . . . that you couldn't tell whether they might be readying for some aggressive act.

If somebody out here did do something stupid enough to start a war or cause an incident, then it was going to be Reice's fault, thanks to Riva Lowe.

Of course to believe that, you had to not believe that the appearance of the Ball hadn't been such an incident, or that the arrival of the ships was the start of a war.

Reice wasn't sure what he believed. About the only thing he was sure of was his unwillingness to add to his list of current duties the job of babysitting Joe South, the Pilot From Before Time Began. *And* Keebler, the grungy fool who still claimed the Ball as his personal property. *And* Sling, who thought he was an operator and had finally maneuvered him-self into a position where an operator's presence was a clear liability.

You'd think, if Creation was giving mankind a heads-up that its time as Master of the Universe was about over, then the folks in charge of humanity's fate would make sure that the people on the sharp end of destiny were the best and brightest to be found.

Not South.

Not Keebler.

Not Sling.

And most especially, not Reice and his happy band of soldiers and cops. Space marines and naval brass, customs bureaucrats and two-bit science officers: Was this the best contact team that the Trust Territory could put together when the Four Horsemen rode into town?

Reice shook his head, and little Reice-reflections moued back at him from his monitors. There must be something he could do to make a difference out here.

Hold the fort. Keep the peace. Ferret out the truth.

He was free to do anything but arrest the perpetrators, unless those perpetrators happened to be humans with itchy trigger fingers.

The real perpetrators, to Reice's way of thinking, were now piloting teardrop-shaped craft majestically in the *Washington*'s wake, on their way to the Stalk.

"Real-time, forward view only," Reice told the *Blue Tick*.

With a sigh of quantumly stored resignation, the ship obeyed.

There in his monitors, the Ball floated. He didn't like looking at it. But it beat looking at his flight path and worrying about sinkholes popping up to suck him up.

And it beat looking at the teardrops headed toward Threshold. The habitat was unguarded, because of orders from their Commander in Chief.

If anything untoward happened, Mickey Croft was going to become the *ex*-SecGen before you could say "Micah Keebler." That is, if there was a civilization left out here to declare anybody an ex-anything.

What Reice wanted, most of all, was to avoid becoming an

ex-Reice. Secondly, if given the option, he'd like to keep the security force under his command from winking out of existence the way the Cummings kid and his girlfriend, Dini Forat, had when the Ball changed colors and the universe puckered up around their ship. . . .

Reice tried once again to push inexplicable memories away. He'd plotted a course right over the spot where those kids had disappeared. He'd been in hot pursuit and, back then, he'd been willing to follow them into Hell itself to bring them back.

When he'd flown over the spot where they'd disappeared, the spacetime had been as normal as a club sandwich in the Blue Mid officers' lounge.

So what was he worried about now?

But then there hadn't been three teardrop-shaped ships popping in and out of Threshold's continuum at will.

He'd seen that much. He'd been locked on UFO-1 when it disappeared. And he was sure it had disappeared, physically. Not used some sort of stealth device. Not moved a centimeter to the left or to the right.

UFO-1, with its unique multi-spectral signatures and its discrete mass, had simply removed itself from this spacetime.

You could do that without violating the laws of physics around here, in the natural world to which Reice was loyal physically and mentally, only by attaining sufficient acceleration to let relativistic effects multiply your mass and alter your relationship to your native spacetime. Then you punched your way into spongespace; not before.

How the hell could anything just remove its mass from the local spacetime without leaving so much as a perturbation behind?

But there hadn't been a waveshift or so much as a gravitational ripple. There'd been no ghost-signature in infrared, even. So maybe the teardrops aren't really physical, he had thought.

But UFO-2 and UFO-3 were each reading as solid as a proverbial house. Or an asteroid. Or a space habitat.

What was solid when it wanted to be, and nonexistent when

it didn't want to be? What came and went at will without traversing linear distance? Bohm-Aharanov transforms hinted that the universe as man knew it was merely a result of a unique set of boundary conditions—everything humans could perceive as real was no more than bits of stuff caught in a narrow band of special-case conditions bound together and maintained on and by the surface tension of an energy sea.

All the three hundred civilizations man had seeded across the stars were living on that surface like so much flotsam, floating on a narrow band of "reality" that couldn't even perceive the rest of the natural world.

If the teardrops could be here, how could they be *not* here without leaving so much as a plume or a trace behind?

Riddles like those could make your head ache. Reice had enough headaches right now.

He had to decide how you could tell if the alien craft was readying for an aggressive act. Or if the Ball was.

The Ball was his job, he reminded himself savagely. That's why he'd dumped his scans of the teardrops on their way to Threshold. If the teardrops made a move, there was nothing much Reice could do about it from here.

In fact he'd been ordered not to do anything about the teardrops, no matter what they did.

Even if they ate Threshold whole. If they positioned themselves around the habitat and somehow created the same set of conditions that had swallowed up Cummings III, his girlfriend, and their ship before Reice's eyes, there was nothing Reice could do about it anyhow. Not even if Mickey Croft had ordered him to try.

So the best thing was to be sure he and his security force were ready to blast the Ball to component atoms with Kinetic Kill Devices if it made a false move.

But you had to know what a false move by the Ball would look like. And he had to admit he didn't.

He also had specific orders *not* to open fire on the Ball, even in self-defense. Even if it started opening up suck-holes and picking off the security complement's ships one by one.

"This sucks," he said aloud. Nobody could order you to commit suicide, not even Mickey Croft. "Head count," he told *Blue Tick*, then listened as, one by one, the ships under his command reported readiness.

Of course that meant, eventually, he was going to hear from Joe South.

South and his antiquated *STARBIRD* were like a thorn in Reice's side that Riva Lowe kept jabbing him with.

When South reported in, Reice bypassed the automated reporting circuit and said, "Hey, South, how about you come on over here and we talk about what's going on?"

There was a pause on the com circuit which lasted altogether too long to be a function of South's ancient electronics and the hijinks that *Blue Tick* had to go through to facilitate coms with *STARBIRD*.

Then South said, "I was . . . just about to go outside and have a hands-on look around." The pilot's voice was more than usually tinny.

The bastard was in a damned space suit. Ready to EVA, Reice was willing to bet.

"The hell you will, without my direct order," Reice nearly snarled. "You get your butt over here, if you need to stretch your legs. I have a burning need to avail myself of your unique perspective and expertise."

South never knew when Reice was insulting him.

Or maybe he did. The pilot said, "Hold it a minute, Reice, okay?"

Reice said, "No way. I'm ordering you to come directly here, right now. Door's open. Coffee's on."

Instead of breaking the circuit South said, "Then I'll have to bring Keebler and Sling with me—or let them go off on their own."

"What?"

Reice told himself that he'd misheard owing to the pilot's infuriatingly low tone. South couldn't have meant what he'd just said.

But then, Riva had told Reice to keep South from doing anything stupid. "If you're telling me that Keebler and that box-jockey of his are up to some stunt involving the Ball, and that you know about it and aren't actively trying to end-run it, you're in for more trouble than you've ever seen, Relic."

There was a long pause, with heavy breathing in it.

Then South said, "You know I'm just getting used to the rules around here, Reice. Let me see if I can't rephrase what you thought you heard: Keebler, Sling, and I were just about to go check the hull of Sling's ship. We're reading a violated seal and we can't find it from inside."

"Tell you what I'm going to do, South," said Reice, trying very hard not to let his voice betray the fury that was making his throat prickle. "I'm going to remember you don't know what the fuck you're doing. And you remember who's giving the orders out here. Got that?"

"Yep. I got that. Once we get this seal patched, we'll be right along—if you've got room over there for three?"

Reice rubbed his face with his hands. The pressure of his fingers on his eyeballs felt good. He tried telling himself that South was trying.

Trying not to be an infuriating son of a bitch.

Trying not to be a classic test pilot sort of asshole.

Trying not to flout authority.

But Reice just couldn't believe it.

He said, "*Now*, South, or you're going to have more to worry about over there than a possible leak or two. I have orders to prevent any untoward action in the vicinity of the Ball. At all costs. Got that?"

"It'll cost Sling and Keebler their lives if life-support—"

"It'll cost you your ship, buddy, if I don't see it and you on your way over here by the time I count ten. That's T-E-N. Now . . . One . . ."

Reice felt as much as heard the com circuit to South go dead.

"Two," he said into the circuit, not caring.

"Three," he said, reaching up to set target-lock-on for South's *STARBIRD*. A KKD up *STARBIRD*'s ass long ago would have solved a number of Reice's problems.

"Four."

Blue Tick shivered a little as she made attitude corrections to facilitate a clean shot up *STARBIRD*'s tail pipe.

"Five," Reice said softly, nearly purring.

His targeting screen blossomed to life, cross hairs centered on the antique ship from the early twenty-first century.

"Six." Reice's voice, despite his best efforts to control it, was almost jocular. He'd have to break off his verbal count-down to let the rest of the security force know that he was firing one disciplinary salvo, and that nobody was to take this single incident as a reason or a pretext to start plinking away out here, but—

"Hold it, Reice, okay? Just hold it. We're on our way."

"Not just you, South. Keebler and Sling in that prefab jalopy of Sling's, too. Or I just keep counting."

This was more fun than Reice had thought he could have out here. "Sev-en."

He was about to switch com channels when South, finally realizing that Reice was serious, began talking fast and promising complete obedience.

"That's better," Reice said, trying not to sound regretful. "Maybe together we can figure out what we're looking at out there."

South's com spouted precise ETAs.

Reice belayed the targeting lock-on and crossed his feet on his control suite's bumper.

Sometimes he liked his job. He hadn't liked it enough lately.

Once he got that hotdog pilot and the Scavenger over here, at least Reice could be sure that, if he wanted to, he could carry out his mission.

Funny how, when those mission parameters had been threatened by South and Keebler, doing the mission had seemed a lot more desirable than it had previously.

Maybe Remson and Lowe were right. Maybe the best thing was to sit here, on guard duty, and make sure nothing untoward occurred. From their side.

As for the other side . . . well, Reice wasn't a diplomat. But he was in charge of keeping anything from busting loose out here.

And he was going to do that.

Just to make sure, he was going to spend the remaining time before the arrival of South and friends talking personally, in his capacity as chief of the security contingent, to everybody on the flight deck of every single ship in this deployment.

Just in case any other fool had some bright idea.

Because somebody would. Every other ship out here had somebody aboard who was using all this standoff time to wonder whether the standing orders in effect were wrongheaded.

It was a natural reaction to inaction, and a natural function of sitting at the sharp end of any possible action.

So Reice wanted to make sure that the other ship commanders, many of them technically of higher rank than he, were "in the loop."

Everybody needed to know that he, Reice, had things under control.

And that he, Reice, intended to keep things under control.

No matter what.

CHAPTER 18

$$\triangledown$$

Prejudice's Ugly
Head

"Cummings the Second has found out about the aliens, Vince.
I'm sorry," Riva Lowe sighed into her office vidphone. Blue
Mid seemed to have shrunken around her, now that there
were aliens on Threshold. Her office with its curvilinear
azure-and-cobalt walls now seemed to be some sort of prison.
She was uneasy, but didn't know what would make her feel
better. Remson was going to think she'd failed. "Vince, Cummings wants to gain whatever trade concessions are possible—
make some sort of deal with the aliens to exploit the new
business opportunities—the usual."

"And you think," came Remson's words, while his thin lips
moved along with them on her desk's vidphone screen, "we
ought to let him?"

"I don't know what else to do. I told you, he's determined
to meet with them. He'll do it somehow."

"He'll have to meet with me first." The tiny image of
Remson's head wasn't a bit less formidable because it was
framed in a minimonitor.

She'd never before felt the brunt of Remson's displeasure.
And she didn't like it.

"Christ, Vince, it's not like I failed or anything. Cummings still wants to take that trip to Earth—and take me with the party." *Remind him of that. Remind him you've got some clout of your own.*

And don't let him scare you. How could anybody make you so nervous without saying a single thing that was overtly threatening?

Riva was afraid the next thing that came out of her mouth would manage to be just the wrong thing. As a matter of fact, she might have said the wrong thing already. Probably had said it. When someone like Remson decided you weren't up to the challenges, you simply stopped being a part of the challenging work. . . .

Riva Lowe would rather be dead than sidelined. She'd put too much into this Earth gambit, and into cultivating Richard Cummings, Jr.

So why didn't Remson say something? Why was he staring at her that way?

She said in a small voice, "I think we ought to meet." *Don't tell me you don't have time to see me. Don't tell me you're too busy.*

Remson said, "I think that's a good idea."

She nearly blithered thanks. Even if he tore her apart when she got to his office, she'd be *in* there. Face-to-face. Able to give the best account she could of herself and her actions. She'd have a chance. He was giving her a chance to redeem herself.

Then Remson added: "Bring Cummings with you. If he wants to meet the aliens, perhaps we'll oblige him."

"No problem," she said faintly. But it was one. No need to tell Remson that Cummings had been bitching about aliens in the habitat without those aliens first having undergone quarantine—about the germs and unknown dangers.

But there *was* a need. "He's . . . Cummings is somewhat xenophobic, so we'll have to expect him to threaten to lodge a formal complaint, as a major stockholder in Threshold."

"But he wants to meet them, right?"

"I think so. That's what I make of what he's been saying, anyhow. I think he feels left out of the decision-making process."

"Then we'll see him first, privately. And play it by ear. How's right after lunch? Call my office scheduler when you have a firm time."

The screen went blank before she could reply.

She got up, got her purse from her drawer, and then paused. She reached down and toggled her way through a morass of offices and schedulers until she'd firmed up the meeting that Remson had decreed.

She had to move things around on her own calendar to do it, so when Croft's office complained she wasn't polite about it.

Then she had a moment to breathe. In it, she decided that she was winning.

She went out, down through the tube station, and waited for her car to come. She *was* winning. She was back in the loop. If Cummings was going to meet the aliens, then that meant she'd get to meet them, too.

Every time she made a step forward like this she was too busy doing the job and protecting her backside to be impressed with herself, or to be honored, or to evaluate the challenge ahead as "progress" simply because she was facing it.

The car slid up to the tubeway entrance, opened its door, and purred. Inside, she'd barely initiated a security block before she was patching through to the psychometry station in Customs.

When she reached the station manager she asked for a report from South's therapist.

The report came up on her car's cam screen: PATIENT IMPROVING. MEMORY BLOCK PARTIALLY REMOVED. SOME VIOLENT SIDE EFFECTS. HOSTILITY TOWARD THERAPIST NOTED. THERAPIST DUMP TWICE DAILY RECOMMENDED IN CASE OF DECOMMISSIONING.

What did it mean? She stared at the red letters. Did the therapist think South was going to trash it?

It sounded like that to her.

So she called her office and told her secretary, "Have South come back in from Spacedock Seven. I want him at these alien meetings. He's the only one who's had contact with— Never mind. Just override any other orders. He's on this Earth junket's roster. I need him here. ASAP."

She wasn't sure why she'd done that, except that she didn't know what to do about the coming confrontation between Cummings and the aliens. The Secretary General's office didn't understand Richard the Second.

Unfortunately, Riva was beginning to think that she did.

Maybe she should assign Cummings a therapist. But he wouldn't stand for it.

The next best thing to a therapist intimate with Cummings would be time to model the NAMECorp CEO on Mickey Croft's psychometric sampler/modeler.

She grinned, as the car accelerated in the tube. She had just enough time to beg modeler time from Mickey, grab some lunch, and change before the meeting with Remson.

Croft still owed her a favor, didn't he?

But when she reached Croft's office and asked to talk to him, she was cold-shouldered.

So she went over to the modeler facility. She hadn't used up the time that Mickey'd allotted her.

She could walk in and use the equipment.

She hadn't been here for ages. The staff had redecorated. Or Mickey had spruced up the place.

Even the lift, when her car sighed open before it, was newly tinted a silver-gray.

Nice. She got in and pushed the indicator for the floor she wanted. The lift checked her fingerprint, and she felt the scanner overhead verifying that she was admissible.

Everything here was very civilized. No guard to ask for her credentials. No need to stick your face in a derma/retinal scanner and steel yourself for the sharp puffs of air against your eyes.

When the lift opened onto the modeler floor, a chime sounded and a soft voice-warning said, "This is a restricted area. Please observe all appropriate security measures. Proceed to the scan gate for further instructions."

All of this was new. Probably brand-new—security instigated in response to the presence of the aliens on Threshold.

As she stepped out into a maroon-and-peach hallway with deep carpet, she could feel the mixed field-scanners going over every inch of her body.

She'd gotten this far without the proper identification. Could she still be fried where she stood?

Could be. The hall was soundproofed. Her footfalls were swallowed up. She couldn't even hear herself breathe.

There were no other doors leading off the hall, and that was new. There had been, once. New, but not remarkable.

The remarkable thing was the presence of a human at the Security Scan Station. Mickey's staff wasn't taking any chances.

"Director Lowe?" said the stern-faced man behind the desk. "We don't have you on—"

"I have some modeler time due me. I thought I'd just use it up while I was in the area." She realized how lame it sounded.

The man looked at her as if she'd gone mad.

She stared back. What was going on around here, anyway?

He looked away from her and punched three buttons, then typed a message, then looked up.

"You can go through, Director. But you'll need to leave your things here. And please change into one of the white suits in the control room before you go into the sampler/modeler room."

"I understand," she said, although she did not.

She hated to leave her purse, even though the man couldn't have rifled it if his life depended upon it: its seal opened only to her touch.

Still, there were things in there that would be difficult to replace. She said, "Don't lose this."

The fellow's chin doubled with officiousness. "We never lose anything, Director."

"I'm sure you don't."

She moved by him, into the room that had once been the external control chamber for the sampler/modeler.

Then she began to understand. There were seven people crowded into that room, looking through the glass at what was going on in the inner sanctum.

And inside, behind the glass, were Mickey Croft and one of the aliens.

Riva Lowe's breath caught in her chest. She'd never seen anything like that alien. She'd seen bioengineered subhumans, designed for mining worlds and terraforming duties, but those had been designed from a human template.

And she'd seen lower forms of life indigenous to planets from three hundred suns. But they were nothing like . . . this.

This was . . . a creature . . . of immense presence.

It had a conical hat or a conical head. It had huge, sad eyes that seemed to float out in front of it and envelop its body, or supersede its body.

The eyes made it difficult for her to see the rest of its shape, because those eyes mesmerized her.

She forgot about putting on the white suit and pushed her way toward the glass.

"Hey," said someone she'd jostled.

She tore her gaze away from the alien, and there was Remson.

She looked up and smiled wanly. "My god," she said.

"Pretty spectacular," Remson said, in a way that made her wonder what he was hiding and what he was lying about.

Obviously Mickey was modeling the alien being, and the model was giving information so classified that nobody but the Secretary General himself was allowed in the room.

So what?

Remson could have told her, that was what.

And why were all the others out here, watching?

And . . . "What's with the white suits, Vince?"

"It's not really worried about our germs, but it thinks we should wear clean suits to protect ourselves from some sort of submolecular non-native pollution."

"What's that mean?"

"Probably that it wants to be alone with Mickey."

"So that's not—"

"Not a simulation, no. They've been modeling . . . history, I guess. Simulating things I've never seen. I don't know what some of the stuff was. Places, maybe. Hyperspaces. Maybe it's giving Mickey a physics lesson. Or maybe he's trying to show it that we're capable of some high technology ourselves."

"Maybe he wants to show it that we're not afraid," she murmured, pressing her face to the glass without thinking, so that she bumped her nose against it, hard.

"Or maybe," said Remson harshly, "he's trying to convince it that we're capable of understanding what it's got to say. Whatever it is it's taking a long time, and they're not talking out loud at all."

"What?"

Remson reached into his pocket and pulled out a transducer with an earpiece. "If you'd be a good girl and get into your suit, you'd find your own comlink to the inside. But don't bother using it. They haven't said a word, either of them, for an hour. They merely look at one another, and the modeled simulations change."

There's nothing being displayed by the simulator at the moment, she thought. Then she looked again. She'd come in here once on her own and modeled a person. You could create a holographically displayed template of a specific individual and ask it questions. It would react and respond very much the way the person might, theory said. So you could ask questions that would prepare you for a difficult diplomatic session. Find out how someone might react to a line of inquiry or to a proposal. Without having to ask and be rebuffed. Without the other person ever knowing that you'd launched such a line of inquiry.

But the thing, if thing it was, in the modeler display area did not resemble a person. It resembled, now that she looked closely, an enlargement of a few excited photons dancing in a microscopic display, with a swirl of iridescent gases in the background.

"What do you think they could be?"

"We don't know. And Mickey's being . . . uncommunicative with us."

She looked up at Remson sharply. "Vince, are you saying . . . ?" He was worried. Clearly.

"I'm not saying anything, here. I'm watching. I'm waiting for my boss to indicate what he wants to do. I'm wondering where to go from here if he doesn't. And I'm wearing my white suit because I was to told to, by Mickey. You should, too."

She went to get it and put it on.

So Remson wasn't angry at her, or worried about her failures with Cummings. He was distracted. Something was happening between Mickey and the alien being that no one was qualified to assess.

That would really hurt Remson. Remson was Mickey's bird dog. Remson was Mickey's right hand.

When the right hand is cut off from the body at the owner's request, the hand dies. The owner lives.

She found a suit. The ankles were elasticized. So were the wrists. She nearly fell over, trying to get it on over her clothes. As she was doing that somebody behind her spoke.

"Look at that. What the fuck is it?"

The sound was so startling in the silence that she nearly jumped. Then she turned to look.

The modeler was now showing a geometry. Or something like a geometry. An embedding diagram. A hypnotist's tool. A mandala. A vista. A place. A space. A hearth and home. Colors beyond rapture.

Stairs that climbed everywhere. Circles that wound in and out of your brain.

And strata of distance that went forever, because you could fly down them with your eyes and your body followed.

She wasn't sure she was still standing where she last remembered standing.

She was whizzing through a kaleidoscoping swirl to a place she'd always been, but never visited.

And then she was right where she'd been before, with her hips in the white suit and Remson shaking her shoulder.

"Let's get out of here. We've got the Cummings meeting to prepare for." His eyes seemed sunken into his head.

So then she had to take off the white suit and scramble after Vince, a huge, solid, stolid shape against which everything she'd just experienced seemed to collide and shatter.

Outside the control room full of observers, he hushed her and led her to the elevator.

They reached it before she remembered she'd forgotten her purse. "Wait," she said. "I left my—"

And then she was zooming down the hallway, headfirst, as if she were flying. She found her hand outstretched for the purse and her body back at the Security Scan Station, in the blink of an eye.

As if she'd really flown that far. And the man there held out the purse to her as if nothing untoward had happened.

But when he bid her good-bye, the words dripped off his lips like molasses.

And now here was the lift, and Remson holding open the door.

This time she'd had no sensation of flying headfirst. But she'd . . . *slid* the distance.

Her stomach was still fluttery from the speed of it.

She opened her mouth again but Remson held up a forestalling hand: *Don't talk.*

In she got, and the lift closed and descended. She felt the wavebath of the lift sensors, checking her.

They recognized her, or the lift would have stopped

between floors. So she was still the same person who'd gotten into the lift.

Wasn't she?

When the tubeway door opened, Remson's car was there. He motioned her inside: "We'll take mine. Send yours along."

Inside, she'd no sooner settled back against the plush than he was slapping drinks out of the bar. The car was already under way, blue flashers strobing, siren screaming so loud she could hear it, even inside.

"What are we going to do?" Riva said. A dumb question, considering all she'd seen.

But Remson said, "Good question. I hear South is on his way back. You ordered that?"

"I thought— Well, South thinks he's seen aliens. . . . Maybe they're the same aliens."

"Good thinking. I should have done it—never mind. We need to get Cummings his interview with these aliens, and soon."

"What?"

"I've got to get Mickey away from it—from them. There's two others we've seen—three, in the formal contact party. The other two seem to appear less often. Of course there could be fifty and we can't tell them apart. At least two more, though. I guess they stay in their ships. This one's the 'Interstitial Interpreter,' according to Mickey. The other two are 'honor guard.' And that's all we know."

"We haven't been on the ships?"

"Nope. Unless you count Mickey's having been on them. But he's not making much sense about what he saw there."

"If what he saw is like what we were seeing in the sampler/modeler how *could* he make much sense, trying to describe it?" she asked.

Remson nodded his head. "That's a good point. But I need to know: How xenophobic is Cummings, really? If we arrange the meeting, is he going to be able to handle it?"

"You were going to chance it, without warning me what

they were like. I just walked in on that little scene back there. You didn't invite me in on that, or anything. . . ."

"Easy, Riva. Seeing them—that stuff—makes people jumpy."

"I guess. But what about Cummings?"

"I told you, I want to separate Mickey from that stimulus. So far, Cummings is just on for a meeting with you and me. We've got to decide if it's safe to let him spend time with . . . one of those things."

"Don't we have to ask the aliens? I mean, will they see anyone?"

"It's a contact delegation," he reminded her. "I want to put South with them and see what happens too—in case I forget to tell you later. As soon as he gets back."

South, with those aliens? She thought she'd object, but couldn't say more than, "His therapy reports say he's beginning to remember what he saw, or thinks he saw, on X-3."

"Good. We're due for some sort of luck, don't you think?" Remson sipped his drink and stared into it—either contemplatively or morosely, Riva wasn't sure which.

"Vince," she said. "You don't think this contact is beneficial?"

"To whom? In what way?" Remson wanted to know.

And she said, "South's all right. Mickey will be all right." And that was foolish, because there was no evidence that Mickey was not all right, or that South's purported encounters with aliens on his X-3 flyby were in any way connected with this.

Remson laid his head back, balancing his drink on his stomach in the car that moved so quickly through the tube. "Riva, I don't understand this at all. I don't like what my instinct is telling me. And I'll tell you one more thing."

"What's that?" she asked when he didn't.

"Mickey thinks he's met the ancestral gods of the human race."

CHAPTER 19

$$\triangledown$$

Classified Information

Mickey Croft didn't understand his staff's reaction to the aliens' presence. Or to Mickey himself, now that he'd come back from his trip inside the teardrop.

The Interstitial Interpreter, who was the only alien to which anyone could speak, was "Mr. Interpreter." He called Mickey, "Secretary Mickeycroft," and Remson, "Assistant Secretary Vinceremson."

The Interpreter was physically present. That ought to have answered some of the questions on the faces of Mickey's people. But it hadn't. Not even now, after a grueling session in the sampler/modeler room, did Mickey see so much as an initial glimmering of acceptance on the faces of Remson, Riva Lowe, or the representatives of ConSec and ConSpaceCom now gathered in his office for an historic tête-à-tête with humanity's future.

Mickey said, "Please tell us, Mr. Interpreter, about the Council and the Unity behind that Council." Might as well begin at what Croft perceived as the beginning.

If the people gathered here couldn't accept even the reality of change as it was currently embodied in the alien in their midst, then evaluating that change was going to be nearly impossible. That was why Croft hadn't balked when Remson had insisted on having an AIP-T—an Artificially Intelligent, Preprogrammed Therapist—at the table. A human emissary might have been insulted to have a four-foot canister of electronics there evaluating its every move and word, and the motives behind its behavior.

But the Interstitial Interpreter wasn't insulted. He wasn't even curious, it seemed. Sometimes Mickey wasn't sure how much of human artifactual spacetime the interpreter could comprehend.

After all, Mickey hadn't been able to make much sense of what he'd seen in the alien ship—at least not the sort of sense that could be translated into comprehensive chunked bits that in turn led to literal assessments such as: "so big"; "so hard"; "so near"; "so dangerous."

Fight-or-flight reactions were still the only ones Mickey recognized on Remson's face. Which was impossibly silly. One couldn't flee facts. Reality wasn't contestable.

The Interstitial Interpreter was here. Here physically. Here phenomenally. Here historically.

Everything else relating to those facts might be matters for interpretation, but the II's presence wasn't.

That was what Remson called the alien when he'd told Croft he was insisting on the AIP-Therapist's presence at this meeting: the II.

Perhaps if everything about this encounter with aliens from another dimension could be reduced to acronyms, then the humans would' have an easier time accepting what they were seeing. "Aye-Aye." It sound affirmative. Mickey had smiled, albeit a bit dazedly, when he'd realized what it was that Remson was referring to.

"It" was the creature who now rose to its feet in a completely human gesture of respect for protocol. Except, of course, that it didn't truly have feet. The footlike appurtenances at the bottom of the skirtlike manifestation, which supported the expected trunk and arms and, of course, the conical head, all shimmered with a sort of evanescence that came, Mickey was certain, from forcing itself to be manifest in the spacetime that mankind knew as its physical realm.

The II said, opening its mouth and manipulating air with that sad, wide orifice, "Secretary General Mickeycroft is wanting a reassurance for the people. Harm is not coming from the Council, we. The Council, we, represents the Unity, it, of smart beings." The II paused and "looked" around.

The II's huge eyes never stayed in its head when it focused on you, Croft knew. They swam around in your field of view, or zoomed forward until they were nearly all you could see. They were full of sadness and compassion and they could swallow you up.

Every person at the table sat back as that gaze fixed on each in turn. Except Remson, who held firm with head high, playing a game of pride and purpose. Lowe dropped her gaze, eventually. But by then her hands were gripping the arms of her chair so hard her knuckles were yellow and red and white.

The ConSec commander muttered to himself and reached for a cigar to stick in his fat face, so that he could blow the apparition away with smoke and fire.

The thin, sepulchral ConSpaceCom general, with medals covering one whole side of his chest, let his eyes dart back and forth and pecked continually at a handheld keypad, taking personal notes for his autobiography.

"All beings smart," said II again, in that aspirating simulation of human speech. "All smart beings. Roving beings. Seeking beings. Self-controlled beings. Growing-up beings. Curious beings. So here we are coming to make the contact, first. Asking hello. Seeking permission to make visitation station, to put at Ball."

"What?" Remson exploded first. "Mickey, you didn't say anything about—"

Riva chimed in: "So the Ball *is* theirs."

The ConSpaceCom general muttered, "Over my dead body. Remson, you and I need a powwow, fast."

The ConSec commander rubbed his eyes, hard, with the

palms of his hands. Meanwhile his mouth said, for the record: "We're formally against any permanent presence of any non-governable force within Trust Territory-controlled space, Croft. And you know it."

Since they were all talking at once, the II sat down primly. It folded its six-fingered hands, with their opalescent nails, before it on the table. And it looked at Croft.

Did they "hear" its intent, these other humans in the room, when the II looked at them? Or was that Croft's privilege alone? He "heard" it not in words, but in washes of emotion: patience, commiseration, and a questioning sense that made Mickey know the II wanted him to speak.

That was fine. He wanted to speak, anyhow. He lumbered to his feet, wondering why his body felt so cumbersome. But it had felt so ever since he'd brought it back with him from his trip within the teardrop. If he hadn't known better he'd have said that, while inside the teardrop, he'd been separated from his flesh and was only now remembering how to be at home in it.

What was happening to him? To them all? He held up a hand and everybody subsided. All of their comments could be sorted out later, on the record, by the conference room's transcription device.

Normally that transcription device would be feeding all comments to the screen set into Mickey's place at the conference table. But there was too much for it to handle. The red letters on the screen when he looked down at it were about five minutes behind the proceedings, back at Riva Lowe's first explosive observation that the Ball and the aliens were connected.

Of course they were. Hadn't Remson and the others realized even that much? Mickey was disturbed, slightly, that he'd not had the time to transfer to staff the most basic of the revelations he'd had while in the teardrop.

Never mind. Nothing was ever too late. Time was more elastic, these days, than it had once been.

When he had total silence and everyone's attention, Croft

said, "The Interstitial Interpreter, our guest from the Unity Council, is asking to set up an embassy, nothing more, out at the site of the Ball." He was trying to be noncommittal, carefully choosing his words. "We are, after all, a United Nations of Earth facility, and one of our functions is to host the embassies of diverse cultures." He was stretching a point: The function of the UNE was to host embassies from the varying cultures of mankind.

"The precedents we are setting here are crucial," he continued, watching Remson's narrowed eyes then Riva Lowe's wide ones, because in those two he expected a degree of support and from those two he could gauge how he was doing. "We're going to need to consult more widely, of course, before we can respond formally to our guest's request."

Now he had to look at the alien. And before his staff, he wasn't sure he dared risk it. So he hesitated, and his glance fell on the AIP-Therapist. Its console was ablaze with lights, including a red one that was unblinking, staring at him as if it were a representative of some AI constituency that he also must satisfy in his negotiations with this alien race.

Then he could delay no longer. Eye contact with the Interstitial Interpreter was always jolting. It carried much more information back and forth than did verbal contact. The huge, sad eyes of the II came flying toward him, demanding and consoling, urging and reiterating.

Had he made a terrible error, in having this meeting so soon? Was he going to fail, before this observer of an alien culture, to grasp the great opportunities it had thought to offer?

Or was he going to fail his own kind in another way and bring among them, prematurely, something with which mankind was not yet ready to live? In peace. In harmony. In understanding.

The way the Unity Council insisted that it was time to live. Croft knew that much. The impatient eyes (hovering so close to his face that he couldn't see the people at his conference table) were unyielding on that point.

He forced himself to blink, and it took all the strength at his command to bring down his lids.

Breaking the contact was as real an experience as turning off a light or flipping a switch. He began breathing again, although he hadn't known he'd been holding his breath. He was dizzy and his ears were ringing.

He was still standing, he realized. He had to say something more. He opened his eyes and, avoiding the II, looked steadily at Remson. "Our guest must be tired. Such a momentous announcement is one we of the UNE must consider in depth. We will reconvene this meeting tomorrow, by which time my staff and I will have a concrete response to the Interstitial Interpreter's proposal."

Have a dimensional gate installed at Spacedock Seven? Have intercourse on a regular basis with creatures whose native spacetime was so different from that of mankind?

Or was it? Croft was so glad to sit down, so relieved he'd found a way to close the meeting, that he didn't realize immediately that the Interstitial Interpreter had gotten to its "feet" once more.

The II said, in a voice that seemed to come from as far away as the beginnings of the universe, "We must very much like meeting the Pioneer who has brought the Ball to your realm. We will like this being, a heroic soul wise and bold. This person, being a privileged person so far as the Council and the Unity is concerned, should be brought to us. We will be feasting him with glory, since this is his rightful prize."

"Oh, Christ," said Remson, and looked at Riva Lowe, who shook her head and made a face.

The ConSec and ConSpaceCom reps whispered together.

Croft didn't at first understand what the II wanted. So, since it was clear that Remson did, Mickey said, "Can you arrange that for us, Vince?" as much to cover the fact that he had no idea whom the II meant as because he wished to facilitate any honoring of a human by the Council. He wasn't sure that any uncontrollable meeting of a private citizen of the human worlds with the II was wise. Not until he and his staff had come up with a position on the establishment of a Unity embassy at the site of the Ball. But . . .

Remson stood up stiffly. "We'll have Micah Keebler brought around within . . . say . . . twenty-four hours at the latest, Mr. Interpreter. We don't order our civilian population to appear here or there. We can only invite Mr. Keebler, who's a member of the Salvagers' Guild—and who, by the way, still claims ownership of the Ball in question."

"Ownership," repeated the II in a sibilant aspiration, and floated away from the table toward the door.

Croft unceremoniously followed, afraid of he didn't know what: Would the II float right through the door, and scare the pants off the security types watching? Would it disappear? Sink through the floor? Float up and through the ceiling? Discorporate altogether?

Mickey's more practiced eye caught the change in the II's substance level. It was more . . . ethereal. Its six-fingered hands seemed to be fanning, almost like the fins of a fish.

He caught up with the II. Perhaps the door would open for it, sense it as physical. Perhaps not. The II had displacement, but that displacement wasn't the sort of mass that the conference room's doors were accustomed to recognizing as a reason to open.

He shouldn't have worried. The door opened and, beyond it, the honor guard stood, waving their censers. The smoke filled the anteroom with a weird multicolored glow.

Nothing the air-cleaning and -conditioning system could do was moving that smoke away from the honor guard. Or from the Interstitial Interpreter, who stepped right into it. Behind the two Croft saw four harried consular staffers trying to pretend that these guests were no different from any other guests.

The II waved at Croft, a gesture reminiscent of a benediction, and the three of them turned as one being to let the staffers lead them off to their quarters.

Croft was beyond wondering about the timing of the honor guard's appearance, or the way the smoke followed them wherever they went.

He was too harried at that moment to worry about small things. But the sight of the aliens in his office complex, wafting down the hallway with humans on the edges of the ball of opalescent smoke in which they traveled, was like nothing he'd ever expected to see.

Remson said, from close behind him, "Mickey, are you coming back in? I don't think you want to let this meeting end here."

Remson was right. Croft shook his head as if the simple gesture might clear it and walked back inside, shoulder-to-shoulder with his trusted executive officer.

Before they took their seats he had time to say, "Vince, you and I need to have some time together," and Remson responded, "God, Mickey, I was hoping you'd suggest that."

So they agreed on taking high tea in Croft's office, once this room was cleared.

But to clear this room he had to deal with what the alien had put on the table.

The ConSec and ConSpaceCom reps were adamant that they needed to consult their own people before they could voice an opinion on the proposed Unity embassy.

Mickey said, "And of course, we'll consult all the UNE ambassadors as well." That was going to take a couple of all-nighters to accomplish, since one had to include the three hundred colony worlds in the case of a decision this momentous. "But let me just state, for the record, that we may not really have much of a choice."

"What do you mean, Mr. Secretary?" asked the Con-SpaceCom general.

"You know exactly what I mean, General," Croft said brutally. "We couldn't stop them from setting up an embassy or any other outpost here if we tried with every iota of force at our command."

He let the ConSpaceCom general and the ConSec commander argue that point until both of them finally ran out of wind.

Riva Lowe and Remson had their heads together. "Riva, do you have something to add?"

"I . . . We . . . That is, we were figuring out how to break the news to the Scavenger."

Mickey Croft grinned. It had been so long since he'd even smiled that the gesture made his face feel unfamiliar. He'd never realized before that when he grinned the flesh under his eyes rose up and occluded his field of vision. Strange.

But: "Tell Keebler that his dreams have come true: He's going to be rich and famous, exactly as he predicted. He is, after all, the man who discovered an artifact from an alien civilization, just the way he claimed. The vid-show rights to his story alone will set him up for life. You won't have any trouble with Keebler, unless you let on that he's doing us a favor."

"I'll handle it," Remson promised. "Riva, I'll need your help, though. Can you join us for tea, in a bit?"

She agreed. Croft adjourned the meeting. He wasn't pleased that Remson had invited Lowe to join them. He'd wanted to really get under the crust of what was happening, and he couldn't bare his soul with the woman around.

But there wasn't much time, in human terms. The two security reps had to be motivated to serve the greater good in a way that was very different from their usual tasks. They had to understand that humanity might have no choice.

If that was the case, Croft wasn't sure anyone ought to know. You couldn't un-happen events. You had to go forward. One way or another, even if the UNE declined to allow the alien Council to send a Unity delegation to take up residence at Spacedock Seven, humanity was now in contact with an alien civilization that in all likelihood possessed power beyond man's wildest imaginings.

"We have to go cautiously, people," he warned them at the end of the meeting. "We don't want any hostile actions, or even a perception of hostility on our parts. No matter how difficult it is, we must behave in as civilized a fashion as we can muster—show our best face."

Show that face to the distant stars. Show it despite all the internal squabbling in the UNE. Show it despite human and subhuman and animal rights violations. Show it despite prejudices and violent upheavals among competing strains of humankind. Show, most of all, a united front—one that was stable and predictable.

One that was in no way threatening.

And show all that despite the aliens' request that Micah Keebler, the crazy, grungy, paranoid old Scavenger, be brought to meet them, there to be honored as a special friend of the Council and the Unity.

What had the II called Keebler?

"The Pioneer?"

If jealousy was what Croft was feeling, then perhaps he could get over it. But he didn't think that jealousy had anything to do with the queasiness he got when he envisioned the Interstitial Interpreter welcoming the Scavenger into the aliens' midst.

This was, Croft thought as he shepherded everyone out of the conference room, one of those days when you wished you could redo everything you'd just done, and come out with a different result.

What were they doing, the lot of them? Were they qualified for this incomparable task? Was anybody qualified for such a momentous undertaking?

He noticed that Riva Lowe was followed by the wheeled and self-powered AIP-Therapist as she left the conference room.

Maybe the AIP-Therapist would have some insights that would be helpful. After all, it wasn't human. It wasn't trying to cover up anything. It wasn't embarrassed by its faults. It wasn't overly conscious of its flaws. It didn't know a damned thing about Original Sin, except what had been programmed into it.

And it certainly didn't care if its god turned out to be less than perfect.

After all, its god was humanity, who'd created its kind out of what was lying around in the Earth's crust.

And humanity wasn't much of a deity.

If it turned out that these Unity beings were being so paternal to mankind for some good and sufficient reason, then that wouldn't bother the AIP-Therapist or its kind.

But it bothered Mickey Croft that he might be the ticket-taker at the first-run showing of Judgment Day. It bothered him one hell of a lot.

CHAPTER 20

$\triangledown$

Contact

"So, Mickey," said Remson, wishing that his boss didn't look so much like someone blinking away a deep sleep, "are we going to ask the Unity Council what they know about the missing Cummings and Forat kids?" Remson put a chocolate-covered tea biscuit carefully on his plate.

Croft frowned and sipped his tea. He didn't want to answer. Or couldn't, quite yet.

Riva Lowe was pouring the Darjeeling, and it was so damned civilized here in Mickey's quarters that it could have been any century, Remson mused, back on Earth—if you discounted the canister-shaped AIP-Therapist sitting at the table, its head just rising over the edge and one red light blinking steadily.

Croft finally said, "We have no proof that the disappearance of the lovers' spacecraft was related to the Ball."

"We've got plenty of circumstantial evidence, sir," Riva Lowe burst out, and then subsided, biting her lip.

Remson pressed the point. "If they're admitting the Ball is theirs, then I think we've got a right to ask. Think about it, Mickey. The kids disappeared in a suddenly perturbed space-time. We've got that on the records. Right near the Ball."

"But we'd be accusing them of something. Or it would look

as if we were, Vince. And I want to avoid unpleasantness at all costs."

"If we don't ask them about it, Cummings will," Riva Lowe said positively. "I've been spending time with him, getting ready for the Earth trip. And I can tell you he's determined to see those aliens. And he's xenophobic."

Mickey snapped his fingers and Remson looked up.

"That's it! We'll invite the aliens to Earth. On the same junket. It'll be—"

"How can we—" Riva started, and stopped.

Remson picked up her thread: "Can we do that? Do we dare?"

"What have we got to lose? If the Unity wanted to land on Earth, we couldn't stop them. I think perhaps they're waiting for an invitation. Sort of, 'I showed you my planet, now you show me yours.' "

"They showed you their *planet*?" Remson couldn't keep the bewilderment, and the disbelief, out of his voice.

Croft nodded. He looked a thousand years old today, as if he'd become a Chinese dowager suddenly. All the skin on his face was loose and creased, and it flapped as he moved his head. "While I was in the teardrop they took me . . . somewhere. There. It's so hard to describe, I can't begin. But I know I was somewhere much larger than the inside of that teardrop-shaped ship. . . ."

"Okay, maybe Earth's the ticket," Remson said slowly. Give in on the easy points. Mickey had taught him that. But Mickey wasn't himself, these days.

Where was the down-to-brass-tacks discussion of how much of this alien pronouncement was misinformation? Disinformation? What about *traps*? Were they friends or foes? Or didn't Mickey care? Was he under some kind of spell?

More than anything, it was this that worried Remson. He'd had Riva bring the AIP-Therapist to monitor Mickey, not the aliens. You couldn't monitor the aliens effectively. You had no template for standard "good" and "bad" behavior against which to judge the II.

But Croft was another issue. And Remson was scared to death for his mentor. "We've got to face the fact that they might have kidnapped those kids. How come they know English so well? And *Farsi*? When they first hailed us, they hailed both in Farsi and English. Cummings III spoke English; his girlfriend, Forat, was a native Farsi-speaker. So maybe they should be accused of something. I know it would make me feel better, to hear their answers to our questions about the kids."

"Cummings will broach it, somehow. If we don't give him the chance, he'll find one. Make one. Bribe one. Or force one. Don't count him out of this equation, gentlemen. If you want a pleasant exchange with these Unity beings, you don't want Cummings aroused." She sat back with both hands on the belly of the teapot, as if her hands were cold and she was trying to warm them.

"Riva's right, Mickey. Even if Richard the Second doesn't charge the aliens with kidnapping, the Muslims from Medina eventually will. After all, the girl's a daughter of a mullah."

Croft sat back, his hands raised to fend off their joint attack. "You have it, children. You have it. But please, don't do your rabid-dog act around the Interstitial Interpreter. I want us to present ourselves in the best possible light. For as long as that's possible." A hint of Mickey Croft's old sardonic humor tugged at the corner of the Secretary General's mouth. "Which may not be long, with Keebler being brought into the picture."

"Keebler," Remson muttered. Keebler's lawyers were still insisting that the UNE's confiscation of the Ball was illegal. "What rotten luck."

"Maybe not," Riva said brightly. "Let's ask the AIP-Therapist what it thinks about Keebler meeting with the II."

The therapist had access to all current therapy banks.

"Why not?" Remson asked, and waited for Croft's reaction, an interrogatory eyebrow raised.

"All right," Croft said. "But it's on your head, my dear

boy, if that AIP-Therapist tells us that we should make Keebler the UNE ambassador to the Unity Council."

Within that shell-shocked exterior the old Mickey was still alive, Remson realized with relief. Then he wondered how chipper *he* would have been, if he'd just been through the traumatizing experiences that Croft had.

Aboard that bubble. Sucked into the teardrop. Aboard the teardrop when it disappeared. Seeing who knew what? Having experiences he couldn't bring himself to relate. And then having to lead the aliens back among mankind. Remson wished he could have been more charitable, more empathetic.

But everybody's collective ass was on the line here. If Croft wasn't up to it, then Remson had better be one hell of a support system.

Mickey needed Remson like Mickey'd never needed him before.

Riva Lowe fussed over the AIP-Therapist's control panel, like a proud mother about to send her child on-stage for its first piano recital. Then she sat back.

The AIP-Therapist's red ready-light turned to green. The green light blinked with its words as it spoke. The words were beautifully modulated, in a nonthreatening female voice:

"Ready to consult," it said.

"What would be the result of letting Micah Keebler, the Scavenger, meet with the emissary from the Unity Council?" Croft asked in a reluctant, half-mumbled way.

"Keebler. Searching. Interstitial Interpreter, according to sampler/modeler data, could be allowed to examine Keebler under supervision. Keebler will be greedy and will try to gain concessions in regard to Ball, considered his property. The result could be informative. No damage to relationship likely to result. Keebler is well within the human curve. The Interstitial Interpreter wants to interact with humans, not just a single human. See South, Joseph."

"What?" Croft said.

Remson said, "Another file. Want it?"

"Oh." Croft knew he should have realized what the therapist meant. He was embarrassed. A troubled look crossed his face. He said, "I'm just tired."

Remson said, "Everybody's tired. We're all making little mistakes. Together, maybe we can keep from making the big ones."

Vince Remson wasn't sure he believed his own pep talk.

He cast a glance at Riva Lowe to see her reaction, but she was already leaning over the therapist. "File ready," she said.

"Okay, AIP-T, let's have the South interface to the Keebler/alien meeting."

"South dreams of meeting similar or same aliens. Probability high that dreams have some basis in past reality. South remembers some alien contact. File is sealed, patient/therapist confidentiality. But patient may relate."

"Patient/therapist confidentiality, my ass!" Mickey exploded, his face red. Then he calmed himself with a visible effort. "I've got to get some sleep." He lifted his tea cup and said from behind it, "Riva, you're South's friend. Talk to him as soon as you can. See what he knows that's relevant."

"I've already asked him to come in. He'll be here shortly."

"Here? Where was he?"

"Out at the Ball site, with Keebler," Remson said before Riva could. Mickey wasn't remembering everything he should. But maybe it didn't matter. Maybe it was what Croft did remember that mattered. "We'll take any data dump you choose to give us from South that sheds light on the Scavenger/alien meeting, Riva."

Somebody had to take charge. If it wasn't going to be Mickey, then Remson had to do it. The worst that would happen would be that Mickey would reprimand him later for being too forward during the meeting.

But this was a crucial meeting. With Lowe and the therapist present, it was an on-the-record meeting. Nobody here had any doubt of that.

"Good," Riva Lowe breathed. "How about taking the Interpreter to Earth?"

"Earth? Planet of origin?" said the AIP-Therapist.

"Earth, planet of origin," she confirmed.

"Insufficient data to assess effect on alien. South data assesses positive."

"Thank you," said Riva Lowe and sat back, triumphant.

Remson didn't quite understand her motives or her triumph until she said, "So, since Cummings is demanding access to the aliens, and Cummings, South, and I are going to Earth in any case, perhaps the most decorous thing to do, as Secretary Croft suggested, would be to take the aliens on a tour as well."

Mickey Croft covered his eyes and gave a mock groan. "I'm surrounded by schemers. I'm giving up." He opened his hands enough to peek at Lowe and Remson between his fingers. Then he said the obvious, in a flip voice: "I'm not up to this. I've been through too much. I'm an old man—too old for this much change this fast. You youngsters are going to have to be my able support in this, my moment of crisis."

Bless him, Remson thought, he's got more grace under pressure than any man I've ever known. In a voice as flip as his boss's, Remson said, "For you, anything. Even a trip to Earth. And you know what a hardship Director Lowe and I consider that to be." Remson smiled at his own sarcasm.

Mickey didn't.

So Remson continued: "But we'll manage. For the greater glory of Threshold and our Secretary General, to bear up. Won't we, Riva?"

"I promise," Lowe said solemnly, "to be the best appointment secretary any alien ever had. With Vince as our travel agent, Mr. Secretary, I think you can look forward to the rest you need."

Croft's hands came down. He sighed. "Yes, children. That's it. A long, relaxing junket to the planet of our hereditary beginnings. Just make sure you bring that AIP-Therapist along, young woman. I may have need of its services myself.''

Remson felt the tension drain out of him. If Croft was suggesting he needed help—even from an AIP-Therapist— then everything was going to be fine.

At least, so far as Vince Remson had the power to assure.

CHAPTER 21

$\triangledown$

Valued Friend, Pioneer

The Scavenger stared at the creatures before him and blinked. The alien threesome didn't disappear. They stayed right there, in the Secretary General's paneled sitting room.

"So this's why ye dragged me in from m' Ball," Keebler said, somewhat mollified but trying not to show it. It was still his Ball, according to his lawyers. He peered around at the Secretary General and his assistant, and at that damnable Customs woman who was pulling Joe South's strings. Keebler grinned as wide a gap-toothed grin as he could.

Then he hitched up his pants and, without waiting for the flunkies to run ahead and make any damn-fool introductions, strode over to the aliens.

He'd known there'd be aliens. There *had* to be.

And here they were.

The three . . . creatures . . . stood up, if you could call it standing, as Keebler approached.

One was bigger than the other two. It had a knobby, elongated skull and pure black eyes as big as pancakes. This one started floating toward him, while the two on either side began swinging some sort of pots with smoking incense in them.

179

Keebler took a step back, despite himself. Then he held his ground. No use letting the aliens think he was scared. There couldn't be anything dangerous here, or that pansy of a Secretary General wouldn't be in the same room with it. Not to mention the woman, Riva Lowe.

Keebler held out his hand and puffed out his chest. "I'm Micah Keebler, member in good standing of the Salvagers' Guild. That Ball out there at Spacedock Seven, it's m' pers'nal property. I found it, nice and legal, salvaged it clean as c'n be. Now iffen yer a-wantin' it back, it's me ye gotta talk to. Which I guess is how come these high-and-mighties here has got me all the way in from the Ball to talk t' you."

Then the biggest alien took his outstretched hand and all the spit evaporated out of Keebler's mouth. His head spun. He saw distant places and faces from his childhood. He saw dreams and lost desires, fond hopes and mother's arms, and all of his family. He saw his cat, the old black ratty thing, with its chewed-up ear, from when he was a kid on Belle Vista III.

And he saw the Ball. Saw it clear as day. Saw it spew rainbows and dance before his eyes. Saw it open wide and swallow him up.

Inside, he was surrounded with cavorting birds singing love songs, only they weren't birds at all. They had faces. Faces like the faces from his dreams. And there were hills and white temples on the hills. He didn't know how he knew they were temples. But they were. They had columns and domes and they felt . . . holy. Peaceful. All-knowing. Reverently powerful. Awesomely content with being.

Then the alien creature let go of his hand. Keebler shook his hand as if he weren't sure who owned it. He wiped it on his greasy coveralls. He looked around quickly.

The Secretary General, his assistant, and the Customs woman were still behind him. They hadn't moved. It was as if no time had passed.

Maybe no time *had* passed.

The alien was beginning to speak: "Micahkeebler," it said.

"I am the Interstitial Interpreter of the Council of the Unity. You have done us a great service, Micahkeebler. We wish to reward you. We must ennoble you. . . ."

"Good luck," Remson muttered.

The alien ignored the interruption: "Micahkeebler, you are the Pioneer for your species. This is you, who are the hero. This is you, who brought enlightenment and the path to other-knowingness to your people. This is you, whom we will praise as bold and far-seeing in our Council."

From beside and behind the big alien, whose wide, sad mouth was trying to smile but not succeeding very well, came the other two.

The one on the Interstitial Interpreter's right reached into his smoking pot and brought out a bar that shone like gold.

He held this out and Keebler, after a look at the other one, reached out to take it.

It wasn't gold. Gold wasn't this heavy. But it was cold, and it had squiggles all over it. Keebler knew it was precious. He said, "Thank y'. Thank y'. But this don't mean I'm relinquishin' m' claim to the Ball, no siree. That Ball's mine, and will be—"

The big alien opened its huge mouth again. The eyes above the mouth were huger, now, than the mouth itself.

The mouth worked, and out of it came words: "The Ball is a gate, a portal. Shall you own a gate? Shall you own a way, a path, a place that is no place? You cannot use the Ball, Micahkeebler, Pioneer, valued friend of our universe, child of our hearts. Take this wand of ennoblement and with it our greatest gifts."

This alien motioned to the one on its left, and that one reached into its pot and pulled out something that looked very much like a gem-encrusted box.

Keebler's mouth had spit in it once again. He licked his lips as he reached for the box. This time when he said, "Thank y'," he meant it.

The sense of the big alien's words was beginning to penetrate. "Thank you, from the heart of the 'Pioneer.' I'm glad

I was able to he'p y'all. I want you to know I consider it m' honor and m' glory to be able to be the first man to open tradin' relations with you folks. Of course as the Pioneer, I know you'll make sure that I'm the guy who ye come to whenever you need to know about people. About what they might need. About what they make that you might need. See, it's a tradin' society, people-society is, and—"

"You will come with us, Micahkeebler, to our home, yes? To be there honored by our kind and to meet other Pioneers, dear valued friends, of our kind?"

"Hell, yes!" Keebler looked around quickly to make sure these Threshold bureaucrats were hearing this.

"C'n you hear this, Sec'etary Croft? You two? I been invited to go see their world!"

"We heard," Croft said in a thick voice. Then the tall, lanky Secretary General stepped forward.

He came all the way up until he was shoulder-to-elbow with Keebler.

Then Croft said, "I must insist that the first emissary from our culture to the Unity be a professional diplomat."

"The hell you say!" Keebler objected. "They didn't ask *you*, buddy. They didn't ask any o' yer diplomats. They asked *me*!" He pounded his chest with his hand.

The big-eyed alien in the front didn't say a word. It looked between Croft and Keebler.

Croft wouldn't quit, though. He said, "We must take this moment to ask the Interstitial Interpreter about the missing ship belonging to Richard Cummings the Third, on which the Cummings boy and his lady friend, Dini Forat, were lost in the vicinity of the Ball. If the Ball had anything to do with their disappearance, Keebler, it's dangerous. And we think that it did. But only the Interstitial Interpreter can tell us what happened out there, to those children."

Croft looked away from Keebler, at the big alien.

The alien seemed to blink. For the first time its eyes seemed to be attached to its face. If you could call what was under its knob "a face." The thing's mobile mouth started squiggling around, and words in English came out of there again:

"The children you talk referring to, Mickeycroft, asked for and received the protection of us. The asylum from you. The safety from killers. Here are these killers. Not with us. We a word and promise to them have given, of safety. Can you so much do for them? Promise safety?"

From somewhere behind Keebler's back came a long, slow whistle. Must be that Remson again, cheeky bastard.

Croft ignored the sound. He said, "Mr. Interpreter, we must keep this matter a secret among ourselves, for now. Understand?" Croft turned to Keebler, and his face was deadly white and tightly drawn: "Keebler, if a word of this business about those kids leaks from here, your butt is mine. Not even our alien friends will be able to help you. I'll bury you in so much red tape you'll never get to open up your trading post to another dimension. Got that?"

"I gotcha, Mr. Secretary. I gotcha. Ol' Micah Keebler ain't no fool. I got the butter, but you got the bread—as the saying goes."

"Good," muttered Croft. And: "May I see that?"

"Ah . . . sure." Keebler held out the box that the aliens had given him. The second present. He hadn't even thought about what might be inside it. It was jewel-encrusted. And so what if those jewels weren't recognizable as any he'd ever seen before? That just made them worth more to collectors. So if it was empty, so what?

Croft took the box in gentle, almost reverential fingers, laid it on his palm, and opened it carefully.

"Lessee! It's mine, ain't it? Lessee!"

Keebler, much shorter, had to stand on tiptoes to peer into the box.

What he saw there took his breath away. Pearls with kaleidoscopes in them. Snail shells that never stopped curling inward. Cut stones with galaxies inside. And more . . .

Keebler snatched the box back from Croft, shut it, and cradled it against his chest. Then he started to laugh.

He laughed so loudly that the aliens stepped back. He laughed until his sides ached. And as he laughed, he crowed to Mickey Croft and his pencil-assed aide and that nasty bitch from Customs: "Tol' ye! I *tol'* you! The Ball was gonna make me rich 'n' famous! An' I was right! Rich 'n' famous! An' this is just the beginning! The beginning, I tell ye!"

Looking at the floating eyes of the foremost alien, Keebler just knew that he was right!

These aliens were going to take him with them, to the place where all this wealth came from! He was going to be their representative, no matter what Mickey Croft said. He could just feel it.

He could feel it the way he'd felt that the Ball was going to bring him everything he desired.

And it had! It had! His Ball was the key to a goddamned new universe, that was what it was! Keebler was going to be credited for discovering a whole new universe!

Now *that* was rich and famous!

As soon as he shook these goons from the diplomatic corps, he was going to find ol' Joe South and Sling and buy both the boys a couple of blue beers, to make up for how nasty he'd been when South canceled the EVA and Sling backed him, and they'd dragged Keebler in here on some pretext about how Keebler couldn't be out there without South to keep watch on him.

Of course, it had taken him a while to find the boys. First he'd had to get out of the alien presence without causing any offense. Then he'd had to sit through a long lecture by Vince Remson, the Secretary General's pet Nazi, about how he had to behave himself and be on call at all times, in case His Government Needed Him.

His government, indeed! The only good government, so far as Keebler was concerned, was a government that didn't bother you.

And that was a government too far away to matter.

Which this one wasn't, by a long shot.

When Keebler finally got out of the diplomatic complex he

was carrying a foolish beeper. A beeper! Like he was some kind of paramedic or artificial intelligence.

Call and I'll be right there, you bet.

Only don't hold your breath, UNE.

Once Keebler was out of the cushy Blue Mid area and down in the Loader Zone, he felt better. But it took some time to hunt up the boys, who turned out to be crawling around the insides of Joe South's antiquated spaceship.

"You two still tryin' to make this salvage resemble a modern ve-hicle?" Keebler hollered down into the hole in the bulkhead behind *STARBIRD*'s flight deck. "Well?"

"Yeah, Keebler?" Sling stuck his head up first. "Whacha want?" Sling still resented Keebler's having called off the bet. But ConSec had interfered. There was no welching involved. There was just . . . no bet. Sling ought to be a better sport. Once he saw what Keebler had with him, he'd forget the stupid old bet. Keebler couldn't have taken Sling's ship from him now, even though he would have won the ship if he'd held Sling to their wager.

Now, "rich and famous" had taken on a whole new meaning.

Keebler put down the sack he was carrying and pulled out a six-pack of blue beer. "Got somethin' t' celebrate, kid. Get Southie up here. I got somethin' a-*mazin'* to show ye both."

South dutifully came scrambling out of the hold after Sling, wiping grime around his face. "What is it, Keebler? I thought you were never going to speak to either of us until the sun went nova." South's expression was mildly irritated, but curious.

"Have a beer, sonny. You too, Sling." Keebler opened two and handed them around.

South shook his head. "I dunno. This stuff makes me feel funny."

"Yeah, but you're more fun when you feel funny," Sling said. "I'll watch out for you if you get a little buzz on."

"You better take a swig, cause you're gonna need it," Keebler opined, hunkering down and reaching into his sack.

When he pulled out the box, Sling swore softly. "What's that, the family jewels?" Sling reached for it.

Keebler snatched it out of range of Sling's grimy fingers. "Keep yer hands off, Sling. This is a gen-u-ine alien artifact, given t' me by a gen-u-ine alien! In person. In the flesh."

Keebler happened to look up right then, in time to see Joe South's face turn ashen.

"Drink up, sonny. Drink up, I say."

South took his beer and walked over to the bulkhead, as far as he could get from Keebler's pride and joy, the alien box, and just stared. He didn't touch his beer.

Keebler didn't get it.

But Sling did. "Keebler, hold on a minute. You sayin' you met the aliens?"

"Yep. Right here. *On Threshold.* In the Secretary General hisself's office! The aliens asked fer me, special. I'm their Pioneer, their special friend. Ain't that a kick?"

Sling said, "Yeah, some kick," and went over to take South by the arm. Keebler heard Sling ask, "You okay, man?"

And South said, "Yeah, I guess. I'm just not up for a party. You know how it is."

Then Sling said, "Keebler, haven't you got someplace to go? Somebody else to bother?"

Keebler cursed them both for stuck-up damn-fool kids, and Sling for a poor sport. He stuffed his jeweled box in his bag, gathered up the unopened beers, and hightailed it out of there. There were plenty of people down in the Loader Zone who'd be glad to celebrate with a fella.

Plenty of people.

CHAPTER 22

$$\triangledown$$

Feeling Different

South couldn't find a single place on Threshold, up here above the Loader Zone, where he felt at ease.

Sol Base Blue, and the Blue Mid slip bay, were military: there at least he knew the rules. Or thought he did. But up here, where the privileged and the civilians called the shots, he didn't fit.

It was just that simple. He kept trying to find a way to acclimate, but he was failing, and he knew it. His hands were shaking. Whenever he was away from Birdy they trembled. And he couldn't stay in his ship forever. He had to work for a living.

Right now, his work was separating him from his ship. He felt like a hermit crab between shells out here on the Secretariat level, where all the brass was.

He'd seen an American flag here once, when he'd been at a diplomatic reception, and Assistant Secretary Remson had been detailed to make South feel like a guest.

But he wasn't a guest anymore. And he was expected to get around by himself. Get along by himself. Make sense out of the way life was lived on the Stalk.

These people who lived on the habitat called it "the Stalk" because it had all these branches and sidebars and spherical living modules that were accessed from a central core. He knew that. But he still got lost all the time, if he strayed from Blue Mid.

There everything was color-coded, and the tubeways took you where you needed to go without your ever having to get off and change cars. Or you could get a private car that would take you right where you needed to be. So he didn't walk around much, except in the Loader Zone.

The Secretariat level was all official buildings, and you had to know which door was which. Or they assumed you already knew.

He got lost so damned much, he was late all the time.

Now he was going to be late to see Riva Lowe at her quarters. He was sure she was going to tell him something he really didn't want to hear. Otherwise why not see him in her office?

Sling had given him a little card that you could use to route yourself: Punch in the destination you had in mind and a schematic came up, showing your position, the route to take, and your destination.

But he kept finding himself off-course. Maybe he *wanted* to be off-course.

Modern life sucked. South was spread too thin. He wasn't doing anything well, because he was doing too much that he only half understood. He felt like a boomerang must feel: forced always to return to the spot it had fled; undergoing an exhilarating rush of freedom, then dragged back inexorably by something incomprehensible.

If he was the boomerang, then the Ball was the hand that kept casting him into the void. No, that wasn't right. Not the Ball. The Ball was the place he kept returning to, and that was all.

How many goddamn times had he been out to that Ball, and been yanked back by the leash at the last minute, before he could touch it . . . ?

He stopped at an intersection and looked around. Buildings rose all around him. These weren't streets, these canyons whose bottoms he walked. Not really. They were just paths into and out of the buildings. Underground was forever, here. There was no surface level. The sense of being deep in a canyon came from the curve far above his head, crisscrossed by frail bridges and tubeways.

On most of the levels you couldn't see the sky at all. Up here, on the Secretariat level, you could. It was a starry night up here, all the time. Eternal night.

Here you knew you were living in a habitat. Down below, where the ceilings were low, you didn't.

He walked through a food court and a plant court, and found the main promenade on this level. As he craned his neck he could see balconies overhanging the courts. He should be able to find the right building. He'd been here before.

Somehow, he'd blundered his way onto the Earth junket. All this man-made living space seemed so oppressive because they were going to let him go home. They were going to let him go home.

Home.

Earth. He knew they had their reasons, and those reasons had nothing to do with his need to see a blue sky and smell real wind and feel real gravity. But he was so afraid they'd take away this chance that he might just blunder his way right out of it again.

He needed Birdy, badly, at moments like this. He needed something to hold on to. He walked around the food court, looking at the stalls, at the shops on the ground level. The people here were all dressed for business: secretaries, government functionaries, clerks, and every other kind of worker bee. Briefcases and book bags. White shirts. Photo IDs slung on neck chains and resting in breast pockets.

His heart was on Earth already. His soul had fled. All but a part of it, which still hovered at the Ball.

The aliens were here. Didn't any of these worker bees know that? Their faces were placid. Tired. Bored. Long-suffering.

What did all of them do, in the great weight of the government complex towering over their heads and hunkering down on top of them?

He tried his routing card again and it showed him where he was again, without a sign that it was losing patience with his incompetence.

He toggled it once more. Everything but details pertinent to his immediate locale disappeared. Nice. He hadn't known it could do that. He started moving through the crowd, looking up now and then, brushing shoulders with people who knew what the hell they were doing.

Don't look around. Forget the kiosks selling everything from tacos to rice noodles. Just pay attention.

He found himself at a pair of closed doors, between two storefronts. They looked like service doors. Beside them he saw a card slot.

He tried the door. It was locked. It said NO ADMITTANCE.

He looked at the card in his hand. It was adamant: the dot that represented his position was blinking, right on course, right where he was. His destination was beyond the door.

He looked for a button to push or a speaker grille: maybe he could talk to somebody inside.

There was neither. You were supposed to know how to get in. Finally he got out his Customs card and ran it through the slot. He heard a click.

He tried the door. It opened when he pulled. He walked inside.

Behind that utilitarian door was marble and dark wood-grain simulation, a lobby with a huge pot of silk flowers, real birds singing in a two-story cage, and a man behind a desk as long as *STARBIRD*'s slip in Blue Mid.

He walked up to the desk and the man behind it said, "Yes? Whom did you wish to see?" as if South couldn't possibly have the right building.

"Riva Lowe."

"Floor?"

He couldn't remember.

"Never mind," said the man. "We'll just check." And he picked up a handset, shielding his keypad from South's eyes.

When the man put down the keypad he said, "Go right up, sir. That lift there."

Inside the lift, he didn't have to ask for a floor or a number. He was automatically deposited where he was cleared to go.

And Riva Lowe was waiting for him in the hallway. Her door was open behind her. She said, "You're late."

And he began explaining until, inside, she said, "Never mind. Help yourself."

There was coffee, and he poured some from a clear container into a glass.

She was already sitting on a long crescent couch. She said, "You'll get the hang of it, just watch. It's not so different from—"

"Earth? You want to bet?" He sat down, as far from her as he could get. He didn't want to spill coffee on her pale rug, or the elegant couch. And his hands were trembling again. She was bound to notice: "Can you tell me what this is about?"

There, he'd said it. Something about these people made it almost impossible to ask direct questions. But he kept trying.

"Certainly." She sat forward and picked up her own glass from the low table, watching him all the while. "We need to know if you're ready for this Earth trip. I need to be able to count on you."

"That's it? Just am I ready? I'm ready. Can't wait." *With any luck, I can lose myself down there and you'll never find me. But then, what would Birdy and* STARBIRD *do without me?*

"Well," she said with a sour smile, "I'm not."

"Excuse me?"

"I need your help, South." She said it as if she didn't believe it herself. "I told you, I need to be able to count on you."

"Yeah, I heard. But . . . help? What kind?"

"We're engineering a meeting between Cummings and the aliens, down there."

"On Earth? The aliens?" South lifted the coffee glass and drank, to hide his expression. He wasn't going to be able to help anybody with aliens. His skin crawled. "Earth, I'm your guy. Anything you want to know, I probably know or can figure out. Aliens—that's another story."

"Good. Obviously, I don't know anything about . . . conditions . . . on Earth. We don't want to make some foolish mistake. With the aliens. Or among ourselves. Cummings knows all about Earth. He has us at a tremendous disadvantage."

"You're worried he'll have the aliens picnic on a hill of red ants? Or hike through quicksand? Or pick poison ivy? What?"

"Ah . . . any of those. Or all of them. Or none. We don't know what the dangers are, as I said. What if he tries to separate us from the aliens? Or to hurt them or scare them? He's xenophobic: he doesn't like the idea of another intelligent race that can give us a run for our money."

"Give us a run for our money?" These people didn't understand what they were dealing with. "Have you . . . seen them?"

"The aliens? Yes."

She had. He sat back from her. Then he put down his glass on the coffee table. "So, what are they like?"

"Like? Oh, that's right, you haven't seen— I have an idea. You tell *me* what they're like. Your AIP-T says you remember."

This was why she'd brought him here. He shook his head. "I can't."

"Why not? What if they aren't the same?"

"Because what I saw isn't what they are. I mean . . . I saw . . ." He closed his eyes.

She said, "You know, your therapy session went so well

that you're scheduled for a pilotry exam. You want that very much, don't you?"

"Don't do this to me." He kept his eyes closed. He was trying not to remember anything.

She said, "According to your therapy reports, you've remembered quite a bit. You think you know something we don't. Why not tell us?"

He opened his eyes then. "You're serious about the exam?"

"After the Earth trip. And if you pass it, which your therapy reports suggest you can, we'll see about getting you the pilot's rating you want so badly. You'll be able to fly anything we have, eventually. But you've got to cooperate with us."

She looked at him expectantly.

He stared back at her, trying to make her drop her eyes.

She wouldn't. He'd never realized how feminine her face was. Yet she was threatening everything he'd done to patch together a bridge of sanity over what had happened to him. He didn't want to remember. The beautiful, misty planet. The rings around it, glowing with soft colors even in the daytime. All his dead relatives, happy as could be. Everything he'd lost, resurrected beyond the farthest stars.

He said harshly, "They show you heaven. They show you everything you want. It's beautiful. I thought I was dead. Maybe I was. Maybe this isn't me. Maybe I'm something they made to look like me. Nothing's real out there. It's all pulled out of your mind. . . ."

Then he looked away from her eyes, because they were beginning to get larger than they should be. They were beginning to float in front of her face. They were beginning to suck at him and tell him things he didn't want to hear.

"Good," she said, as if soothing a child who'd had a nightmare. "Good. Now, what else do you remember?"

"I . . ." He stood up.

Her eyes dragged him down. His body seemed to melt onto the couch. He could barely hold his head up enough to look at her. "You . . . don't think that's enough?"

"Not if there's more, Joe."

She wasn't the same person he remembered. Or *he* wasn't the same person he remembered.

"Well, there isn't any more. What do you want from me?"

"The truth."

"What truth? You tell me something: You saw them. Do you feel the same? Do you think you know what happened to you? Haven't you got the goddamned sense to be scared?"

"We're not frightened, Joe."

He didn't like the way she said that. He'd learned out at X-3 that you couldn't trust your senses, or your memories. A suspicion chilled him, and the old terror it raised in him gave him strength. "You did see them? You were with them, the aliens? Near them? Did you touch them?"

Somehow he wanted her to say she'd never touched them. He'd been in his ship, in his suit, safe inside *STARBIRD*, the whole time. He'd been inside his suit, helmet down. He'd been curled up on his bunk, and the auxiliary life-support function had been engaged. Sealed in his suit. Double-sealed in his bunk. Triple-sealed inside *STARBIRD*'s hull.

Life-support had never been violated. He'd never let them inside. He'd been—outside. He'd been standing in the rubble of his ship and his life-support had failed him. His climate-control system had died. His suit had melted off him, leaving him naked under lavender skies.

And there they'd been, floating at him. All of their care and all of their overwhelming need making him die and come alive and die again and be everywhere he'd ever been, with everyone he'd ever loved.

Then everyone was there, all alive. All happy. All under lavender skies with rings in them.

None of X-3's planets had had rings.

He was shaking all over, and she was still looking at him with too-big eyes that were too dark and had too much pupil in them.

"Answer me," he whispered after a million years had

passed. "Did you touch them? Did they touch you? Were you in the same room with them, without a suit?"

She came toward him across the couch and he nearly cowered back from her. "Don't be afraid. We took all the necessary precautions."

"You did, didn't you—you touched one." He shook his head. He said pityingly, "Now you'll never know what's happening to you."

"We know what's happening. We're setting up consular relations. We're extending our guests every courtesy during their stay in the Secretariat. . . ."

"You let them inside Threshold?" He slumped back, wishing he didn't have to breathe. "They're breathing this air, and you're recycling it throughout the habitat? You're letting them pollute everything?"

"Shh, shh." Somehow she was holding him. He was shaking so violently he hardly felt her. Her hand was cool on his forehead. "They're in a sealed section. We know what the dangers might be. We're taking every precaution."

"And on Earth? How are you going to protect—" He stopped. He'd almost said "the Earth."

But it was too late to protect anything from whatever the aliens could do. Whatever had happened to him was going to happen to others. If he'd crashed on X-3's fourth planet the way he half remembered, and they'd put him and Birdy back together again, then maybe it was all right. But it didn't feel right.

It felt wrong.

He wanted her to let him go, but she didn't. She was rocking him and talking to him, and he only partially understood what she was saying.

She'd give him his pilotry rating, if he played along. He knew it for a certainty. He didn't understand why she was doing this to him.

And then she was over on the far end of the couch again and he was slouched back against its back. She was prim and proper.

He wasn't shaking as badly as he had been. "Tell me," he said hoarsely, "how we can get you and your people prepared for the Earth trip. I'll do whatever I can. I really want that pilot's ticket."

"I'll get the itinerary," she said and stood up.

It seemed to him she didn't walk but *slid* out of sight and back. It was as if space had folded around her.

He was afraid of her now. More afraid of her than he'd ever been of the memories in himself. But he wasn't going to let that stop him.

"We've both seen things," she said when she came to rest on the couch again, "that few other people have ever seen. And yes, I know there are . . . weird effects. I've felt them."

At least she was admitting it.

"But this is an opportunity or a problem—it's mankind's choice which. Our SecGen's been in their ship. He's . . . different."

"*You're* different," he croaked.

She tossed her head and looked at him, hard. Her eyes were all black for an instant, and huge.

"Maybe you're different, too," she said. Now her eyes were normal, and beautiful, and concerned. "But we have to face this situation to evaluate it. Your expertise is going to be invaluable."

Had she said that to him before?

Or was he living through the same moment twice?

He wanted to bury his head in his hands, but he couldn't. He said: "They gave Keebler a box. He touched them, I bet. He breathed the same air they breathed. He sure as hell touched the thing they gave him."

"Gifts. Yes. It couldn't be helped." She leaned forward once again and her lips parted. For a long time no words came out of them.

Then she said, "We're what we are. There's no going back. Help me do what we've got to do. I promise you, you won't regret it."

"I'll get to try to qualify for my test pilot's ticket, right?"

"I said so. And we're getting you to Earth. You wanted that."

She was offering him the stars. She was offering him a trip home. But her words seemed to come from everywhere, and he wasn't sure if he could handle what she was asking him to do.

Then he thought he could. After all, he was going to try to open up the Ball, wasn't he? Crack the egg. Find out what was inside.

"Okay," he sighed. "Let's see what you've got there. If we're going to make omelettes, you people had better be ready to break some eggs."

She looked at him askance. Of course that wouldn't make any sense to her. But she was beginning to make sense to him.

And she was the same person she had been. He was almost sure. If she was dangerous to be around, then that danger wasn't much to worry about.

Not to somebody who'd been on X-3. Not to somebody who was going to Earth in the company of aliens.

He'd fled them so far. He was nearly exhausted. He wished bitterly that they hadn't come after him, followed his trail, or homed on his beacon.

But they were here. And everything was going to be different from now on, not only for Joe South but for the whole human race.

Why couldn't he seem to make Riva Lowe understand the danger?

The threat?

Somehow, much later, she was in his arms and they were on her bed. He couldn't imagine how it had happened. He couldn't remember coming in here. Time was . . . folded, a fan with different colors on each flat surface.

And there were lifetimes in the folds. And choices beyond his ability to make.

Eventually he slept there, in her arms. And in his dreams she gave him the stars.

But he hardly recognized them. They were scattered on a field of colored gases that swirled together like the clouds on X-3. And all around the universe were rings of another universe that had exploded, and died.

CHAPTER 23

$$\triangledown$$

Blowup

Bringing the Customs woman and her party to Earth had been a bad idea, Cummings admitted to himself as the third of three ships landed on his bluegrass meadow.

Seduction and manipulation of a pretty Customs official was one thing. This major diplomatic incursion was quite another.

Still, once started upon an enterprise, Cummings always followed through. He had determined to learn what he must about the Ball and its relationship to the disappearance of his son and heir. He felt no less determined now.

Real live formidable aliens were another matter. Alien rights were a sore spot with Cummings. His companies were always running afoul of regulations designed to protect alien species from the depredations of corporate mankind.

He was pretending that he was interested in forming a trading alliance, or at least an understanding, with this new race.

He could pretend along with the best of them. He was, after all, the Chief Executive Officer of the most powerful corporate entity among the stars. But his skin crawled at the thought of an alien power that would need delicate handling.

He watched the ships come down and the horses in nearby pastures snort and scatter. Birds stopped singing, frightened by the descending ships.

Vertical-landing craft would do the least possible damage to the meadow. But damage there would be. The meadow would never be quite the same. Cummings culled deer in these woods, and fox, and the occasional wolf. He knew that the smells and sights and sounds of this intrusion would send the animals running for cover.

Perhaps they were right to run. But Cummings couldn't run. He must stay here and protect his rights. His preserve. His tenure as master of the known worlds.

Who the hell were these aliens, anyhow? And where did Mickey Croft get off, trying to hide news of their arrival from him?

He waited where he was. They could see him. Let them come to him, on his hillcrest. He'd thought of coming to meet them on horseback, but that wouldn't do. The aliens couldn't be expected to ride horses, even if the horses could be expected to carry aliens.

So they would all walk the two miles back to the cabin.

Cummings purposely had not brought a car. Part of the original purpose of this visit had been to show the ecological purity of this place to the Threshold bureaucrats.

He wished that original purpose were still important to him now.

But it wasn't.

His spies had told him too much about what was going on in the Secretariat, and out at Spacedock Seven, for him to be able to think about anything but his lost son.

Cummings watched the landing party assemble outside the ships. He could tell the aliens right away. They were the ones with the funny-shaped heads and the skirts and the gliding gait.

Well and good. Bring them on. NAMECorp—North American Mining and Exploration Corporation—had eradicated competing alien species before.

Of course it had done so quietly, and had done so only when the competitor species was relatively helpless. But a planet ripe for the taking was a prize too rich to be ignored.

When you found one, if it had a primitive species whose ascendancy there would complicate export or which was hostile but relatively weak, you did what you had to do.

What Cummings would need to do about this purportedly "superior" alien life form remained to be determined.

He watched them straggle up the hill toward him, and waved when one of the humans pointed his way.

Here he was, yes. By his leave, they set foot on the hallowed ancestral ground. No shooting deer, this time, even with cameras. Cummings's skin crawled at the clear alienness of the three guests from the Unity Council.

No planet named. No coordinates, that anyone knew. No star-fix whatsoever, to identify the provenance of these creatures. Cummings had paid a great deal of money to ascertain that no one knew even the basic facts about this race.

One knew they were powerful. Oh, yes. One knew that. Cummings had had people doing covert scans of every imaginable type on the ships. Three teardrops, from Planet X.

He'd had his spies crawling the Secretariat records to find and make copies of all the exchanges between the aliens and the human diplomatic corps. That attempt had been only partially successful.

But Cummings thought he knew enough. He needed to know more, but now was the time to find out, face-to-face, what he could.

Up the hill came Riva Lowe, with the antique X-ship pilot, Joseph South. South had grown up on Earth. That was his only reason for being included in this party. Next came Michael Croft himself, and his assistant Remson.

Croft was deigning to honor this adventure with his presence. Cummings was not honored.

He felt that his hospitality was being strained. Perhaps to the breaking point.

Still, Croft was the elected Secretary General. These aliens were UNE guests. And Cummings, rightly, was hosting them on his turf.

He was calling the shots. Just as he liked it.

The pilot was the only one of them who really knew how to walk on grass. An uneven surface tended to mildly befuddle habitat-dwellers. They didn't know how to look out for burrows or potholes. They weren't used to looking where they were going. The pilot had the woman by the arm.

Behind her Croft and Remson came, flanking the alien trio. One in front, two behind. The two aliens behind were carrying pots that smoked fitfully in the breeze.

Cummings found the presence of the pots annoying. But what could he do about it now?

He hadn't said, "Don't bring anything smoky."

But this was the Earth, hallowed ground. One didn't chance starting fires.

He decided that he would have the aliens put out their smudge-pots, or whatever those were that they carried.

He put his hands on his hips and called down, "Greetings, Director Lowe. Commander South. Would you have those aliens put out their fires? We can't risk a spark getting loose."

Then he waited to see what would happen.

The two paused, conferred, and Lowe trotted back to discuss the matter with Secretary Croft.

Everyone stopped in their tracks.

The foremost alien looked up the hill.

Cummings could feel its gaze fix on him. The eyes were large. Cummings could see them even from here. Then the foremost alien came whizzing up the hill by itself.

Floating. Almost flying. Skimming the ground. Faster than anything could walk or run.

The creature was nose-to-nose with him. It had a conical head and a wide mouth. Its eyes seemed far too big for its head. It said, "Honored host, we must bring our ceremony to you without interference."

"Sorry. House rules," Cummings said, and crossed his arms.

Then he realized how heavy his arms were. Behind the first alien, the others were hurrying up the hill.

Lowe. South. Remson. Croft. And the other two, with their smoking pots.

He heard Croft's voice say, "There's no fire in these pots, Richard. Not the way we understand fire."

And surprisingly, Cummings heard his own voice say, "Fine. No use getting off on the wrong foot. We'll make do." He was really tired of standing out here. He wanted to go to the house. He didn't want a problem over nothing.

Disaster seemed only a breath away and he didn't know how to forfend it, because events in the future seemed as fixed as events in the past.

Where was his will? Where was his purpose?

In the alien's eyes, it was drowning. He looked for his son there, and what he saw made him want to weep. Or to strike out.

When Croft's hand came down on his shoulder, it was as if Mickey had awakened him from a deep sleep.

He was still standing nose-to-nose with the alien.

Nobody else had moved.

Mickey said, "Can we go inside, wherever that may be, Richard? Or do you wish to make this an outdoor event?"

Cummings backed up three paces. He couldn't take his eyes off the first alien. Had it spoken to him?

His life was a toilet. His reason for living had gone to dwell in the eyes of the alien.

He turned his back and said, "This way, folks. My humble cabin awaits."

Mickey fell in beside him as he led the way up the hill.

Mickey was saying, "You could have sent a car, couldn't you?" He was beginning to puff.

"You could have warned me that these . . . guests . . . were in town, Mickey."

"Now, Richard, can we be sensible?"

"I don't know. I wish I did know. Can we?"

"I hope so, Richard. I truly hope so. This is a momentous occasion."

"Aren't they all?"

"For the whole human race. I want to make this clear: We're confronted with very wise and powerful beings, and we must tread carefully. The human race has a sad record where care and diplomacy are involved."

"You ought to know. You're the diplomat."

Croft sighed deeply and said, "Can you tell me what you want to talk to these guests about? Your staff has been most insistent on this meeting."

"That you'll soon find out. Now go tend to your guests. I could have done this on Threshold, if your staff had been even marginally accommodating."

Surprisingly Croft didn't answer, just paced him in silence, breathing hard and falling back pace by pace.

Cummings, furious for a reason he only dimly understood, picked up the pace. Let them rough it. Let the chips fall wherever they might.

These creatures were some kind of mind-benders. That was clear enough. Well, they'd come up against a mind that didn't bend easily. They could take their smudge-pots and their Halloween hats and sit on them, for all he cared.

He would have satisfaction out of this visit.

He would.

When the "cabin" came into sight over the hill's crest, only South, the pilot, had experience enough to whistle at its beauty.

The sound made Cummings feel slightly better. Here he was, hosting quite a different party than he'd anticipated. So be it. He was a gentleman, and he would make the best of it until the moment for gentlemanly behavior had passed.

Then he would see what was to be seen.

Three servants came scurrying out of the house and down the stairs. As arranged, they bore hot toddies with them.

When the aliens drank the toddies, perhaps they'd die of some unforeseeable reaction to alcohol.

But no such luck. The aliens refused the drinks with elegant good manners and Croft's party sipped theirs, remarking on the delicious flavor, as Cummings led the way into the big, rambling manor house.

When Cummings sat down in his library, lined with ancient books, and saw those aliens there, he knew his patience had reached its limit.

He sat forward, interrupting Joe South's quiet recitation of Kentucky lore, and said: "Let's not mince words."

He kept his eyes away from the largest alien, the one Mickey called the "Interstitial Interpreter."

The other two were standing behind the big one, and their pots were still smoking.

"I want to know," Cummings said, "if the Interstitial Interpreter will tell me what has happened to my son."

For a long heartbeat, silence reigned.

Then Croft said, "Richard, you promised. . . ."

Riva Lowe said, "I wonder if we can begin this meeting on a less contentious note, somehow."

South said, "Christ."

Remson said, "Mickey, I told you so."

And the Interstitial Interpreter said, "If you wish an unpleasantness to be said here, this is not our wishing. If you are wanting your son again, back, then you must be patient."

Cummings leaped to his feet. He pointed at the alien who'd spoken. He nearly shouted: "You heard him! They have my son! They're kidnappers! They're kidnappers! I want them arrested and held! I want to swap them for my boy! And I want you to support me, Croft, or I'll have your job!"

Then, somehow, the Interstitial Interpreter was in front of him. He couldn't avoid the huge, sucking eyes. Or perhaps the eyes alone were in front of him. He was so frightened, suddenly, that he nearly went to the bathroom in his pants.

He couldn't understand how the Interpreter had gotten so close, so fast.

His stomach turned. He was going to be sick. Vertigo overtook him.

He must have sat down. He found himself on his couch, with his head between his knees and a cold compress on the back of his neck.

Riva Lowe was saying, "It'll be fine. The rest of you go on. I'll be right with you."

Cummings croaked, "Child-stealers. They didn't deny it. What did they do to me?"

"They didn't do anything to you, Richard. We think you may have had a mini-stroke. Please just be quiet. We've sent for a diagnostics kit from one of the ships. The SecGen is taking the party back up now. There's no reason for them to stay, not with you so clearly ill. We're sorry. We didn't realize you were in such poor health."

He tried to raise his head, but her hand was on the compress on the back of his neck, pressing firmly.

"Help me," he said, and then didn't know why he'd said it.

"What?" she asked.

"I said, God help me, I'm going to create an anti-Unity bloc of such formidable vehemence that those aliens will never be allowed to set foot on a UNE possession until my son is safe and sound in my arms. And the Forat girl, too. I'm going to call her father tonight."

"Please don't make trouble, Richard. It'll just be harder for all of us."

Now he did sit up. The compress fell from his neck.

The woman stepped back.

"Young lady, don't you ever presume to tell me what to do. I'm going to fight the SecGen tooth-and-nail on this. There'll be no friendly relations—no open, legal relations of any kind—with these disgusting alien criminals until my son is home safe and sound. And that goes for everybody I can access: no trading missions, no scientific exchanges, if you think you can get around me that way. No contact. Clear?"

"Clear, sir. But we can only hope you'll reconsider."

"Surely. The day after my son is returned to me. Now get

out of my sight. Take your aliens and get off my Earth. They're despoiling it."

Without another word, the woman left. The sound of the door closing behind her as she left seemed so final that Cummings was suddenly terrified that he'd done the wrong thing.

Had he closed the door on negotiations that might have gotten his son back?

But those aliens had recognized his hostility. He could feel that much. And they were frightening in the extreme.

No, he'd done the right thing. He was sure of that now, as the strange weakness left his body.

He got up and made his way to the window, using furniture to support himself as he moved through the room.

Stroke, did they think? Cummings was sure it was no stroke that had overcome him. Those aliens had done something to him.

And now that whatever they'd done was wearing off, he was even more determined to do something to them in return.

They would not come into UNE space unopposed. Not if Richard Cummings the Second had anything to say about it.

And he did. He had, if truth be told, a great deal to say about it.

He would start saying those things this very day. The anti-Unity bloc would be fully fledged by the time Croft and his aliens returned to Threshold.

Couldn't Croft tell they were dangerous?

If not, then Croft himself was due to be replaced.

CHAPTER 24

▽

Winning One

The digital examiner said, "Take your seat in the simulator, Commander South, and indicate when ready."

The simulator looked like a flight deck on giant springs. The flight deck and the springs were attached to a superstructure dependent from the ceiling. If somebody had cut up the ship that South had piloted to Earth and used its forward section for a simulator, the result might have looked like that.

The Pilot-Competency Test Vehicle sat in the middle of an open space whose walls were lined with stuff that looked like egg crates and other stuff that clearly performed a monitoring function.

When he climbed up the ramp to the forward section and hit the air lock switch, the ramp raised itself up and formed the hatch of the outer air lock. He remembered his instructions:

Microgravity conditions in effect. Vacuum flight rules must be observed. Failure to follow safety procedures can result in injury or death. To abort sequence, press ESCAPE. *To restart sequence, press* RESTART. *2* RESTARTS *allowed. All attempts count toward final score. 0 points for sequence ending in crash parameters.*

When the light turned green and the hatch opened, he was

inside an unfamiliar spacecraft that resembled only slightly the one he'd flown to Earth for Riva Lowe.

Well, this was it. He'd been trying to get this chance for so long he'd lost track of how long.

Pass/fail, was what this was. He trailed a hand over the AI copilot bank, potentiating it with a caress as he headed for the pilot's throne.

He'd done this for real, on the Earth junket. He hadn't crashed the in-system cruiser they'd given him, because nobody had remembered he wasn't qualified on it. He'd done the vertical landing before he'd ever tried the vertical takeoff. So far as he was concerned, he was now qualified on VTOLs.

So this pilotry exam was going to be a piece of cake.

Sure it was. If he'd crashed the real thing—between Threshold and Earth, in the asteroid belt, or on the home planet's venerable surface—then he'd have been dead for real. No RESTART in life.

They gave these pilots three chances to come through this simulation with their physio-simulators reading ALIVE.

Well, South had been through a lot more, and his real-time physiological meter was still ticking.

So some days you win. Maybe it's the law of averages. But South knew better. You hardly ever won when you didn't expect to win. But if you went around expecting everything to fall into place for you, you were disappointed most of the time.

He used to have a better attitude. Can-do thinking had to precede perfect performance. And he really wanted to perform perfectly, because Riva Lowe had given him the chance.

And because he didn't know any other way. The suit he was wearing was quicker and more intimate with his body than his own. Its interface with the autopilot was so fast that South found himself talking to the autopilot as he powered up the ship.

Or the simulated ship. It felt real, quivering under him. The vibration of real-time separation came up through the soles of his boots as a display grouping flared on his monitors.

Seven, plus or minus two, data streams were all that the human mind could process at a time. This AI processed three times that much and fed the pilot what he needed to know for the arbitrary decision-making process called "human judgment."

He liked Birdy's way better. Birdy just showed him what he wanted to see. He didn't really understand why he needed turbulence patterns and infrared density schematics: one way or the other, you had to traverse the distance.

But then a second "ship," another simulation, cut across his flight path and he felt the one under him buck. He lost a point for not anticipating the chop from the vehicle a hundred miles ahead of him, and finessing his course to avoid it.

By the time the simulator had stopped acting like a bucking bronco, he had more respect for it.

It was going to throw everything it could at him, he realized.

Okay, let 'er rip. Birdy, I wish you could see me now.

He kept reminding himself that he'd done this for real and brought the in-system cruiser back safe and sound, without a dent or a fried circuit.

The simulation wanted him to park and take on a fragile cargo without EVA.

You played that one close to the chest, leaning on the AI, hoping the simulated locks would mate before some unpredictable perturbation of the simulated magnetic field tried to rip the two simulated vehicles apart.

Gravity was always the big problem. The AI whispered to the back of his brain as if it were trying to help him cheat. It liked him, maybe.

He'd been around too many AIs not to believe they were quirky. This one seemed to want him to come through with flying colors.

Maybe it was a friend of Birdy's.

He smiled at that thought, and crooned softly to his copilot as he worked. Ancient Earth folk in the deserts of Egypt had believed that Nut, the sky goddess, was a woman who arched herself over you, and your planet, protectively.

The AI of this ship was like that: She was all around him.

And they were hitting it off just fine.

He narrowly avoided an uncataloged piece of space junk heading their way at a quarter C. But they didn't crack an attitude thruster seal doing it.

He sat stolidly through a possible fuel leak, and ran diagnostics until the problem went away like a skeleton dropping down over you in a fun house.

Then there was more parking—this time, parking on a steeply curved gravity well with eccentric orbit-matching for rescue of a derelict in a degrading planetary orbit.

In life, he'd have EVA'd to do this little job. But you couldn't EVA from a simulator. The exterior hull readings gave him hot near-space, as if this planet were so close to a nasty little sun that you wouldn't want to risk your testicles out there, even with one of these newfangled suits.

So they made a perfect parallel parking job, and transferred the appropriate piece of simulated equipment.

Sort of like a flag race: you had to bring back the flag. Next came gravity-intense landing, which he'd already done on good old Earth.

Outside the simulator, all of its sensors were trying to tell him, was the home planet. But he'd been there. He knew that a simulation wasn't the real thing.

When he'd touched down there in Mickey Croft's fancy-ass consulate boat, part of the entourage of the aliens, he'd wanted to run off into the woods.

But he couldn't. Not just because of Birdy.

Because he didn't belong here, either.

The air was so clean he could hardly breathe it. When he'd been on Earth, the sky wasn't nearly that blue. Now you could smell the oxygen and all the plant perfumes. It was too heady.

Worse, it was lonely.

There were only a few people on Earth. He'd known it. But he hadn't known he could "hear" it. He could sense the absence of minds around him, busy thinking and scheming. He could feel the animals peering at him, thinking: interloper; dangerous visitor; predator; despoiler.

He had wanted to leave. He hadn't wanted to muss anything up.

But the grass had felt so good. And Riva Lowe had been so transported by the experience that he'd just followed along like a good little functionary, watching the privileged have their spoiled-brat fight over whose will was going to prevail.

When he'd seen Cummings's house he'd had a very old urge to do something, anything, to mess up Cummings's day.

In that instant one of the aliens had decided to stare him down and make him remember what was really going on, during that trip to Earth.

Nobody should have been there but the people who originally belonged there—the ones from South's time and their descendants, he'd thought.

Those aliens sure as hell shouldn't have been there. Cummings was a fool.

In that library, with those old books and the smell of flaking leather bindings and mildew and rotting paper, South had known there was no way to ever undo this trip: the aliens had been on the home planet.

Maybe they'd been here a dozen, a hundred, a thousand times before. Maybe they'd been here when people hadn't been around to wonder whether they should be here.

But they still didn't belong here.

If there were too few people on the Earth, there sure as hell were three too many aliens.

So he'd found himself on Cummings's side. At least Cummings kept the old books, lived in a house made of honest logs—even if it was the size of a hotel—and knew what a rag rug was for.

But in the end, as with all human endeavor, factionalism

and polarization became more important than the crisis at hand—in this case, the aliens' presence itself.

To everybody but South.

On the way back to the ships he had said, "You ought not to do this," to the backside of one of the honor guard.

And it had heard him.

It turned sorrowful eyes on him. It opened its whale-sized mouth and swallowed him up and rocked him and crooned a lullabye to him and told him that families always fought when they had reunions.

Then the aliens had gotten into the consular ship and he and Remson had taken the other two. Rising on a gout of flameless power coaxed from an A-potential driver coil that South didn't yet understand, he had found himself more worried about the ride his single passenger was having than the effect of his words, or his trip, or the ship's power displacement, on the world he was leaving behind.

He'd had his chance to cut and run. He'd found out he wasn't a back-to-nature freak. He'd miss the life men had made among the stars too much.

Or at least, he'd miss Birdy and *STARBIRD* too much.

So now, as he brought the simulated craft back toward its apocryphal docking tube and waited for Sol Base Blue to clear him to bring her in and park her inside in a narrow slot, he wasn't really worried.

The testbed he was flying wasn't half as hard to fly as the testbed that his life had become.

You had to remain calm. You had to look all the possible screw-ups in the face and thread your way through tiny gaps in disaster's plan.

It was nothing new. It was what he did best.

When he sat back with a sigh and looked at all the green lights on the strange console, he wasn't even sweating.

These guys didn't know from "for real."

If he'd been asked to take a written test on A-field drives, he might have been in danger of failing.

But he'd done more with less, and lived to tell about it, than the testbed had asked of him today.

He got out of there without having once had to RESTART, without having crashed or bent a single simulated fender, and with a feeling of new beginnings as he waited for the lock to cycle.

When the simulator had assured him it was safe to deploy the ramp and walk down it, he almost expected a crowd of happy friends to be waiting to meet him.

But that wasn't in this universe. That was in the past. Or in the future.

In this present you went back to the equipment bay, racked your test suit, and exited through the examination/registration area, where you got a temporary ticket.

Just like that.

He was holding a card that allowed him to fly anything Threshold had in stock, a Class 4 license. The machine that dispensed it told him that a second, permanent card would be forwarded to him in six months, barring complaint or accident.

That was it. No brass band. No clapping hands but his own.

So he went to see Sling, in Sling's shop. The aftermarketeer was hard at work, his braid sticky from chewing on its tip.

He pushed back his goggles and extinguished his torch, stepping away from the workbench.

"No shit? Well, we ought to go break some traffic laws or something, South."

South said, "That's what I wanted to talk to you about."

"Oh-oh, here we go again. Now you want more power in that ship of yours, right?"

"Something like that. I flew one of the UNE's in-system cruisers, and it was downright amazing."

"At this point," Sling said, coming around in front of the workbench and sitting on it, "there's not much I can do for *STARBIRD*. You'll never make that crate into a zero-pointer with major torque. The hull just isn't up to the stress."

"She's the only ship I've got. And I can't afford—"

"Look, why don't you think about taking everything you

like about your old ship—what you think of as *STARBIRD*, and as Birdy—and migrating those things into a new super-structure? New hull. New drives. Old friends."

"That'd cost . . ."

"Yeah, you bet it would. But it's what you want, and you ought to admit it. Otherwise, keep that ship of yours for fun and go fly the UNE skies as a pilot for hire."

South shook his head. His mouth was dry. "I'm still Customs."

"But now you don't want to leave the woman who did so much for you. God, South, you're an ancient person, you know. You're not with the modern world, here."

"So? Maybe that's good. Somebody's got to shake things up."

"Now I suppose you want to shake things up some more, to make Customs and UNE happy, and go take that black box and get into the Ball. Otherwise, I don't know why you're here tellin' me all this."

"You still have it? The box?"

"I built it, remember?" Sling waved a hand in front of South's face. "Tell me you're not serious. I wasn't serious. I mean, not really serious. Ever. The black box probably won't do a hell of a lot. I was just scammin' Keebler. But I don't want to scam you, South. Who needs to get into that Ball, anyway? You don't need to do anything like that, and I don't need the heat of helping. Why don't you just go borrow some money on your contract, or on *STARBIRD*? Then we'll start working on a transfer to another hull."

"You haven't asked me about my trip to Earth."

"Ain't it classified?"

"Yes and no."

"Well then, how can I know what to ask you? You're even weirder than normal today, you know?"

"I know. It was a weird trip. Would you know where the Scavenger is?"

"Why, you want to borrow money from him now that he's rich and famous? Now he's got those jewels and all?"

"Nope. Just wondered if he was around."

"Far as I know he's not out at the Ball with a black box—at least, not with the one I made. That's here. I'm not a cop, like the rest of you." Sling was herding South toward the door. "If you want to migrate your astronics to a better hull, you let me know."

"Or if I want to try a black box on the Ball?"

"Or if you want to do that, yeah. Of course somebody's got to pay me for some of this. I been working for you guys too long without a paycheck."

"I'll see what I can do," South promised.

Outside, the Loader Zone closed in on him. He didn't feel like celebrating any longer. Maybe he'd been kidding himself about why he'd come here.

He hadn't been fooling Sling.

The Ball was still out there. The aliens hadn't marked it "off limits." He turned around and jabbed at Sling's doorbell until the aftermarketeer came to open it.

When he left there, he had the black box with him.

CHAPTER 25

▽

A Friend Indeed

Riva Lowe was losing patience with the Scavenger, when the receptionist informed her she had Joe South waiting to see her.

South wasn't scheduled for today, but she couldn't have been gladder for the interruption.

The Scavenger's jeweled box was on her desk, between her and the green-toothed, greasy old man.

She flipped it shut, closing the lid on the twisting, scintillating jewels and the things that perhaps were more than jewels. Things that Keebler thought were living. Things he wanted to lease—not sell, mind you, but lease—to the UNE for study at an exorbitant price.

First, of course, he had to get the gifts through Customs.

And she wasn't at all sure she wanted them on Threshold. She wasn't sure why she didn't want them around, loose, or sold off, split up. It was, after all, Keebler's box. But this was, equally, her office.

And her call. She said, "I've got Joe South waiting outside. If you're finished, Mr. Keebler . . ."

"I'm not finished, little lady. Not finished by a long shot. That is, unless yer givin' me the paperwork nod I need to do as I please with m' property. I need ye to clear the contents o' this here box through Customs. Why do y' think I'm all the way up here? You let Southie on in. Maybe he c'n talk some sense into ye."

"Fine." She was annoyed. This greasy curmudgeon not only never washed, he never treated her with even the modicum of respect that her actual power ought to demand.

"Iffen I can't get yer permission, li'l lady, then the Pioneer, Valued Friend o' the Council of the Unity, is goin' to hafta tell them aliens how y' been mistreatin' me."

She wanted to tell Keebler to shut up. Instead she told the receptionist to send in South.

"Now it's a quorum," she said as he entered.

Had she and South really . . . ? Yes, of course they had. So now he thought he could come up to see her whenever he chose, no appointment necessary.

As he saw Keebler he shot her a frankly interrogatory glance. Proprietary, as if he were a husband questioning her judgment.

She ran a hand through her hair. Those aliens had turned her nice orderly life into a free-for-all.

"South, would you help me explain to Mr. Keebler that— no matter what his lawyers say, and no matter what his friends, the aliens, say—there are certain technicalities involved in admitting heretofore uncategorized substances into Threshold? Such as the substances in this box."

She tapped the box.

South started toward it. So did Keebler. Both men reached the box on her desk at the same time.

"Southie," Keebler said. "You been a valued friend. How about I give ye—"

Keebler opened the box. Out of it he took one of the jewellike snails that almost seemed to move. He held it up. "—give ye this here token of m' esteem. Come on, South, hold out yer hand."

South said, "Look, Keebler, I don't want anything. . . ." But he held out his hand.

Keebler put the snail shell shape into it and then turned on

Riva: "Ah-ha! See? You ain't objectin' when you see me givin' a treasure to a friend of yourn! I don't hear no talk o' the technicalities involved now. No I don't."

She sat back down and resisted with difficulty the impulse to cover her ears with her hands. "Mr. Keebler, I was just about to say you can't distribute any of these items. Not for free. Not under any circumstances. Joe, put that back."

The order snapped out of her mouth and took physical form. It lashed around the room as if it were trying to find a way out. It wrapped around South's neck like a snake. She shook her head and the vision faded.

South was putting the snail back in the box. It glowed with a blue/red/green/yellow light.

He closed the box. She took a deep breath and started to speak.

South spoke first: "Keebler, why don't you go take a bath? Get a couple beers. Count your blessings. Prep for a vidshow. This stuff's all logged in, right?"

"That's right, sonny. An' appraised and in-sured, to boot."

"Then what have you got to lose?"

"Well, Southie, c'mere. I'll tell ye what." Keebler crooked a finger mysteriously.

South went over into the corner and huddled with Keebler, leaving her sitting there, clearly excluded from the confidence. She was affronted, so she tapped a key that would change the acoustics of the room slightly. One had certain requirements, in her job.

Keebler was whispering to South: "Y'see, sonny, that stuff—it comes and goes. Sometimes there's more of it. Sometimes there's less. The wand brings it back, mostly, if the box empties out. But I wanta sell it while it's still in this continuum, or whatever you want to call it."

"Uh-huh," South said commiseratingly. "Well, it'll be around for your trip to the aliens' universe. Which is probably where it's slipping off to, anyhow. Don't worry, Keebler. It's safe here. I promise. Now let me and the lady talk, okay? I'll find you later."

"Do I hafta leave m' property here?"

Riva Lowe took a deep breath and said, "Mr. Keebler, I'm going to tell you one more time: These items which you keep claiming as your property are unique and as yet unclassified as to suitability for importation into Threshold. If you—"

"But I didn't import 'em. The aliens did. I didn't see you givin' them your Witch-of-Endor hard time."

"—if you must have physical possession of these items before we make a decision, then we won't be able to study them well enough to make the sort of decision you'd like." She continued doggedly. She would treat this fool better than he deserved, because Mickey wanted her to. Because he had alien friends in high places. And because, damn it, South was watching. That shouldn't have mattered. But it did. "If you insist on having physical custody, we will deliver the items to you aboard your ship. As long as you keep them aboard ship, Mr. Keebler, and don't try to smuggle them into Threshold or into any other UNE-controlled territory or space, then you're beyond our jurisdiction."

"But that's not fair!" Keebler whined loudly. "We'll see what the Council of the Unity has to say about this!"

"Fine." Her temper, long straining at its leash, slipped its collar and was gone. "Good. You do that. Try to pressure me. But get out of my office. And *leave those things* here until you come to your senses." *Or until Mickey truly loses his and lets those bits of Somewhere Else loose on the habitat.*

Keebler stamped his foot like an enraged child. "Get outta m' way, Southie! Outta m' way, I say!"

South moved aside and Keebler charged the door, which withdrew hastily from his path.

When it had closed in the Scavenger's wake, Riva Lowe put her head in her hands and slowly let her splayed elbows separate, so that head and hands sank gently to the desk top. She closed her eyes and merely breathed.

Then she heard South say, "Sorry. He'll get over it. He's not really a bad guy, under all that bluster. Honest."

South! How had she forgotten that he was still here? She

sat up jerkily and resumed a cool, authoritarian demeanor. She hoped.

The pilot was sitting on the edge of her desk. How dare he?

No, he wasn't. She imagined it. He was over by the office couch, looking at views of Earth she'd chosen before she'd been there. How could she have thought he'd dare to sit on her desk? How could she have chosen those views of Earth?

Who cared, anyway, about Earth? It was dirty. It was made of dirt. There were bugs in the dirt. And flying ones in the air. They got in your nose. Little bugs. Thousands of them. A plague of nearly invisible bugs. "Gnats," she'd been told. The atmosphere of Earth reverberated with the chirping of insects. It was nerve-wracking. She couldn't imagine how people had built up the romantic image they had of the planet. Like any planet, it was full of things eating each other and trying to bite you. It was completely uncontrolled. It was noisy. The atmosphere blew around at odd times. The climate was uncontrolled. The surfaces weren't level. Creatures went to the bathroom in the grass and you stepped on the offal. Flying ones went to the bathroom on you as they passed overhead.

Something had gone to the bathroom in her hair and on her shoulder. There had been black-and-white . . . stuff . . . all over her. South had thought it was funny.

South was—still here. Still in her office, waiting patiently for her to notice him. She said, "And what was it you wanted, Commander South?" She was uncomfortable beyond measure with the memory she had, so disjointed, of having cuddled him, slept in the same bed with him—maybe done more with him.

And he was definitely proprietary. Why did a little bit of sex change a relationship?

Why, now, was he not behaving toward her as he always had?

He said, "Came to show you something." He turned from the view of Earth and tossed a pilot's license onto her desk.

So? So what? She'd known he could pass the exam. That was never in doubt. Qualifying him to take the exam had been the difficult part.

But of course, he didn't understand that. She said, "Wonderful. Congratulations."

"You bet. I'd like to take you out, to celebrate."

Had he forgotten that he worked for her? He was her junior, her subordinate. But he was, of course, a man. She said, "I'm snowed under here."

"I'll wait. Maybe I can help."

She looked at her watch. It was late. Time to go home. He was here because he expected to take her home.

Now what was she going to do?

"I can't leave." Then somehow she was at the closet, and she knew she hadn't walked there.

She'd zoomed there.

His head was still swiveling. He said, "I'm going on a little trip. I need to clear it with you, maybe. Or at least give you a heads-up. And I don't want to do it here."

Or had he said that before she'd gone to the closet?

She got her briefcase and filled it, saying, "I hope it's something Mickey's going to like." The room started whirling, streaming by her. Then she was sliding through the reception area. Nobody was there to notice.

South was right beside her. He had something in his hand: Keebler's box.

"Mickey will like it, I promise," he said. "I also want to get a little advance. I need to get my ship a couple more upgrades. Since this may be my last chance for some—"

He stopped. Stopped talking. Stopped physically.

She stopped too, with difficulty. She felt a jolt, as if her need to stop had had inertial consequences.

Now they were at the lift. What was happening? "How—" But she couldn't ask if he was aware that spacetime was sliding and jolting around them. All of this distortion was happening inside her skull. Wasn't it? "W—why'd you take that? You shouldn't have taken it."

South looked at the box in his hand. "Couldn't leave it there. Not safe."

"How do you know that?"

He pushed the lift button and shrugged.

"Not safe for what? For who? For us?"

"You like this timeslip?"

She didn't want to meet his eyes. But she did, and everything started to twist around her as if she were in a maelstrom. The next thing she knew she was sliding down the curving sides of the lift, and he was with her.

Talking calmly: "The stuff from there's screwing things up some. Better not leave it in your office. If you ever want to find it again."

His voice came from a deep well. At the bottom of the well was her personal Customs car, with its AI driver.

The well poured them both into her car from above, as if it were a convertible.

She grunted when her buttocks hit the bench seat. She was panting. "This is—it's got to stop."

He put the box on the floor, between his legs, and looked at it. "I'm not so sure that it has to. Or will." He turned to her in the car. "I want to go open the Ball. Maybe I should take Keebler's box with me. Maybe we don't want a lot of this stuff floating around Threshold."

Floating. Bad choice of words. The tubeway was running together outside the car windows, and the car was behaving as if it were a sponge vehicle. It was popping in and out of the tubeway, making progress in leaps and bounds, as if it were attached to a deadbeat second hand on some giant clock.

It seemed like years since he'd said he wanted to go into the Ball. Matter-of-factly. They'd wanted to try that once, before the aliens changed everything. . . .

"I can't let you."

"Can't let me what?" he asked.

Maybe he hadn't said anything about the Ball. Maybe she'd imagined it. She enunciated clearly: "Try to open the Ball. Take Keebler's gift out there."

"I don't have to try. I did it once before. And I don't need Keebler's animal farm. Just don't let them get loose. They might multiply."

"They?"

"The creatures in the box."

"They're not."

"Not what?" Outside, the tubeway stopped flickering into being and there was total blackness. She said, "God, where are we?"

"Probably somewhere we don't want to be. Think of where you do want to be. Don't think about the inside of the damned Ball. Especially if you don't know what's there, okay?"

His voice sounded very serious, very far away.

She thought about her apartment. Him, in it, in her bed. She didn't know if it was a good thought, or an appropriate one, but it certainly was a clearly defined one.

And they were sucked there. She was wrestling with sheets that had wound around her.

He was still fully dressed. So was she. And there was Keebler's box in his hand. "See?" he said, with a dark triumph. "Told you."

"It's the box, doing this?" she gasped.

"It's stuff from their spacetime that's alive—stuff in the box; more than the box itself." South picked up the box from among her maroon sheets, and opened it.

She hadn't really looked inside. At first you saw gems, and then you realized that the glowing things were moving. Climbing over one another, or through each other. And that inside them, other things were moving.

She remembered seeing microphotography of exotic things like this, things that lived inside other things. But there were galaxies spinning in one of the gems. Riva thought that if she could just stop it from spinning, her head would stop spinning.

"Don't," South said harshly.

She pulled her finger back.

They were standing in the tubeway, and the car was purring

beside them. He shut the box with a snap and handed it to her. "I'm going."

Had they been tangled in her sheets, with the box between them, a moment before?

"I—good luck."

"Just transfer some credit to my account, okay? I've got to buy some stuff. Tell Mickey I think this is the only way."

She opened her mouth to ask, "The only way to what?"

But he wasn't there. He hadn't left. She didn't see him walking away. He simply wasn't there. She was standing by her car with Keebler's box in her hand.

Guiltily, she stuffed the jeweled box into her briefcase, dispatched the car, and took the lift straight up to her apartment, without stopping in the lobby.

When she got there she went into the bedroom to put away the briefcase, with the contraband stowed inside.

Her bed was a wreck. Maroon sheets were tangled and humped. She'd made the bed this morning.

She knew she'd made her bed. She always did.

Without putting the briefcase away, she went back into the living room and sat down. She clutched the briefcase against her stomach and closed her eyes and concentrated, very hard, on making things be just the way they always had been.

She wanted the moments to proceed one after the other, without any skipping or flipping or twisting. She wanted everything to be predictable. She wanted events to occur in a stable realm of physical reality.

She wanted a cup of coffee.

She'd have to make one.

But of course, she must have made one.

She reached up and took the glass of hot coffee from where it hovered before her face, in thin air.

Don't get hysterical. Call Mickey. And get rid of this damned box.

Maybe she should give it to Keebler.

Let Keebler have it back.

Of course, that was it: Give Keebler back the box.

This was Keebler's gift, not hers. Not anyone else's. Threshold would only be safe from Keebler's gift when it was back in his possession.

How stupid she'd been.

She reached into her briefcase to get the box.

It wasn't there. It was gone!

Don't panic. She got up, very slowly. She imagined every step she must take to cross the room and call Security.

The box was gone. *You can take one step at a time.* She took one step at a time.

But then she got excited and slid the rest of the way. South knew she'd been exposed to the aliens without a suit. Everybody had on Earth, South included. So what?

He was paranoid.

She had the receiver in her hand. She told the handset she wanted Remson.

When Vince's face blossomed in her monitor, she told the flower with the Remson-faced center: "Vince, we've got to give the Scavenger back his box. I mean, I think I did do that. We've got to get those gifts, and Keebler, off Threshold. Now."

CHAPTER 26

$$\nabla$$

Compromise

Standing above the crowd in the main function room of the Secretariat, Croft said, "Vince, Cummings is raising so much hell about his missing son that I've decided to talk to the aliens about it now—before they leave."

His assistant replied, in a low voice, "I must agree that's probably wise, sir. Cummings has done a good job of poisoning the atmosphere in here. Nobody down there, not even an Epsilonian lady who hopes to weave Unity jewels down the fur along her hump, wants a Unity embassy here. Not even out at the Ball. If there ever was consensus in this body, we've got it now."

Croft sighed heavily. He'd tried everything he could think of to block Cummings's attempt to sabotage the establishment of a Unity mission. To no avail.

He was so tired from trying he could barely think. But there was no rest for the wicked. This endless ambassadorial function was turning out to be one of the most perilous— and draining—of his career. A few ice sculptures of teardrop-shaped vessels, and the occasional alien anecdote, had done nothing to allay the fears of the worried diplomats whom Cummings had stirred up.

Nor had honesty helped. Or pressure. Or promises of

advantage. Now his Secretary General's bag of tricks was nearly empty. And the situation before him had improved not one whit.

And it was a "Situation" with a capital "S." Growing worse with every passing moment. Growing more volatile with every contact Cummings made down there on the embassy floor.

Yet Croft couldn't bring himself to truly enter the fray—to perambulate through the crowd and by so doing clearly and openly contest with Cummings for adherents. He wouldn't do it.

It would do no good. If he tried he'd manage only to support suspicions, exacerbate doubts, and give credence to Cummings's accusations. He must remain calm. Or at least maintain a semblance of calm. Do nothing out of the ordinary. Appear to be in control.

That was a joke. He'd never been less in control of events, or of himself, in his entire life.

Remson said, "I had a call from Riva Lowe. She's released the Council's gifts into Keebler's custody. And Keebler has agreed to keep the gifts on his ship and not disperse them, for the nonce. I talked to him myself. He's mollified, if that's any help. He's not screaming for his lawyers, anyway."

"Good," Croft said softly. Not because he cared about the Scavenger's incessant threats of legal action. Not because he worried that the gifts from the Council to their Valued Friend had some ulterior purpose or posed some hidden danger, the way Lowe did. But because Vince had worked hard on the Keebler problem. "Good work, Vince."

Never punish loyalty. Never forget that people need to be praised for their successes.

Mickey Croft would have traded Keebler and his gifts—a hundred Keeblers, all with gem-encrusted boxes from Beyond—for a mere glimmering of an idea that would solve the problem before him.

If the UNE refused to allow the Council of the Unity to

establish an embassy—if, as a body, the civilized worlds rebuffed the Unity's overture—then what?

Croft held tight, with both hands, to the balcony's polished railing, as if he might float away otherwise.

Sometimes, Croft knew, his staff thought he asked for their opinion and then went ahead with whatever he'd decided to do beforehand. Was Remson concurring with Mickey's plan out of resignation, or did he truly believe that Croft was right to talk to the aliens about the Cummings problem?

Croft wasn't sure he was right. He was bleary-eyed, he was so tired. Maybe there was some other way. Maybe he was missing an obvious shot. He said, "Maybe we should let the aliens mingle with the guests." But he didn't believe it.

And Remson didn't answer. Vince pretended he hadn't heard.

There'd been some question as to whether Mickey himself was fit to mingle with these guests. He knew he was not quite up to his normal range of activities.

He wanted to sit down. To just sit down here and cross his legs and forget about everything.

The world started to melt, and he propped it back up by controlling his desires.

He wanted to see the aliens. He needed to see them. There shouldn't be this much disruption of human activity.

He found himself saying, desperately, "Things have to proceed, for humans, from the past to the future, in an orderly way."

As he said it the balcony disappeared and the Interstitial Interpreter was looking at him mournfully, shaking its conical head.

So he tried harder, wondering how he'd gotten here and whether Remson was still back there, downstairs, wondering where he'd gone.

The honor guard was at work with its pots. Good. Things would be less difficult, when the pots were smoking. Mickey had learned that much.

The Interstitial Interpreter was speaking: "We are causing grieving. We are causing difficult moments. We are leaving, now. We are not being sad for you. We are not wanting confusion. Not fear. Not much unhappy people."

"Leaving?" Had he known that? Of course, Croft had always known it. "You can't . . . I mean, you mustn't think that Cummings and his ilk represent the will of all mankind. I wanted to take you among the gathered ambassadors, but—"

"Fear, you are full of. And hold back a need." The Interpreter's eyes were going to crack open Croft's skull and suck out the truth. "What is need, this day, Croft?"

"I . . . must tell you. In order to demonstrate good will and secure the permission you wish for an embassy at the Ball site, you'll have to return the Cummings boy and the Forat girl—unharmed."

"Unharmed, no problem," said the Interstitial Interpreter. "Returning, their choice. What if they wish not to return? Can we guarantee against killing them? Can we convince killing is not about to happen? Children mistreated. Children unhappy here. Children happy, our place."

"We must guarantee no killing," Croft said desperately. "We will guarantee it. And you must show the children to the parents. So they must come."

"Only if they agree, the children, must they come, Mickeycroft. No one must do anything unwishing. Likewise, for your people. Not happy, us? We will go our place. You will be what you want: alone in small universe."

"No, no," Croft said. "Please. I don't think what's happened can be undone. Nor forgotten. Nor ignored. The status quo ante can't be reinstated, in any case. And I'm right, aren't I?"

"Correct. This is unavoidable. Everything observed by observer changes both observer and observation. Simple law. You know this law."

He knew that law, all right. Croft was seeing things, around the edges of his vision. He ignored the phenomena as best he could. He was different than he had been before his encounter with these beings. So were most of his staff.

Too bad Cummings hadn't become different—at least, not different enough.

"Mr. Interpreter, we have our laws. Kidnapping is against our laws. So are other acts of which you can be accused by the frightened and the greedy. You have to help us prove that you're not inimical."

"Am imical. Or not. All point of view. Unity allows room for diverse opinioning, yes? As UNE? So not stay, this mission. Send other mission, later time. Enough change for one millenium, could be."

For one millenium? No. Croft hadn't gone through all this to be cheated of seeing the matter through to its conclusion. "You've got to continue to help us as we try to forge a permanent bond," Croft said.

Now, in back of the alien, the room around them was dissolving. Croft was seeing raw spacetime, scattered with blots of majestically wheeling nebulae. He said over the cosmic wind: "We've got to find a way to continue the contact. To have continuity."

"Pioneer, Valued Friend, will come our place, an emissary from here. Can bring others. No fearing ones need join. But can make places for more visitors. More Valued Friends. But never wish divisions cause. Too many divisions, now. You are children of your children, Mickeycroft. Cannot squabbles bring to other spaces."

Croft was falling through raw space, all alone, forever. As he looked up, he could see the skirts of the Interstitial Interpreter above him.

When he landed without a jolt beside Remson, right where he'd been before, he was hardly winded.

Vince said, "Mickey, are you all right?"

"Certainly." A little ride through a vacuum that may not have happened—what was that, compared to the crisis he had on his hands among the diplomatic contingent? "Let's go find

Cummings and tell him that if he's a good boy, we'll get him in contact with his son. Perhaps that will shut him up."

"Is that where you went? To check with the II about the kids?"

So he *had* been somewhere. At least, Vince had noticed his absence.

Somehow, that relieved Mickey mightily. The trick was, these days, to figure out what was really happening and what only seemed as if it were happening.

Come to think of it, maybe things weren't so different than they'd ever been.

As he walked down the long, curving staircase with Remson, in search of Cummings the Second, Croft was more worried that the Interstitial Interpreter and his party would withdraw because of hurt feelings than he was that Cummings couldn't be reasoned with.

After all, Cummings was human. He was a father with a missing son. And now that contact with that son could be promised, Cummings ought to come into line.

If, after that, damage control couldn't prevent a withdrawal by the Council of the Unity, then perhaps that wasn't all bad.

Everyone was so frightened of the Council representatives, perhaps the best thing they could do was to withdraw. Show everyone that no invasion was imminent.

Croft chuckled aloud at the thought.

Remson said, "What was that, sir?"

"Nothing," he told his assistant. If the change in Croft's perceptions of spacetime continued, and if that sort of skewed perception spread, then some sort of invasion had already taken place, hadn't it?

Croft stepped off the staircase and into the crowd, in search of Richard Cummings, an enemy of the right size and a threat of the right proportions for Croft's human brain to assess and combat.

When he found Cummings he was brusque: "Richard. We're getting you a message from your son. A meeting is possible, if the children agree. The kids are afraid they'll be killed—that the death sentence pronounced on them by the girl's father still holds. Now, will you stop all this foolishness?''

Richard Cummings stepped away from the camel-lipped dignitary he'd been exhorting. He puffed out his chest and said, "Mr. Secretary, I want to see my son. See for myself that he's alive and well. Know he hasn't been brainwashed. Then I'll begin to believe that *you* haven't been brainwashed—perhaps. Until then, I'm holding my cards pat."

Croft said, "Stand by for a few hours then, Richard. You're about to see what a few motivated bureaucrats can really do."

With Remson in tow he headed for the door, past the ice sculptures of the alien teardrops. Remson said, "Was that wise, sir?"

And Croft replied, "I have no idea. But I can't help but think that, having gotten into this Unity matter this far, our best hope lies in continuing on. If the aliens pull out, leaving us with only unresolved questions, and with missing humans known to be under their control—then what?"

Remson stopped and his eyes widened. "You don't mean it. Not *war*? How could we possibly wage—let alone win—a war with creatures such as they?"

"Look at Cummings. Listen to the talk. We still have a massive amount of force deployed around the Ball site. I'd hate to underestimate Mr. Cummings. I'd hate to find out that those ships have been given orders to fire on the teardrops—or on the Ball, if no message from Cummings's son and the girl is forthcoming."

"Damn, Mickey . . ."

"Yes. Damn," said Croft, already moving through the door and into a long, difficult night.

CHAPTER 27

$\triangledown$

Lonely Vigil

Reice had been out here circling the Ball so long he'd almost forgotten about the sinkhole lurking somewhere along his orbit.

Hell, he'd been over the place where those kids had disappeared more times than he'd been to the bathroom in *Blue Tick* since the security cordon had been formed.

Not only had he not been sucked into oblivion, all the ships traveling in *Blue Tick*'s wake had passed over the spot just fine.

The Ball hadn't changed a bit. It hadn't displayed so much as a single green or yellow stripe. It hadn't sent a spark of color off into space. It hadn't moved. It hadn't signified any awareness of their presence.

If Reice hadn't remembered so well his headlong chase of the Cummings boy and Forat girl through here, he'd have been wondering whether the UNE wasn't making up scare stories.

But he knew what had happened to him. He ran his data files every now and again, to remind himself that vigilance wasn't a sometime thing. You had to be vigilant all the time.

Especially when you were bored silly. The problem with being on the sharp end of a confrontation that might or might not come was that you got bored silly. You worried. You concocted scary scenarios to keep yourself alert. Then you got used to your job. You rotated through your workday and you slept your way through your dark time. You talked to the other guys in the other ships. You swapped every scummy joke you knew, and then you tried making up new jokes.

But eventually, ennui set it. If something were to happen now, Reice was sure, the security cordon out here would react no quicker than if it had been awakened from a sound sleep.

You couldn't keep guys from getting bored when all they did was fly around in circles. The most exciting thing you think of was going home.

The ConSpaceCom contingent was running a war game based on the teardrop ships attacking Threshold, but it was a piss-poor war game. There were no parameters to attach to the enemy's capabilities. So Reice wasn't playing. He had better things to do with his time.

Or so he said. But that was a lie. He was bored stiff. So bored, in fact, that he was even talking to his AI.

So when South made contact, Reice had to work hard to keep the pleasure out of his voice. He had to pretend that he wasn't starved for news of what was going on back home.

You couldn't get any nitty-gritty news out here because of security constraints. All you heard was the regular vid broadcast, and that was pablum for the worker bees.

"South," Reice couldn't help but ask, "what's shakin' back there?"

"Not much. I need permission to cross into those coordinates you're guarding, though. I want to send you my course, my orders, and my projected ETA. Okay?"

That woke Reice up.

His feet came off the console and hit the floor. "How about you just tell me what you can, while you're dumping that data?"

His fingers flew, potentiating a secure channel so that *STARBIRD*'s ancient coms could dump to *Blue Tick* in something like a secure fashion.

South's voice came back to him, doubtful and distant, as if the pilot weren't talking directly into his mike: "I'm about to do what you know we've been lookin' to do. Take a box over to the site. Mickey wants to know what's in the Christmas present."

Trust South to drop names and throw his connections around. Mickey this. Mickey that. Only when Reice's irritation at hearing South use the SecGen's first name had begun to fade did the rest of what South was telling him penetrate: "You're going to try that box, right?"

"Right."

"And what am I supposed to do if you uncork the genie from the bottle?"

"I have no orders for you on that." South's voice was now clipped and very clear. "Repeat: no action, no deviation, despite results, has been recommended, so far as I know. We just want to see what happens. I heard Mickey wants to use the results to solve a few problems back on Threshold—calm folks down."

Folks weren't going to get real calm if, when South used that box, a sinkhole opened up and sucked the entire security contingent through into some limbo, leaving Threshold unprotected. "You know I've got to confirm these orders with my command chain."

"Then you'd better get to it," South said without a hint of bend in his voice. "I'm cleared for this. I have a timetable. I expect you not to shoot when I come by. South, out."

Just like that. South was turning into a real monster. Reice pulled up the data dump, looked at it, and then hesitated.

His finger was already on the automated patch that would put him in touch with ConSec Command.

But South's data was slugged with high-security encodings and dissemination blocks. The only place Reice ought to be verifying this mission was with the SecGen's office.

So he started doing that. It took some time. While he was telling various horse-holders he needed a verbal confirm-or-deny on some very sensitive intelligence, he began wondering what the hell was going on back there.

The only thing he found out, prowling around the comlinks, was that the UNE Security Council was planning to meet to discuss the whole matter of the alien contact.

So for sure, Croft wanted this data by then. Ammunition.

Suddenly, Reice wasn't jealous of South. Or angry at South. Or even annoyed by South.

The SecGen was sending South out here to the Ball because South was expendable. If South crashed his antique ship, or died out here trying to do whatever that black box was purported to do—or even disappeared. . . . Well, South was a Relic. South couldn't be expected to understand modern equipment. Anything that happened to Joe South could be crossed off as an accident aided and abetted by ignorance.

For all Reice knew that idiot Relic had *volunteered* for this duty.

Probably had.

Sure as hell would have.

Reice felt suddenly responsible for South. He had found South in the first place, in his ancient ship, drifting around outside the space lanes. Reice had brought South in. Helped the ancient out whenever he could.

Maybe that help hadn't always been given with the most grace and charm, but grace and charm weren't Reice's strong suit.

Hell.

Reice stabbed a button and said, "Customs Special? This is *Blue Tick*. Hey, South? Good luck, you hear?"

The com crackled and South said, "Yeah. Thanks, Reice. Good luck to you, too."

Reice almost cut the circuit. *Infuriating son of a bitch.* Reice didn't need luck. He had competence. He also had the whole security contingent flying formation behind him, to back him up. So he said, "South, just tell me one thing: Did you volunteer for this duty, you crazy Relic?"

For a long time the com stayed silent. Just when Reice was certain that South wasn't going to answer, the pilot said, "Yessir, you bet. You see, none of you button-jockeys from the future seem to remember a whole lot about what doing this kind of job is all about."

"What kind of job is that, Relic?" Reice demanded.

But by then South had broken the connection.

Reice couldn't get him back on the horn. It didn't matter. Reice could track South so close that when South farted Reice would know about it.

The fool Relic thought he could play high-security radio-silence games with ConSec? He had another think coming.

Anyhow, if South spontaneously combusted out there somebody ought to have it on the record.

Blue Tick came to full alert, all her surveillance modes trained on *STARBIRD*.

If Secretary General Croft wanted the results of this attempt to pierce the secret of the Ball on the record, then he was going to get it.

In spades.

That way, if there was any glory to be had here, Reice would get a piece of it. He called around and spread the word that the Relic ship and pilot were coming through the cordon, all nice and cleared, and everybody was to ignore that it was happening.

If, later, there was a fire order to be given, because South turned loose some terrible menace with that damned black box of his, then Reice would be ready to sound the alarm—when and if he needed to.

It was too early to get everybody in every ship out here all lathered up. People who'd been this bored for this long didn't need much coaxing to get their balls in an uproar. If somebody got antsy, or thought he saw things and jumped the gun, South and his antique ship might get hurt.

Reice was at pains to make sure his contingent understood that this little visit of South's was just some on-site recon, and nothing to get excited about.

That took some doing, since South's was the first spacecraft allowed to pass through the orbital plane Reice's cordon had been guarding since they'd come on-station.

So he had to be very clear, and very commanding, with the ConSpaceCom contingent, which was getting its first news of this change in standing orders from Reice.

"We're just watching. We're still waiting. Nothing's changed," he told everybody in plain, simple terms.

For now, that was all you could do. Wait. And watch. And wonder.

Reice sat forward, hunched over his control suite, doing just that.

You had to give South and *STARBIRD* credit for guts, anyhow. Or maybe it was plain stupidity. There was a saying that if you needed a hero, you just had to paint a good man into a corner.

South's corner was filled with one big, shiny, silver Ball.

CHAPTER 28

$\triangledown$

Send You a Letter

Richard Cummings the Second came striding into Croft's inner office as if he were Destiny itself.

Croft hadn't been sure, until he'd been advised that Cummings had entered the building, that the NAMECorp CEO would come at all.

Then Mickey would have gone to him. But Cummings didn't need to know that.

Croft sat behind his fossil-bearing desk of polished hematite and spread his arms expansively. He wasn't going to get up to greet Cummings.

But then he was up, in front of his desk, pumping Cummings's hand.

Damn, it was hard to function this way. Mickey tried to focus on his words and control his expectations: "So glad you could come, Richard. I really needed to see you where I could control peripherals. Please sit down."

Cummings stepped back from him, narrow-eyed. Had the NAMECorp CEO seen Croft slide around his desk? Cross the distance without moving?

If he had, would he pretend he hadn't?

Cummings said, "This better be good, Croft. I'm going to

have your scalp over this alien business. And to be truthful,
I can't wait."

Cummings had been in the presence of the aliens, too. He
was in the seat that Mickey had indicated, looking at his hands
on the arms of the overstuffed chair as if he weren't sure he'd
decided to sit there.

Croft took careful, predetermined steps forward. "I want
you to know that we've moved heaven and earth to satisfy
your conditions." Wrong words, surely.

Cummings looked up at Croft as if he weren't quite sure
why he was here. He definitely hadn't gotten over finding
himself in that chair.

Had Mickey done that to Cummings, somehow? Made him
take a seat?

No time to find out. No time to wonder, either, or they'd be
playing musical chairs for one of those awful intervals where
everything sequential folded up and reality became a ball of
aluminum foil you couldn't unfold without tearing it to shreds.

Cummings said, "I told you, Croft, I'm not interested in
anything but word from my son. If you and your flunkies
haven't got that—"

"But I have got that. That's why I wanted you to come
here." *Move slowly. Try to keep your attention on Cummings.
Walk around your desk. Sit down.* Slowly.

"Good," said Cummings disbelievingly. "Then let's see it.
I wish you wouldn't waste my time, Mickey. You can't possibly have anything substantive this fast. Not fast enough to put
your spin on the Security Council meeting tomorrow. And
I'm here to enjoy letting you know that I know it."

"Richard," said Croft, safe in his chair, "just watch the
monitor, please."

And Croft touched a button on his desk top to start the
vid.

Behind Croft's desk, on the big screen set into the wall
for command briefings, a likeness of Cummings the Third
appeared.

Richard Cummings III said, "Hi, Dad." The face of Rick Cummings was full of mischief and not a little hostility. Beside him sat Dini Forat, the Muslim girl with whom young Cummings had fled his father and her father and all the conventions opposed to their marriage.

Croft stole a look at the older Cummings's face. Richard the Second looked as if the wind had been knocked out of him. He looked, in that instant—old.

His eyes seemed sunken. They were too bright not to be holding back tears.

The son was speaking from the vid screen: "We were told you're making trouble, Dad. So Dini and I want you to know we'd like you to quit it. We're happy here. We're not going to be happy if you use all your tricks to get us home and then try to split us up." The youngster reached out and put his arm over the girl's shoulders. His face was stony. "So lay off, okay? You lost this round. Everybody loses, once in a while. If we have guarantees from you, we'll come for a visit. But you're not to cause any trouble. The Council's promised to protect us from you. We're holding them to it."

A furry creature, reminiscent of a raccoon, jumped up on his lap, stared at the camera, and climbed onto Rick Cummings's shoulder.

Dini Forat said, "Father, this is a message for you, too. We were in danger from you. Now we are safe. Our home is beautiful. Life is full. We will come to see you, and Mr. Cummings, only when we have guarantees of safety. And of honorable intentions. If you do evil, we will not come."

The screen went blank.

Richard Cummings was rubbing his eyes. When he took his hands away from them, they were red. "If this is some kind of joke, Croft. . . . If you've faked this. . . ."

"Don't be ridiculous, Richard. Why would I bother? How could I? Those children both look a year or so older than when we last saw them."

"I . . . noticed." Cummings was trembling.

Croft sympathized. He'd been doing some trembling himself lately.

At least the sequence of events was staying predictable. Croft kept his mind focused on the step-by-step process of the meeting in progress. "Richard, you know as well as I do that the speed at which we received the communication you asked for is beyond our technology. If we could acquire that technology alone—be able to communicate so quickly over such vast distances—what would it be worth to humankind?"

"A lot." Cummings said dully. He was still shaking off the shock of seeing his son.

Croft mercilessly pushed his advantage: "And if that is just a foretaste of what the Council of the Unity has at its command, what then? Do you want to rebuff them? Open hostilities we might not be able to withstand? Why make an enemy? Or another enemy. Your son doesn't seem too thrilled that you've interrupted his honeymoon." Croft's words were brutal, but his career and more were at stake.

Cummings shuddered slightly. He looked away from the screen above Croft's head and said, "Have the Medinans seen this?" His words spilled out of his mouth very slowly, like a waterfall of alphabet, and puddled in his lap.

Croft concentrated as hard as he could on getting out his next statement. But still, part of his mind was half praying, *Please, don't let things fall apart. Don't let the moments disappear, or get scrambled. Don't let the floor dissolve, or the Council show up. Not now. Not till I'm done.*

And he said: "The Medinan embassy is in receipt of a copy of this video letter."

Cummings said, "Well, I'd like to know if they think that their Forat girl seems . . . different. My son seems very different." His face was turning red, flushing. "That's not the boy I know."

"You're not saying this is a fake?" All around Cummings's head Croft could see whirling spirals, as if Richard Cummings's skull was smoking. "Because that's ridiculous." Had they said these words before? "We' checked with the psycho-metric modeler, which verified this as an actual video of your son and Dini Forat."

"No, that's not what I mean. I mean they're . . . different. *Changed*," Cummings growled. "If those aliens have hurt them. . . ."

Who wasn't different, changed, from contact with the aliens? "You're a bit different yourself, Richard, than you were last year." Croft stood up very carefully, and watched his feet as he took step after step toward Cummings.

"They're different, I say."

The carpet was waving, as if it were a miniature forest. There were things crawling in it. Colored things. Things like snails. . . .

Focus on Cummings's face. Look into his eyes.

"You asked for a message from your son. You have that message. Whether you wish to see your son or not, is up to you."

"Of course I want to see my son!" Cummings thundered, and stood up.

He towered over Mickey, and for an instant Mickey was afraid.

Then Cummings was five feet away, and looking from his balled fists to Croft in bewilderment. "What? What's happening?"

"You're agreeing to stop arousing anti-alien sentiment."

"The hell I am! I never agreed to anything like that! I want to see my son! You're beginning to sound like you're in league with these kidnappers!"

"And I want you to bide your time. We're doing everything in our power to negotiate a peaceful resolution to this crisis. The Council is willing to produce the children, so long as no harm comes to them from their parents. That doesn't say much for the way you and Dini Forat's father treated those children. Do you understand me? Your children are afraid of you. They think harm will come to them if they come back. They still fear for their lives at your hands. And they must be guaranteed safe passage by my government. Is that clear? They'll visit. But they don't want to stay here. They can't be forced to stay here. Do you agree to abide by those conditions, Richard? Otherwise, no matter what you do, those children aren't willing to come to Threshold."

Mickey's mouth seemed to be breathing fire.

Cummings must not have noticed. He said heavily, "Fine, Croft. I agree to await the return of my son. I'll see for myself, then, what's to be seen."

And Cummings stormed out the door.

Croft made his way back to his desk and nearly collapsed in his chair. He was shaking all over. His knees were quaking.

The Council had agreed to produce the children. But both Cummings and the Medinan embassy had doubts that the message tape showed their missing citizens—or at least, showed them unharmed.

Mickey hoped to hell that the Council of the Unity really had a living Richard Cummings III, and Dini Forat, to produce.

Otherwise, the damage that Croft had done today to his own—and to the Council's—cause was incalculable.

Now he had to find the strength to take that information back to the Interstitial Interpreter. How did you say to the II that he'd better not be lying, or even stretching the truth in any way?

Croft couldn't imagine how he was going to do that. But he must. Everything he'd worked so hard to secure hinged now on the appearance of a couple of wayward teenagers who'd disappeared under mysterious circumstances, out near where the Ball now was at Spacedock Seven.

CHAPTER 29

▽

In the Ball

South found it hard to leave *STARBIRD* alone and derelict, floating empty in space, even though Sling's new upgrades would improve her survivability if he bought it out here. He told himself she was parked, safe and sound, where somebody—Sling, if nobody else—would be sure to salvage her if South never came back.

But he didn't believe it. Nobody would want *STARBIRD* but him. His ship would end up scrapped, or chopped for parts. He felt awful about it, hanging there in his suit between the ship and the Ball.

He could see himself reflected in the Ball, he was so close. A nondescript human in a space suit with a Manned Maneuvering Unit strapped to his back and a black box in one hand. Unremarkable. Nonthreatening.

He hoped.

"Birdy," he said into his open comlink, "I'm going to jet over there now and make contact." Birdy was with him, sort of, as long as he kept his com channel to the ship open.

He could hear his harsh breathing in his helmet. His nose was stuffy. Hell of a note. His breath rattled up and down his nasal passages, and his mouth felt as if he'd been eating glue. But he was going to get this job done.

Get it over with.

Face his demon.

Face down his fear.

His climate-control was humming happily. "Spec scans," he told Birdy, and his helmet's heads-up display quadranted to bring him multispectral views of the Ball in infrared, UV, and electro-optical, as well as real-time.

In real-time, the Ball was waiting quietly for him to approach. He'd read a book once about a boy who tamed a wild horse that wouldn't let anybody else near it. When the kid finally got close to the wild stallion, the horse had just stood there and waited for the boy to touch it.

But he was no kid, and this Ball was nothing of his world.

So he jetted around it awhile, grateful for the illusion of control he got from rolling his thruster track-ball under his palm or tapping fine course corrections onto his wristpad.

He could fly around out here all day and all night, a moth just smart enough not to dive-bomb the flame.

Or he could get it over with. Bite the bullet.

The lower-left corner of his visor displayed a blinking red dot: a signal from Birdy that somebody wanted to talk to him.

He'd told Birdy not to patch anybody through. He didn't want to be pulled back at the last minute. He didn't want to have a pre-game argument with Reice. He didn't want Riva Lowe to start second-guessing him. He didn't want any incomings whatsoever.

He told Birdy to queue the message, and any follow-up. He'd deal with it later.

Better hurry. Before somebody found a way to stop him.

"It's you and me," he told the Ball. He tapped his forward thruster control, and physics gave him a gentle shove toward the silvery sphere that had been making his life a living hell for so long.

The sphere seemed to ripple, as if he'd disturbed the surface of a pool of water between him and the Ball.

And it began to change color.

A purple wave ran across it, like the edge of night over a

planetary surface. Or like a shock wave seen from an aircraft high in the sky.

After the purple leading edge, a red band came rushing. Then yellow. Then green. Then indigo, then . . .

South heard his own voice in his helmet saying, "Now's the time for the black box. Push the button and watch the show. Sling, I hope the hell you knew what you were doing. . . ."

For the record? Not really. Because he wanted Birdy to know he was still okay.

Because he wanted to make sure he could still hear his own voice.

He still had the forward thruster control depressed. If he didn't let up soon he was going to crash right into the color-rippled surface of the Ball.

Crash hard.

He held the black box out in front of him like a shield. Like a rifle. He turned it on.

And he didn't let up on his forward thruster.

"Okay, Ball. Open up, says me." His whisper was harsh. His teeth were locked together.

If he was right, the Ball was going to make its own decision any time now. . . .

He remembered the first time it had opened up for him. If it didn't do that in the next few seconds, he was going to hit that silver/pink/gold/lavender surface pretty damned hard.

The rainbow surface, quadranted into display modes by his helmet, disappeared. His heads-up went totally blank. Black. Featureless. Systems failure?

He tried breathing. His life-support seemed to be working. What a time for his helmet to go down. "Birdy?"

No answer.

"Real-time," he gasped. Maybe the suit could still hear him. It was still keeping him moving forward.

For an instant more the world around him was totally black. And then he could see through a clear faceplate.

Into a crevice in eternity. Inside a Ball that was opening wide to swallow him whole.

He let off the forward thruster.

He engaged reverse.

Nothing happened.

He said, "Shit, wouldn't you know?" as he sailed past the outer edges of the Ball and the universe he knew and loved disappeared from sight. Ahead was—what?

A swirl of colors. A maelstrom of texture.

A mist, or a pressure seal, or a giant eye.

His thrusters wouldn't respond. He was headed straight into it, deeper and deeper.

He desperately wanted to see behind him. See if the Ball was closing up. He tried throwing his weight to one side in an instinctive gesture. No good.

Made sense. He was nearly panting. He tried his thruster track-ball once more, saying "please" under his breath.

And it responded. His MMU kicked him in the pants and he spun at dizzying speed.

He couldn't find the opening he'd come in through. And then he could. It was closing behind him.

He still had the black box in his hand. Everywhere he spun, everywhere it pointed, the Ball roiled as if it were being stirred.

He couldn't make sense of anything he was seeing, he was spinning so fast. All the swirls were so agitated, it was as if the Ball were dizzy, too.

He reversed his thrust, carefully.

Then he shut off the black box. There was no use wasting power. And it seemed like wherever the black box pointed, the colors were the most disturbed.

Colors trying to tear themselves apart. A whirlpool trying to form a center of calm. Lots of stones falling into water and making rings that extended until they banged into each other . . .

The black box blinked yellow: standby.

His reverse thruster slowed his own spin. He stabilized himself with a final tap. And the colors around him steadied.

Whirlwinds eddied. Storms subsided. Planetary eyes blinked and opened wide. Clouds parted.

He floated, absolutely still, above a place. A portal. A gate. An arch of lions with roaring mouths wide. A curve of dragons whose spread talons kneaded the threads that kept space-time taut. A ship was around him for one instant, a huge and busily humming ship full of lights with streaming tails and machines happily at work generating a pulse and a wave that he could feel running through him.

Then the ship was gone. The huge, circular ship with the command stations and the view stations into everywhere.

The portal of lions was gone. The dragons knitting space-time were gone. And the boundary conditions of perception were those he could live within, once again.

He was floating above a place, and it was so familiar his heart ached.

White temples, on green hills. Lazy meadows brushed with flowers. Dark groves full of life.

He tapped his thruster, wanting to turn again. He needed to see something else. If he kept looking that way he'd see his family, his girlfriend, his parents.

And rings in a lavender sky full of clouds. He'd been here before.

He wanted to know about the Ball.

He said, "Come on, Ball. Where are you?"

He needed to see beyond his mind's attempts to show him something acceptable.

He needed to see that gate again. See those lions, or whatever they were. Shake those dragons by the clawed hands and come up with some kind of report. . . .

Report on what?

Everywhere? Nowhere.

He saw a man in a space suit floating in the heavens. He saw a sky of violet fleeced with salmon clouds, and himself silhouetted against them.

Okay. Clouds. He hit his forward thruster. What was beyond the clouds?

He hit that thruster harder than he'd meant to, or else gravity was slight here.

The white temples below began to run together. Circular shapes darted up from them and danced around him. Amoebas in the sky. Plasma creatures cavorting with him in midair.

If they touched him he'd sputter out of existence like a match head when struck.

He wanted to cry out, but he knew Birdy couldn't hear him.

The clouds were all around him now. Cotton candy on a summer afternoon at the county fair looked like that, once it had begun to melt in the sun.

He was afraid he'd get stuck in it.

Then he was through the clouds, facing the portals again. Lions as large as moons, with open maws.

One lion yawned, and the suction nearly sent him spinning down its gullet.

Between them there was a wavery space and he headed for it, cursing under his breath the whole time and barely hearing himself.

Mickey Croft, I hope this does you some good.

He hit the wavery stuff and bounced. Madness might have brought him to these invisible trampolines, strung between jungle animals sunning themselves under an infrared starscape.

He was spinning again. He hit his thruster reverse manically, slowing himself in jolts.

And there it was again, as he slowed: the controls of heaven. The flight deck of eternity. An empty cockpit whose windscreen looked out on a thousand starscapes.

Curving inward, the flight deck was folding back on itself, toward its center and the spot where the portal of lions led to the dragons of spacetime.

What the hell could he tell them, if he ever found his way out of here?

Out of here. Out of here seemed like a good idea. He could see the curve of the Ball itself now. This was where the hardware was. The rubber met the road here, curving around infinitely and creating itself into reality as it did so.

He followed the curve of the inner edge of the Ball. In places he could almost see through it. It was latticed with lines that resembled laser beams seen through dusty air. He saw a dark spot and he liked it.

It resembled a familiar sky. It looked as if it could lead him home. It had that been-away-too-long, welcome-home feel to it.

So he headed for it. The navel of existence. The belly of the Ball. The doorknob of creation.

You couldn't get to it in a straight line. That had been his mistake—thrusting straight ahead. You had to circumnavigate; slide along the sides; slip down into wherever you wanted to go.

He was nearly there, nearly at the black spot that promised peace and a relief from all this color, when he remembered he was trying to get out.

He gritted his teeth and powered up the black box, aiming it straight for the spot into which he was sliding as if he were sliding down into a gravity well.

Round and down; round and down.

The spot began to stretch. It got tall. It got long. It spread itself wide and it opened up.

It split. It spit him out. Straight out. Not on a vector. Not around and around.

But *out.*

Out past the walls of the Ball, which were as thick as an atmosphere. Out past the place where machines hummed and vistas were screened on walls that curved too many ways.

Out into his nice, calm spacetime.

He was gasping for breath and spinning again. As he spun, emanations from the black box in his hand sprayed the Ball. Once. Twice. Three times.

He shut off the box and everything stopped.

He stopped as if he'd used his thrusters. The Ball stopped spewing colors.

It was only a silver Ball, closing. Closing on color. Closing on somewhere else.

He heard a pinging in his ears and it was Birdy, trying to reestablish contact.

"Yeah, Birdy, I'm okay." He let her dump the two messages he had waiting while she fussed over him, tweaked his life-support, and coaxed him back toward the ship.

If he'd been unconscious she'd have remote-controlled his thrusters and brought him inside that way. Nice retrofit, Sling.

Birdy was bossy, overriding his manual control, but he didn't argue. He was too tired to try asserting man's primacy over machine.

His AI brought him back to *STARBIRD* unerringly, as gently as you please.

He had the black box hooked on his belt. Ought to call and tell Sling it had worked. But he didn't. *STARBIRD*'s lock was open and waiting.

For an instant it scared him: another black maw with red strobing colors inside. But it was just Birdy, wanting to mother him so bad she was pushing the air lock's limits to get him home quicker.

Inside, a green light lit so fast he couldn't quite remember how long it ought to take that lock to cycle.

Birdy wanted him out of the suit so she could spec it. He obeyed. Safety precautions were something he was lucky to be able to think about.

Once he'd racked the suit for Birdy to examine, he sat naked on his bunk with his head in his hands and tried to sort it out. Mickey Croft's message said, "Check in and report, ASAP."

ASAP. As Soon As Possible. He rolled all the way onto his bunk and pulled his knees up to his chest. The doubly safe life-support partition came down. The bunkside astronics came to life. Birdy knew what he needed. He needed to be safe a little while.

Then he could call Croft and tell the SecGen, "Yes indeed, that sure is a portal out there. A gate to somewhere, no doubt of it. Just what the aliens said it was, sir, for sure."

That was what Croft needed to hear. What he wanted to be able to claim as verified intelligence.

As for the Ball being something *more* than just a gate, well . . . they wouldn't want to hear that, back on Threshold.

Anyway, South couldn't figure out, for the life of him, how to even begin to tell them about that ship out there. Ship. Gate. Portal. Spacetime bubble. Dragons, all the way down.

You go out to do a job and you find yourself at the wellspring of eternity. You see secret things, things that maybe have to do with the mystery of reality—or existence—itself.

Except there weren't any words for what he'd seen. What was he going to tell Croft? "I saw the boundary conditions of perception. I saw the substructure of the universe, sir. I saw what's holding everything together. And let me tell you, sir, it's dragons all the way down.

"That is, once you get past the lions."

Report that, and he'd earn himself a lifetime of therapy.

So he'd better come up with a cogent report, and fast.

He straightened out, sat up in his bunk, and said, "Birdy, what did you make of that exploratory?"

STARBIRD was an X-class ship. She was meant to explore the unknown and keep a running log of what she found.

He looked at the record the ship had made and eventually he chuckled. "Okay, let's send that. With this additional message: 'Ball confirmed as nonthreatening. Inside devoid of weapons. Emerged unharmed.' "

He put his hands over his eyes. Birdy's record showed South floating into and around the inside of a featureless space, while the Ball opened and then closed. Then nothing but a closed-up Ball. Then the Ball opening, South jetting out, and the Ball closing again. Mostly her log showed an empty space inside the Ball, its expanse broken only by South playing with a black box while he used his MMU to do lots of three-sixties on different orbital planes and axes.

Wouldn't you know it?

Once he'd verified that Birdy had sent the message, he said, "Okay, Birdy, let's go home."

He meant Threshold, but Birdy knew what he meant. Curled up on his bunk, he let the AI do the piloting. He was way overdue for a little nap.

Birdy would wake him if she needed him. He needed to sort out what had happened to him. He'd been there before, to that place with the lavender skies and the rings you could see through the clouds even in daylight.

He hadn't realized it was so easy to get there. Or so easy to come back alive.

He kept seeing visions of the Ball and what was inside, but this time he wasn't afraid of the memories.

After all, he'd just done one hell of a test flight. Never mind that he hadn't taken a ship with him. Next time he would. Once he found a way to make sure that where he'd gone was a place and where he'd returned to was the same universe he'd left.

Birdy thought everything was nominal. He got back into his suit once it had checked out, and ran a self-test through his physiomonitors, just to be sure.

According to every available readout, Joe South was as normal as could be.

When he was convinced that Birdy was right, he returned Riva Lowe's call, to see if he could conduct a sequential conversation.

She looked as perturbed as the local spacetime, when he popped up in her monitor.

He tried to pretend he didn't notice, and made a dinner date.

Maybe he'd tell her about the lions and the dragons. But he didn't think so. She and Mickey Croft and the Threshold bureaucracy had their hands full with the Council of the Unity, three teardrop-shaped ships, and the Ball.

One thing South knew was that you couldn't run away from change—not this kind.

He'd tried. And look what had happened.

He said to her, "How's the everyday world,' back there?"

She knew what he meant. She said, "Survivable."

He'd settle for that. He always had. He said, "Hey, anything you walk away from's okay, right?"

"Right," she told him. "I'm glad you walked away from this one."

But they both knew there was no walking away from the Ball or anything else the aliens had brought.

So there was something she wasn't telling him.

When he gave up trying to find out what, he broke the circuit and tried to get some more sleep. But he couldn't.

There were all sorts of things in his dreams now. Things that made sad-eyed aliens seem run-of-the-mill.

When he got back there'd be plenty of time to find out what Riva Lowe was hiding. One thing about Threshold these days was that you had all the time in the world—to make a decision—

Or a mistake.

The trick was figuring out which was which.

CHAPTER 30

$$\triangledown$$

Follow Your Dreams

Mickey Croft was choosing volunteers to accompany the Scavenger to Unity space. His office had never felt so empty as it did while he looked over the roster of qualified personnel.

He'd never felt so ambivalent about a task in his life. He was sad for himself, that he couldn't go. Relieved that he didn't have to try to justify going personally.

He was happy for humankind, that representatives of a better quality than Keebler would be going as guests of the Council. He was unhappy that Keebler, Valued Friend, Pioneer, couldn't be dissuaded.

The Council couldn't be convinced to break their word to Keebler. Their word was their bond. Croft had become convinced of that.

After the effect of the message from the missing children had rippled through the diplomatic community, almost everyone else had become convinced of it as well. Even Cummings was now content that his son was alive.

The NAMECorp CEO was busy making preparations for the return of the runaways. Mickey had already been invited to a gala reception in their honor.

By then the Council would be gone. He hadn't been able to dissuade them from that either. So he should count his blessings that he was being allowed to send a skeleton staff— the beginnings of a diplomatic corps.

He flipped through the roster desultorily. He was waiting for the arrival of his preferred choices. If they turned down the mission, refused their appointments, then he'd go to his designated backup team.

Croft had had a long time to weigh the pros and cons of sending Remson. In the end, Mickey simply couldn't bring himself to spare Vince.

You didn't cut off your right hand.

So Vince was off troubleshooting Richard the Second's plans for a gala banquet and the announcement of NAME-Corp's primacy in relations with the Unity—all based on his son's prior contact.

Better Vince than he. Croft was having trouble with both his temper and temporal effects. He was too stressed to deal directly with Cummings, after what Cummings had tried to do to him.

Croft looked at his hands on his desk top. White hands, wrinkled and aging. Beneath the hands was the hematite of the desk top, where a school of fossils darted forever.

Sometimes he saw the tiny organisms move. Sometimes they had flesh on their petrified skeletons. Sometimes he didn't know how he was going to carry on.

But he would. This was too important a moment for mankind. A step forward, surely. But a step into what?

He still wasn't certain that the provisional permission he'd gotten for the Unity Embassy out at the Ball site was wise.

But when had mankind been wise? When did he get anything worth having without risk? And when had man ever been able to turn back the clock?

No new world, opening up, was without its dangers for the explorers. He felt his kinship with ancients who'd opened trade routes and continents. Terrible things and wonderful things come in the same package. You found a new land, or a new world, and you brought cultural upheaval, plagues, social unrest, conflict, technological pressure, disruption of every kind.

Progress was disruption. Chaos had a methodology. It could be modeled. The result of that modeling showed that things tended to get complicated, and that progress often occurred through the abrupt destabilization of norms.

The destabilization of the norms of reality as they were known in a pre-Unity cosmos would lead humans into great discoveries. And there was no way to avoid those discoveries. There was no way to avoid the truth.

The fossils that intermittently swam fully fleshed in the hematite on Mickey's desk proved that.

"Send them in," he said, when his receptionist told him that the candidates had arrived.

Riva Lowe was ashen, scrubbed and prim. Commander South was recovered from his trip inside the Ball, as far as Mickey could see—except, perhaps, for the dark circles under the test pilot's eyes.

"Sit down," Croft told them. "I assume you've guessed why I called you here?"

The woman said, "No," but Mickey saw the word "yes" come slipping off her lips.

South didn't sit. He hovered behind the woman, looking as if he wished he were somewhere else.

So Croft said, "Then I'll be blunt: We wish to send a contact team with some official standing along with Keebler—to the Unity. Director Lowe, how would you like to be our first Ambassador to the Unity?"

"Secretary Croft . . ." The woman's face went even whiter. "Yes," she said. "I guess I thought it would be this. I mean, I'm honored. . . ."

South was looking at his feet.

"Commander, we want you to take this mission as Ambassador Lowe's Deputy. Can you see your way clear to accepting?" Hit them hard and fast. No time for second thoughts.

South was moving very slowly, very cautiously, toward Mickey's desk. And then his face flew up to Croft's. Their eyes were inches apart. South said, "You want me to watch Keebler, is that it?"

"We want someone experienced," Mickey said, and a deep sadness drenched him. It was all he could do not to embrace the younger man.

Croft's best choices for this remarkable adventure had turned out to be a test pilot from the distant past and a woman whose main qualifications were a certain amount of physical . . . resiliency, and an affinity for change.

His reasons for choosing them didn't seem to matter so much, now that Croft's cards were on the table.

South turned his head and said to Lowe, "Don't go because of me."

So he was going to accept.

And Lowe said, "I wouldn't miss it for anything. I might as well go where . . . the action is," she finished lamely.

Maybe she'd meant to say, "go where I'm normal." Or perhaps that was Croft's own emotional spin, laid on her words.

He said, "Thank you." He could never have ordered anyone to step into one of those alien teardrops. He could never ask anyone else to go through what he'd been through. Or to live with the aftereffects.

So these two, who were each somewhat changed already from contact with the aliens, had been the obvious choices.

Still, when Croft raised his eyes to say something more eloquent, they'd already left.

Or they'd left long ago.

And when he found himself sliding and floating through a ceremony of minimal pomp, out in a parking orbit parallel to the Interstitial Interpreter's teardrop of a ship, he wanted more than anything in the world not to go aboard the alien vessel. Not again.

Not ever again.

And his wish was granted. The Interstitial Interpreter knew

how he felt. Those huge black eyes that floated before him told him to be calm. Everything would be fine. The Valued Friends would soon be home again.

Then the II receded and Croft saw Keebler, strutting around with his wand and his gift box, telling bad jokes and pumping hands before he stepped into the air lock, helmet under his arm.

Riva Lowe stared at Mickey as she came by and said, "Thank you, Mickey. I won't disappoint you."

He kissed her cheek, and her flesh was scalding hot.

Then South shook his hand. The contact made the *Washington* disappear. Suddenly Mickey was floating toward the center of the Ball, where all the threads of the universe came together.

South dropped Mickey's hand. The ship around him reappeared as contact faded.

"I'll bring her back safe and sound, sir," said the test pilot from the past.

Mickey Croft, looking at South, believed without doubt that the pilot would do exactly that.

Keebler's voice called from the air lock, "Ain'cha comin'? Southie, get yer butt inta this lock. History's a-waitin'."

Remson, coming to take Mickey by the arm, said, "I guess nobody'll argue with that."

Then the Interstitial Interpreter stepped between Croft and the closing air lock. On the Interpreter's right and left, the honor guard's pots were smoking.

The smoke filled up the cabin with a mist full of light and, in that light, all of Mickey Croft's doubts and fears disappeared.